**"A DOOR HAS BEEN OPENED....
A DOOR YOU CAN'T CLOSE."**

SHADOW

PAWLIK

VALLEY OF THE SHADOW

 TYNDALE HOUSE PUBLISHERS, INC., CAROL STREAM, ILLINOIS

Visit Tyndale's exciting Web site at www.tyndale.com

Visit Tom Pawlik's Web site at www.tompawlik.com

TYNDALE and Tyndale's quill logo are registered trademarks of Tyndale House Publishers, Inc.

Valley of the Shadow

Designed by Dean H. Renninger

Edited by Sarah Mason

Published in association with the literary agency of Les Stobbe, 300 Doubleday Road, Tyron, NC 28782.

Scripture taken from the New King James Version®. Copyright © 1982 by Thomas Nelson, Inc. Used by permission. All rights reserved.

This novel is a work of fiction. Names, characters, places, and incidents either are the product of the author's imagination or are used fictitiously. Any resemblance to actual events, locales, organizations, or persons living or dead is entirely coincidental and beyond the intent of either the author or the publisher.

Library of Congress Cataloging-in-Publication Data to come]

Pawlik, Tom, date.
  Valley of the shadow / Tom Pawlik.
    p. cm.
  ISBN 978-1-4143-2679-5 (pbk.)
  I. Title.
  PS3616.A9573V35 2009
  813'.6—dc22   2009005439

Printed in the United States of America

15 14 13 12 11 10 09
7   6   5   4   3   2   1

*For Mom and Dad,
who've gone on ahead*

VALLEY OF THE SHADOW

ACKNOWLEDGMENTS

I cannot help but first thank God for His continuing, manifold, and undeserved blessings in my life. Primary among these is my beautiful wife, Colette, who is more than I could have ever hoped for. She is my life partner, my sounding board, and my best friend. She is truly a wife of noble character and everything Proverbs 31 describes (less, of course, the maidservants).

My beloved children, Andrew, Aryn, Jordan, and John: the words of a thousand novels could never express my love for you or the joy you bring me.

To my editor Sarah Mason: Thank you so much for your diligent work and creativity. Your input has been invaluable. It is a joy to work with you!

Stephanie Broene: Thank you for your encouragement and support. And for shepherding this book through that shadowy valley to publication.

Dean Renninger: Thank you for lending your considerable talent to create yet another cool and creepy cover.

And to the rest of the team at Tyndale—Karen Watson, Babette Rea, Vicky Lynch, Cheryl Kerwin, Jeremy Taylor, and the entire sales staff: Thank you all very much for this second opportunity and for your tireless work behind the scenes. It does not go unnoticed or unappreciated.

I would also like to say a word about my dear parents, Karl and Ruth Pawlik, who have gone on through that magnificent swirling vortex into the presence of their Savior. Throughout my life, they had a wonderful manner of both encouraging my artistic aspirations and grounding my feet firmly in practical matters. And they have passed along a rich spiritual heritage. My only regret is that neither of them lived to see my books come to print. At least not with mortal eyes.

Which brings me to my parents-in-law, Gerald and Judy Eckert. Thank you for adopting me into your family and for raising such a wonderful daughter. She has blessed me in more ways than I can count. I only hope I can do as good a job of raising my own children as you have done with yours. And to Judy, a natural-born publicist: thank you for your love and enthusiasm.

As to the writing of this book, I owe some technical thanks to Ellen Hanson, an ER nurse who has a few stories of her own to tell. I am also blissfully indebted to Todd and Sherry VanRyn and their family, who have been such a blessing to me over the years. I would have surely given up long ago were it not for their selfless encouragement. May your Loaves and Fish be truly multiplied. There are of course numerous other friends and family members who all complained that they were left out of the acknowledgment section in the last book. Consider yourselves duly noted here.

I would also like to thank Jerry Jenkins and the staff at the Christian Writers Guild for their vision and ongoing efforts to help new authors grow and succeed. And finally, thank you to my agent, Les Stobbe, for his continuing wisdom and counsel.

PROLOGUE

"**Nine-one-one.**"

"There's two guys—two kids in a car." Jim's voice was shaky. Out of breath. "I think they've just been shot. I saw another car tear off and . . ."

"Sir, where are you located?"

"I'm—I'm on the corner of Jefferson and West. Just a ways down on West. I think it was like a drive-by or something."

"Are they conscious?"

"No. No, I think they may be dead." Jim's breath rasped over the phone. "Oh, man, there's blood all over."

"Sir, are these children?"

"No . . . I think they're maybe teen-agers."

"Is the car unlocked? Can you get to them?"

"Uh . . . the window's shattered. The driver-side window."

"Can you tell if they're breathing?"

"No. I don't think . . ." Jim leaned into the window, scraping the cell phone against the metal frame. "I can't tell. I don't—he's not breathing. The driver's not breathing. Man, they're just kids. They gotta be no more than seventeen or eighteen."

"Sir, I have the police and paramedics on the way."

"I'm checking . . ." Jim hurried to the other door. "I'm checking on the other side. The other kid."

Jim fumbled with the door handle. He could hear a siren in the distance. The passenger door opened and the boy tumbled out, limp. Jim dropped the phone and caught him. Pulled him out of the car. Laid him on the cement. The boy's head flopped and rolled. A cherry red stain spread across his gray Nike T-shirt. Jim felt himself gag. He'd never touched a dead body before.

He picked up the cell phone. "I'm on the other side. I got the other kid. He nearly fell out when I opened the door."

"Is he breathing?"

Jim bent and listened. He watched the bloody chest for movement. It was motionless. "No. I—he's not breathing."

"Sir, are you able to perform CPR?"

"What?"

"I can walk you through it. Until the ambulance arrives. Are you able to perform CPR?"

"I, uh . . ." Jim stammered. He'd taken a course back in high school. That was twenty years ago already. "I—I can try."

The operator walked him through the steps. Clear the airway. Administer mouth-to-mouth. The kid had been smoking; Jim could smell it. He pushed on the boy's chest, not sure if he was pressing too hard or not enough. He prayed silently.

He glanced up into the car. The driver was slumped forward against the steering wheel. Blood was pooling on the seat. Dripping onto the floorboard.

Jim could help only one of them.

"Somebody help me!" His voice echoed down the street. Cars rolled by on Jefferson. But nobody turned down West. He was half a block down. Too far down. They couldn't see him in the dark. No other pedestrians approached.

The siren grew closer. Jim worked through another set and breathed in two quick breaths. His heart was pounding, yet he found himself strangely calm.

"Jesus, please help me. Help this boy."

Five minutes ago he had been sipping a beer at Frank's Tap around the corner on Jefferson. He'd had his own problems to worry about then. They seemed like pretty big ones at the time, but he hadn't been in the mood to pray. He'd been too angry.

A Chicago police car pulled hesitantly onto West, spotlight sweeping the street. Jim stood and waved and the squad car rolled toward him. He went back to CPR. He could hear the car doors open and close. Two officers moved slowly. Cautiously.

Jim was careful not to make any sudden moves. They'd heard a report of gunfire and probably had their own weapons trained on him. He glanced up, squinting into the glare of flashlights. They lit up the sidewalk around him. Jim looked back down and gasped at the amount of blood.

He'd better explain. "I was coming out of the bar." His breathing was labored. "Coming back to my car over there. I saw a black sedan pull away. It just tore off. Then I saw these two kids in the car here. I saw the window shattered. But I didn't hear any shots. No gunshots."

One of the officers knelt beside him. "I can take over."

The other cop was shining his light into the driver-side window. "This one's not breathing either." He spoke into his shoulder radio, relaying information to the dispatcher. He described the scene, then opened the door and pulled the driver out.

Jim sat back and caught his breath. His forehead was dripping. He could hear more sirens now. Getting closer.

A second squad car arrived and, shortly after that, the ambulance. There was a flurry of lights and activity. A second ambulance was on its way. The medics unpacked their gear. They seemed to work without emotion, speaking to one another in tight, clinical phrases.

Jim's head was swimming. He'd never been this close to death before. Well . . . except for once.

The second ambulance arrived. A row of spectators had gathered, watching from the shadows. Jim just shook his head. Sure, now there was plenty of help.

The medics unpacked more equipment. They had cut off the boy's Nike shirt, exposing his chest. Jim could see a bullet wound near the shoulder. One of the medics checked for an exit wound and set about packing gauze around it.

They had an oxygen mask on the boy now and a medic squeezed air into his lungs. The other listened with a stethoscope, then turned and reached for the portable defibrillator. Flipped a few switches, pulled out the paddles. "Charging," he said to his partner.

The medic laid the paddles against the boy's flesh. "Clear."

Jim heard a click and soft hum. The boy's body stiffened for a moment, then fell limp again. The medic checked for a pulse. Finally he nodded.

Jim's eyes widened. He couldn't contain himself and blurted out, "He's alive?"

But they ignored him and continued giving the boy

oxygen. Three cops gathered to help lift the boy onto a stretcher and wheel him to one of the waiting ambulances. Jim watched them go, then remembered the other kid. The driver. Had they been able to save him too?

Jim moved closer for a better look. But they had covered that boy with a sheet already. Jim felt his stomach tighten. The kid was just a faceless shape lying on the asphalt under a blue sheet. Jim couldn't even recall what he looked like.

One of the officers pulled Jim aside. "Good thing you happened along when you did or they'd both be dead."

Jim stared at the sheet.

The officer held a notepad. "Sir, I'm going to need to ask you a few questions."

Jim nodded.

"Let's start with your name."

His name? Jim couldn't take his eyes off the sheet. Or the body underneath it. Thoughts started peppering his mind like crows diving for corn. Swooping down and flitting away. What if he had pulled the driver out first? Would that kid have been in the ambulance now instead of under a sheet? Why had he even gone to the passenger's door in the first place? For that matter, what if he had just stayed at the bar for another beer like Danny had wanted? Or what if he hadn't gone to the bar at all? What if he'd stayed home with his wife instead? She had asked him to stay. She'd said they needed to talk. They had a big decision to make. But he'd just wanted some air. To clear his head and have a beer. There were so many tiny decisions that night. So many choices that led him here.

"Sir?" The officer's voice broke into his thoughts. "Can I get your name?"

Jim blinked and nodded. "Uh . . . Jim," he said. "Jim Malone."

VALLEY OF THE SHADOW

FREEZING. Devon Marshall was freezing.

Darkness enveloped him. Thick and heavy, wrapping around him like a blanket. He could feel its weight pressing in on him. Squeezing him. Smothering him. And far off in the darkness, he heard sounds. A deep rumble mixed with a jumbled, muddied squawking. The noises were muffled and distant but growing steadily louder. Like a train approaching: the thunder of the engines and the clacking of its wheels on the tracks.

A pinprick of light blazed in the darkness. Tiny at first, but getting closer. Every second it grew larger and more intense. The sound roared now as the light rushed toward him and then . . .

Everything exploded into chaos.

Light and sound washed around him like a giant whirlpool. He could feel himself spinning inside it. Being buffeted and pulled along by a current.

And he was still freezing.

Lights flashed in his face. A dizzying array of reds and blues. Light and darkness. Shadows loomed over him and moved about. He tried to focus on the shadowy images as they swirled around him. Then he recognized them.

People?

He was surrounded by people. Actual human beings! They were speaking to one another. Devon could hear distinct voices but still couldn't make out the words. And the voices sounded worried. Anxious.

Devon's vision was becoming clearer. Several people with uniforms and badges hovered over him. An ambulance was parked nearby, and two police cars, their lights flashing.

Paramedics? And cops? Was there an accident somewhere?

His mind was a jumble of thoughts and he tried to recall what had just happened. Images flashed through his mind. Terrifying ones. Disjointed and vague memories of huge, empty buildings. Skyscrapers. An entire city, void of life. A dull, overcast sky. Gray, faceless creatures reaching out hands with long, bony fingers like enormous spider legs.

And a farm out in the middle of nowhere . . .

Terrell. Where was Terrell? They had been together just a few days ago. Or had it been only a few minutes?

Devon tried to turn his head but couldn't. Something was holding him in place. He struggled to move but was too weak.

He had to get out of here. He had to find Terrell.

He could hear the voices better now. One of them called for help. Something about a stretcher. Legs and feet shuffled out of view, then back in again. More lights.

Not far off, a row of strangers huddled together, watching. Devon scanned their faces, and one of them caught his eye. One face seemed out of place in the group. One man was standing off a little ways by himself. Standing in the shadows, staring right at Devon. His face seemed to draw Devon's gaze toward him, as if pulling him down into a pit.

It was long and narrow. Pale skin almost glowed against the shadows behind him. His cheeks were gaunt and sunken. And his eyes . . .

His eyes shone a pale yellow. But they seemed hollow. Then he smiled. His thin, puckered mouth expanded into a wide grin. Rows of brown, rotted teeth dripped with black saliva.

Devon couldn't take his eyes off the man. Then someone passed between them and he was gone.

Suddenly Devon felt himself moving. Floating. He could see several people standing around him. Cops and paramedics. They slid him into an enclosed space where white light surrounded him. Two people climbed up beside him.

What was going on?

Devon heard doors slam shut with a thud and a click. A moment later, he could feel himself moving again.

His eyes widened and his breathing grew more rapid. The crowd. The paramedics. The cops . . .

They were there for him!

They had put him into the ambulance!

One of the paramedics leaned close. He had reddish brown hair, green eyes, and a broad, freckled face. " . . . what

I'm saying? You've been shot. . . . going to be all right . . . Cook County Memorial . . . understand?"

He was pressing something against Devon's chest. Devon glanced down. Now in the light he could see his shirt was cut open and drenched in blood. A large, white piece of gauze was taped to his chest.

Devon looked back up at the medic and his breath caught in his throat.

The man's face had changed. His eyes glowed yellow. His lips parted in a twisted grin, showing dozens of teeth. Dark and rotted, all jammed together in his mouth. Black liquid, like tar, dripped onto his chin.

"The door is still open," he croaked. His voice was gargled and deep.

"Leave me alone!" Devon squeezed his eyes shut. "Leave me alone! Leave me alone!"

He felt a hand on his forehead and opened his eyes again. The medic's face had returned to normal. The guy was working on Devon as if nothing had happened.

Devon tried to slow his breathing. His chest burned and a sharp pain knifed through his ribs with every breath. He struggled for air as darkness began to close in around him. Sounds grew muffled. The medic's voice sounded urgent but began to fade. Devon could feel them moving around, trying to save him.

And he could feel himself slipping away.

2

CONNER HAYDEN FOUGHT his way
through the woods. Branches
snapped at his passing, disintegrat-
ing into puffs of dust, as if every drop
of moisture had been sucked out of
them. Tendrils of mist curled around
his legs like serpents seeking to pull
him to the ground. He could feel their
weight as he struggled to walk. But
he had to press onward. He had to
keep going.

He had been here before.

Darkness fell around him like a
thick blanket, almost smothering him.
His chest pounded as much from the
strain of his movement as from the fear
rising inside him.

He knew what was out there.

But he heard no voices this time. No ghostly whispers from the dark, save one. One single, moaning plea.

Help me!

His breath came in steamy puffs. The passing branches lashed at him like razors, slicing into his hands and face. The trees seemed to lean their gnarled limbs into his path, blocking his way and closing in again behind him. He would never find his way out.

Please, someone help me!

"Mitch!" Conner hissed through his teeth. For two months Mitch Kent's face had haunted his dreams. The thought of the young man he barely knew, trapped inside this place—trapped between life and death—gnawed at him day and night. Conner had to help him. This was his sole mission. This was the reason God had saved him. Brought him back from the dead. Back from the edge of the abyss.

A light flickered between the twisted branches. Conner lowered his head, threw his arm across his face, and plowed through. The trees seemed to claw at him like a swarm of angry cats. He almost thought he heard them hissing as if not wanting him to pass. Trying desperately to keep him from moving forward. It was the only way he could tell he was headed in the right direction. It seemed to be the one place they didn't want him to go.

Conner stumbled into the clearing and found himself staring at the old cabin. Again. It stood weathered and barren, the roof sagging under its own weight. A dull, orange light poured out from the crusted glass of the single window in the front.

He stepped closer. "Mitch?"

Help!

Conner peered through the window. The cabin was empty,

just as he remembered it. He cracked the door open and slipped inside. And winced. The odor flooded his nostrils like an overflowing sewer. He turned toward the door, gagging. His head swam from the stench. This was not what he remembered.

Conner gathered himself and inspected the interior more closely. The wood-burning stove poured out a sickly orange light. But there was no heat.

"Mitch, where are you? It's me. It's Conner."

Something thumped against the wood. Conner spun around. The doorway stood open and empty. Nothing moved in the darkness outside.

There was a second thump and a sharp crack. The entire cabin shuddered. Then something burst through the floorboards directly in front of him, splintering the wood. An arm reached up. Blackened flesh dangled from the bones. Maggots poured from abscesses in the rotting skin. A skeletal hand gripped Conner's ankle like a bear trap. He couldn't move. The stench flowed up stronger now, overpowering him. His eyes rolled back, and the cabin seemed to sway beneath him. Conner tumbled backward onto the floor, but the hand kept its grip.

A second arm burst through the boards and clutched his hair. Then two more crashed through, pinning his shoulders to the floor. Conner screamed. . . .

He sat up straight. Chest heaving.

The cabin dissolved into the shadows of his bedroom as Conner gasped for breath. Cold sweat soaked his T-shirt. He felt something stir beside him.

Marta rolled over and reached for the nightstand lamp. "Connie?" Her voice was hoarse with sleep. She sat up and slipped her arm around him, pressing her hand lightly against his sternum. She held it there as she rested her cheek on his shoulder. "Was it the dream again?"

Conner could feel his heart pounding under her hand. He sucked air into his lungs, deep and slow. He had to control his breathing. He had to calm himself. Finally he nodded. "Yeah. The same one."

"Can I get you anything?"

"No." His heart rate began to slow. He rubbed his eyes and lay down again. "I'm all right."

He closed his eyes but could still feel Marta's stare. She was worried about him; he could tell. More so than usual. In the two months since his heart attack, he hadn't made it through more than three consecutive nights without having that dream. But he'd only described it to her in vague terms. He didn't want to give her the details. He didn't want her to press him with questions about his "experience" during the heart attack.

Because he hadn't told her everything.

"Something's bothering you," she said.

Conner yawned, trying to shrug off her insinuation. "D'ya think?"

"I mean there's something else. Something you're not telling me. I can tell when you're hiding something, Connie. I always could."

Conner glanced at the clock. "It's three. Let's talk about it in the morning."

"You know I'm going to keep pestering you." She leaned against him and trailed her finger through his hair. "I can be very persistent."

Conner tried to roll onto his side, but Marta pressed her weight harder against his shoulder, pinning him in place. He chuckled. "Believe me, no one knows better than me."

Marta stared at him for a moment, one eyebrow raised. Then she leaned over and flicked off the light. "Just so we understand one another."

Three and a half hours later, after Conner had showered and sat down for breakfast, Marta slid a plate of toast in front of him. Conner downed his orange juice and spread some jam over the toast. He could feel her stare again and wondered what she would think of him if he told her the truth. What would she do if he actually told her everything?

She'd want him to see a shrink. . . . No, the old Marta would've had him see a doctor. This one would want him to speak to their pastor.

Conner had been going to church with her for the past five weeks—since they'd gotten officially remarried—and she'd been pestering him to set up a meeting with the pastor. Conner's journey to his newfound faith had been dramatic to say the least, but he was still an independent thinker. He didn't want somebody else telling him what to believe. He wanted to discover it on his own. He needed to figure it out for himself. It wouldn't seem real to him otherwise.

Conner bit into his toast, avoiding Marta's gaze.

"So anyway," she said after several seconds, "I think I've had about enough of this."

Conner stopped chewing and looked up. "Enough of what?"

"Of you keeping all this stuff penned up inside you. What's it going to take for you to figure out that you can talk to me? A heart atta—? Oh, wait . . . that's right."

Her sarcasm was improving.

Conner started to laugh and that at least felt good. "You'll think I'm going crazy."

"Going?"

"Very funny." He paused, taking another bite of toast to buy himself some time. "Actually, I have been wanting to tell you something. It's just that . . . well, it all sounds a little . . ."

Marta lifted an eyebrow. "Crazy?"

Conner sighed. "The night of my heart attack, I told you how I found myself standing at the edge of this cliff. This huge chasm."

"I remember."

"Well . . . what I didn't tell you was how I got there."

"What do you mean?"

Conner drew a deep breath. "When I was dying . . . I didn't actually know I was dying. I didn't know what was going on. I was in my study that night when I saw this weird storm out-side—big black clouds rolling across the sky with lights flash-ing inside them. It wasn't like any storm I had ever seen before. Then I blacked out, and when I woke up the next morning—or what I thought was the next morning—I found myself all alone. Everything seemed as real as this does now. But Rachel and you . . . and the entire world had just . . . vanished."

Marta frowned. "I don't understand."

"There were buildings and cars and trees, but no other people. I drove around town, but the entire city was deserted. It was like I was the last man on earth. Then I saw these things—these creatures watching me. Following me. For a while there I thought they were aliens."

Marta leaned forward. Her frown was deepening but she didn't say anything.

Conner went on. "I finally met up with some other people who'd all had the same experience I did. They had seen the storm too and woke up the next morning all alone."

"So that's what that list of people was all about. That you had asked your assistant for?"

"Yeah. Mitch Kent and Helen Krause. And Devon Marshall, Ray Cahill, and . . ." A slight shudder rippled down his spine. "And Howard Bristol."

"You actually met them? spoke with them?"

"Yes," Conner said. "They were as real as you are right now. I swear. But we were all dying. My heart attack, Mitch's accident, and Helen's overdose. Devon had been shot. But Howard . . . Howard wasn't what he seemed."

"What do you mean?"

"He saved us from some of those creatures. They were attacking us. They had dragged Ray Cahill off into the darkness. And they were coming for us, too. But Howard showed up and saved us. He took us to his farm and we thought we were safe. But he was . . . working with them. Or maybe he was really one of them . . . some kind of being that could make itself look like a friendly old farmer."

"And when they dragged people away," Marta said, "these things . . . they brought them to that chasm?"

"That's where they brought Helen. A bottomless, black abyss, and I would have ended up there too if they hadn't revived me." Conner closed his eyes. After several seconds he regained his composure. "But Mitch isn't dead yet. He's in a hospital in Winthrop Harbor, hooked up to life support—his body is, anyway. But his . . . his soul is still in that place. Howard called it the Interworld. Mitch is still there with Howard. And he doesn't even know what's really happening to him."

Marta leaned back and bit her lower lip. She didn't say anything for what seemed like an eternity.

Conner spoke up again. "So that's it. Now tell me . . . do you think I'm crazy or not?"

Marta's eyes traced a path around the kitchen. Conner

could tell she was trying to process the story. She looked like she was trying to understand . . . or decide if she believed it.

Finally she shook her head. "It's just . . ." She seemed to struggle for words. "I mean, I've heard of people having near-death experiences. But never this detailed. Nothing like this. This just seems so . . . so unreal."

"But it was real." Conner grew solemn. "I didn't believe it myself at first. I kept telling myself it was just a hallucination. But when Nancy came with my list of names, when she found those people—people I had never even met before . . . I knew it was real."

Marta folded her arms. "That's who you've been trying to get in touch with? Mitch's father? That's what you've been so worried about?"

"I know it probably seems like I've lost my mind," Conner said. "I hardly know Mitch. I don't know anything about him. But I can't just leave him there. I know what's waiting for him if he gets disconnected. I've seen it. If they let him die . . . Marty, I can't get it out of my head. I can't stop thinking about it."

"But what can you do about it? It's not your decision."

Conner shrugged. "I don't know. But like Rachel told me once, God brought me back for a reason. He saved me for some purpose, and I think it's to try to help Mitch. I think He wants me to save Mitch."

"But how do you know that? How are you supposed to save him? What are you supposed to do?"

"I don't know." Conner slumped in his chair. As though a weight had just been dumped onto his shoulders. "That's what's so frustrating. I feel like God wants me to do something, but I have no idea what it is or how to do it. And in a way, I feel like I'm getting angry at Him all over again. Why doesn't He just come out and tell me? Why does everything have to be so difficult?"

"I know you've been trying to avoid this, but why don't you talk with Pastor Lewis?"

Conner started to protest, but Marta cut him off. "Please? We'll go together. This is something neither of us has any experience or knowledge about. Please, Connie? Let's at least try."

"I'll think about it." Conner glanced at his watch. "I need to get going."

He'd been back to work for three weeks already. But he found he was having trouble getting into a routine. He was also finding it difficult to concentrate.

He could no longer view his job the same way. There were things he used to do, tactics he once had no problem with, that now caused him a sort of inner turmoil. He wasn't the same man he had been. He found he was developing new priorities, new values that were beginning to conflict with his old ones.

And he knew it was only a matter of time before it would affect his job.

Conner packed up his laptop and went out to the car. He had to get to the office.

But there was something he needed to do first.

VALLEY OF THE SHADOW

3

MITCH KENT STEPPED onto the back porch and stretched. Thick, tattooed arms reached toward the overcast sky, forcing an expansive yawn. He twisted at the waist, rolled his head, and then eased his burly frame into one of the lawn chairs.

A tall, gray-haired man strolled up from the barn. He seemed irretrievably gaunt, like a dry stalk of November corn bent by the wind. But his face bore a wide, yellow-toothed grin.

"Mornin', Hoss." He spoke with a slight bucolic twang. His voice was soft and gravelly, as if he were constantly on the verge of laryngitis. In an odd way, the sound of it both soothed Mitch and grated on his nerves.

Mitch nodded. "Morning, Howard."

The old man squinted at the layer of gray clouds. "Y'know, we gotta make another run for gas today."

"Mmmm . . ." Mitch groaned. "Let me check my schedule. I think I may have a conflicting appointment this morning."

Howard chuckled and leaned against the porch railing. "I know it ain't your idea of fun, but you don't really want us to run outta gas, do you?"

"Heaven forbid."

Howard laughed harder. "Better get some breakfast. I'll get the truck ready."

Mitch rose, shuffled into the kitchen, and pulled out a box of stale crackers and a jar of peanut butter. Twisting off the lid, he peered inside and sniffed. They were nearly out. They'd need to stop for food on the way back.

He ate, downed four glasses of water, and trotted out the door as Howard pulled up in the old milk truck.

This had been their routine for nearly five years. Mitch had struggled to keep track of how long it had been since he'd first come to the farm. It was just after he'd met Conner, Devon, and Helen. Nearly five years ago.

It felt like an eternity.

Howard, for his part, was bearable at best. Mitch had grown accustomed to the old man's hygienic idiosyncrasies and quirky jocularity. But it was his insufferable optimism that Mitch found most wearisome. It seemed the farmer could put a positive spin on any event, no matter how dismal. Every cloud had its lining. Every trial, its lesson.

Like the night several months back when they were rudely awakened by the shrieks of an old woman—Noreen, or something—who'd arrived at the farm the day prior. She had wandered away from the compound that night, no doubt seduced by some vision of a loved one promising that the answer to all her questions lay within the brooding forest out yonder. Her bloodcurdling screams echoed for several minutes, growing more distant until they eventually stopped. Mitch had to cover his ears. He'd warned her repeatedly not to pay attention to anyone who might try enticing her out into those woods. Especially after dark.

And to that tragedy, Howard's only comment was that at least now they knew the creatures were still out there. They had been experiencing a dearth of visitors and alien activity at the time. Normally someone would happen by the farm at least once or twice a month. By car or truck. Many of them on foot. They'd stay for a day—two at the most—and then just disappear. A few into thin air. But most would fall prey to, among other things, a woeful lack of discernment by following an enigmatic vision into the darkness.

They had gone several months without a guest until Nadine, or whatever her name was, had stopped by the farm. In fact, Mitch had started to hope that perhaps this whole alien ordeal was finally over.

But it wasn't. Much to his despair. Mitch sank further into despondency and Howard . . . well, Howard continued to look on the bright side.

And so the months wore on. Long weeks of dismal gray solitude, punctuated by brief periods of terror. Oh, and once a week, they would spend the better part of the day siphoning gas from abandoned vehicles and empty gas stations. All to keep the generators running and the lights burning at night.

This was their routine. This was their life.

But Mitch was growing weary of it. All of it.

Some time ago, he'd developed a keen interest in books, but even that had started to grow stale. He'd begun reading at first just to pass the long hours of tedium, starting with pop fiction novellas and working his way up through more arduous tomes. After the first two years on the farm, he'd amassed quite a literary collection during their weekly jaunts into town. Besides fiction he had also dabbled in biochemistry, astronomy, and philosophy. He would always make sure to stop by a library or bookstore to pilfer an armload of anything that caught his interest. Though *pilfer* wasn't exactly an accurate descriptor. More like *confiscate*, *impound*, *sequester*.

He'd also collected several dictionaries, a set of Encyclopedias Britannica, and something called a thesaurus.

The truck rattled and squeaked as they drove along. Mitch slouched against his window, watching the drab landscape roll past while Howard whistled a cheerful tune.

"It's time for an oil change again," Mitch muttered, noting that the engine was sputtering a bit. Howard had certainly made use of Mitch's skills as a mechanic during their time together. Mitch didn't mind, though. It kept him busy and passed the time.

Howard interrupted his tune to reply. "I think there's still plenty left in that quick mart over on Highway 20. Remind me to stop by on the way home."

"And we also need more food. I noticed a paucity of peanut butter this morning."

"Paucity, huh? I just picked some up last week." Howard snorted. "Boy, you're eatin' me outta house and home. Where d'you put all that food anyway?"

"It would seem my appetite is rapacious."

"I think I liked you better before you started all that reading."

They rolled into Harris, a small town just thirty miles south of them. They had come across it only two weeks ago, so there was still plenty of gas left to siphon. Mitch had stopped wondering why the gasoline in all these abandoned vehicles had not gone bad yet. There was no telling how long they had been sitting there dormant. And after a time, gas just went bad. But thankfully they never had any issues. The gas always seemed to work just fine.

They spent the next three hours canvassing the whole northwest quadrant of the town, working their way toward the quaint downtown business district. A variety of shops and stores lined the wide main street. Howard had compiled a shopping list and was headed for the hardware store. Mitch, however, spotted a small bookstore down the street and said he was going in for a peek. Howard muttered something about not being surprised and waved him off.

Mitch entered the darkened store and listened for any odd sounds. The aliens generally kept to the shadows, so one never knew what one might find in a darkened building. But the place seemed quiet enough. The musty scent of old paper filled the shop. Enough daylight filtered through the front windows to allow Mitch to scan the shelves as he strolled up the aisle. He ignored the magazines, the weight loss and the workout books. He paused for a moment at the how-to section for anything that might prove helpful, but nothing caught his eye.

Next he came to the fiction aisle: romance, romance . . . more romance. Historical romance, suspense romance, Western romance, romantic comedy. Coming to the end of the aisle, Mitch was turning to go down the next when he stopped in his tracks and let out an involuntary gasp.

Another man stood in the aisle before him.

He was a slender black guy, just over six feet tall, probably in his thirties, Mitch guessed, with short-cropped hair and a goatee. He wore plain faded jeans and a black T-shirt. And sunglasses.

Mitch blinked. Sunglasses? He hadn't seen the sun in five years.

"Who—who are you?" Mitch stammered, trying not to sound startled.

The stranger removed his glasses. His brown eyes held an intense, almost wild look. "You need to leave that farm," he said. "You have to get away from him."

DEVON MARSHALL ROLLED out of bed
and stood up. His eyes fluttered as the
last shreds of sleep drained away, rolling off of him like drops of water. The
wake-up buzzer blared through the concrete corridors, rousing the occupants
of other rooms. He'd have ten minutes
to get ready for breakfast. Ten minutes
to wake up, wash up, and get dressed.

He leaned on the tiny rust-stained
sink and peered into the cracked mirror. It reflected a distorted image of his
face, like broken halves of the same
kid staring back at him. But his gaze
seemed empty and hollow. Not unlike
how he felt.

As juvie facilities went, the Chicago

Juvenile Corrections Center on the city's south side was about as bad as it got. Overcrowded and understaffed, it was often more dangerous here than out on the streets.

They had transferred him two weeks ago after his case had been adjudicated. Illegal possession of a firearm, possession of a controlled substance, possession with intent to sell. The list of parole violations went on. It hadn't mattered to the court that he'd been shot. It hadn't mattered that he'd almost died. And it hadn't mattered to them that the only friend he'd ever had in the world was gone.

Pain sliced through his ribs. Devon winced, placing his hand against the wound on his upper chest. It had healed over but was still tender. The first bullet had entered his upper left pectoral, cracking a rib and piercing his lung. The second bullet had only grazed the back of his left shoulder. He must've ducked or slumped forward. Had the second shot also struck his chest, he'd most certainly not be standing here now.

It was all just dumb luck. Whoever had shot them had not stuck around to make sure they finished the job. Maybe they were sloppy. Maybe someone had scared them off. But Devon couldn't recall who the shooter was or anything else of that night prior to being shot. And the things he did recall, he desperately wished he could forget.

But that part haunted his dreams. The storm. The gray, faceless monsters reaching out grotesque, spidery hands. He could see Terrell's face, flushed with a purple tinge, screaming for him as the creature pulled him out of the store. He could feel the alien's elongated fingers tightening around his throat.

And then there were the hallucinations. The tall, thin guy with pasty skin and yellow eyes glaring out from under stringy black hair. Devon would see him every so often in a hallway or the cafeteria. There one moment. Gone the next.

He woke up most nights drenched with sweat, heart pounding, feeling as if someone were choking him. And he would hear voices in the dark whispering words he couldn't quite make out. He didn't know if they were real or just his imagination. But one thing he did know . . .

They weren't going to leave him alone.

He fell in line for breakfast. *Head down, eyes forward. Just stay out of trouble. Stay clear of any scuffles. Don't look anyone in the eyes.*

He had no one from his "community organization" inside. There was no help, no support. Nothing.

He was completely alone.

After breakfast, Devon went to the common area. He still had an hour before classes started. A dozen or so other kids, mostly younger, sat at tables, reading or talking or trying to play checkers.

"Marshall, you got a visitor."

Devon heard the voice, but his eyes remained unfocused on the room. He'd taken a seat apart from everyone else and fallen into a half-dazed funk. He was finding it harder to concentrate lately.

"Hey, Marshall, you hear me?"

The staff guard was large, round, and dark. He took a few menacing steps toward Devon and waved him over.

Devon got up. The guard led him to the secure visitors' room. Dismal gray walls and scuffed beige tiles. A long countertop and a sheet of thick glass split the cramped room in half with video cameras on both sides. A speaker system allowed kids to talk with their POs or lawyers. Or on rare occasions, their parents.

A man in a suit was waiting for him on the other side of the glass. Some white guy. His head was down, like he was reading something.

Devon sat down, thinking it might be the public defender or his probation officer. Then the guy looked up.

Devon stiffened and swore.

The man held up his hands. "Whoa . . . Devon, it—it's all right. It's me." He spoke excitedly. "Do you recognize me?"

Devon slid his chair back a few feet. "Who are you?"

"It's all right; it's all right." The guy leaned forward. "It's me, Conner. Conner Hayden."

Devon shook his head. He couldn't believe that he was seeing this face. "I don't . . . I don't believe you."

"It's crazy, I know. But it was real. That night. The night you got shot. Everything you experienced. It was all real."

"I don't want to talk to you."

"Listen to me." The guy wouldn't quit. "Just listen to me. I was having a heart attack that night. At the same time that you were shot. We were both dying at the same time. We both had the same experience. But we didn't know what was happening."

"Who are you? Why are you doing this to me?" This had to be some kind of trick. Maybe this was the guy who'd shot them. Who'd killed Terrell. Devon slid his chair back farther. "What do you want?"

Conner went on. "And you remember Helen and Mitch? They were real too. Mitch is in a hospital up in Winthrop Harbor. He got in an accident on his motorcycle that same night. He's been in a coma for the last two months. I swear it's all true!"

But Devon was shutting down. This was too crazy. They were doing something to him. Playing some kind of game with him. Maybe trying to get to him. He stood and backed away. "Just stay away from me, you hear me? Stay away!"

"Devon, please. Give me a chance to prove it to you. You don't know the whole story. You don't know what was really going on. I can help you."

Devon turned and pounded on the conference room door. "Get me outta here!"

The guard unlocked the door and poked his head inside.

Devon pointed back at Conner. "Dude's crazy. I don't wanna talk to him."

The guard glanced from Devon to Conner and back to Devon.

Conner knocked against the glass. "Devon, I just want to try to help you," he said. "I can help you."

But Devon shook his head. "I'm done here. Let me out."

They brought him back to his room, where he sat at the edge of his bed, staring at the floor. Snatches of memories raced through his head, like he was standing in the middle of a busy street with cars flying past on either side and he could only catch glimpses of their occupants. Fleeting images and voices. Some of them terrifying. A lake and a farm. A gray sky. Mist rolling in from a forest.

He could almost hear the whispering again. Words he couldn't understand. He stood and peered into the mirror. One half reflected his own harried countenance. But the other . . .

Someone was standing behind him!

Devon spun around. The tiny room was empty. He shot a glance to the mirror again. It was empty now too. But he knew what he'd seen. A tall, gaunt man. Long black hair. Dressed in an old overcoat and dirty trousers. Like a vagrant. Yellow eyes, glowing. Brown teeth, grinning at him.

Devon's heart thudded against his ribs. He'd seen the guy before!

A door has been opened, Devon. . . .

Devon felt the words inside his head. But they weren't his thoughts. It was as if someone else were in the room with him. He peered at the mirror, but his reflection looked strange somehow. His eyes were empty. Solid white. Void of any life or soul, they gazed back at him from a face that felt familiar but looked completely alien.

Devon leaned closer.

The image in the mirror mimicked his movement. But a smirk was spreading across its face.

Devon froze, unable to look away. His reflection grinned at him, lips peeled back. Jaws opened. Black saliva, like ink, dripped from rows of pointed teeth.

A door you can't close.

The image in the mirror lunged forward and Devon fell back onto the floor.

5

MITCH STARED AT THE STRANGER.
The bookstore was silent except
for their breathing. Finally Mitch
said, "Get away? From who?
Howard?"

The stranger nodded. "Yes.
Howard. And that farm. You need to
leave. You're not supposed to be here."

"Not supposed to be here? Where?
Indiana?"

"You're not in Indiana, my
friend."

"I'm not your friend, pal. You don't
even know me." Mitch struggled to
regain his composure. "What say we
start with your name."

The stranger glanced around the

bookstore as if making sure they were alone. Then he said in a low tone, "You can call me Nathan."

"Nathan, huh." Mitch put his hands on his hips. "Where exactly are you from, and how do you know me?"

Nathan moved to the front windows and peered outside. "That's not important right now. What is important is that you believe me. You need to leave. The longer you stay on that farm, the harder it's going to be for you to get back."

"Get back?" Mitch said. "Back where?"

"Back where you came from."

Mitch's jaw tightened. "Dude," he said through his teeth, "you're about five seconds away from tasting my fist. You better start making sense."

Nathan turned back to Mitch, a spark of anger flashing in his eyes. He leaned into Mitch's face and hissed in staccato beats, "You. Are not. Supposed to be here!" He pointed out the window. "Not on that farm. Not in Indiana. Not anywhere here!"

"Fine." Mitch backed up. "Where am I supposed to be?"

"He's trying to keep you here," Nathan went on, ignoring Mitch's question. "He overstepped his bounds, and he knows it. But the longer you stay, the harder it's going to be for you to leave."

"Overstepped what bounds? What are you talking about?"

Nathan rubbed his eyes. "You really don't have a clue where you are?"

Mitch was getting tired of the circular conversation. "If this isn't Indiana, why don't you enlighten me?"

Nathan looked around the store a moment and then motioned for Mitch to follow him. "C'mon."

The guy was searching for something on the walls. He

wasn't looking for books, just shaking his head and muttering to himself. Mitch followed to the back of the store, where Nathan slid a big, gray shelving unit away, exposing a section of bare wall space. He stepped back and looked it over, as if sizing it up for something. Then he produced a small object from his pocket and held it up for Mitch to see. It was a piece of chalk. A thick blue stalk, three or four inches long, like the kind kids used to draw on sidewalks.

Mitch shrugged. "What?"

"You seen any strange things the last few years?"

"One of 'em right now."

"Funny," Nathan grunted. "I mean hallucinations. People . . . weird stuff. Stuff you can't explain. Stuff from your past, maybe? Old memories?"

"Maybe," Mitch said. "What about it?"

Nathan pointed around the room. "This place can take your memories and bring them to life. Your thoughts, nightmares. Your worst fears can take on a life of their own. It can give them form and substance."

"Dude, the aliens are doing that. They love to mess with our heads."

"Yeah, right. Aliens. But you've seen it, right? You've seen stuff you can't explain?"

Mitch shrugged. "Yeah."

"Well, I bet you haven't seen this yet." Nathan proceeded to draw a large circle on the wall with the chalk. About three feet in diameter. Then he stood back.

Mitch stared at it, waiting for something to happen. After a few seconds he raised an eyebrow. "And . . ."

"Shh." Nathan held up a hand and listened.

Then Mitch could hear a soft hissing sound. Wisps of smoke began wafting out from the chalk line. It looked to

Mitch almost as if the chalk dust was burning its way through the drywall. He frowned. "What's that?"

The hissing grew louder, and soon smoke was pouring out along the entire perimeter of the circle. After several seconds it seemed to stop. Nathan put his sunglasses back on and smashed his fist into the center of the circle. The drywall cracked and crumbled away.

Shafts of intense white light sliced through the cracks in the wall. Mitch swore and stepped back, covering his eyes. Nathan pulled the pieces away, and more light shot through the swirls of smoke that lingered in the air.

Mitch could barely see anything. "What is it?"

"Here." Nathan nudged Mitch's arm, holding out another pair of sunglasses.

Mitch could barely see them but managed to slip them on. They blocked the light a bit, enough for him to see a glowing, rippling surface beyond the drywall. It looked like water. Like the surface of a swimming pool standing vertically behind the wall. Defying gravity.

Mitch stared at it, his breath gone. "What . . . what is that?"

"A window," Nathan said. "Just a window. Can you see anything?"

Mitch hesitated; then, drawn by sheer curiosity, he leaned closer. At first he couldn't see anything through the rippling surface. He held out his hand but couldn't feel any heat coming from it. He touched it with the tip of his finger. It felt like solid ice, though it seemed to move like liquid. But his finger couldn't penetrate the surface.

"It's cold," he said. His voice was barely a whisper. "Freezing." He peered at the glowing surface. "I . . . I can't see anything."

"Look closer."

Mitch squinted. He thought he could see something beyond the watery surface. A series of dark blotches, distorted by the waves. But he couldn't make out what they were. He continued to gaze through the hole and eventually the images began to congeal, to form a picture. An entire scene was taking shape.

VALLEY OF THE SHADOW

6

CONNER PAUSED OUTSIDE the main
entrance to the detention facility,
mentally kicking himself. He had
been too eager. He had spent the
last two months tracking Devon
down through the court system,
waiting for the right chance to see
him. And now he had blown it by
just blundering in like that. He had
shocked the kid. He should have
made the initial contact by phone,
but something inside him wanted to
have the first meeting face-to-face.
He should have known better. Conner
shook his head. He wasn't thinking
straight anymore. He should have
known better.

The morning air was crisp, but the late October sky was hard and blue. Cloudless.

Conner started down the steps and passed another man coming up. A man who looked familiar somehow, dressed in jeans and a leather jacket. A beefy, blue-collar type. Conner frowned, stopped, and turned around.

The other man had turned as well. Now Conner placed him. He did know the man after all. "Jim Malone?"

Jim nodded, extending his hand. "Conner, right? How are you? Good to see you up and around."

"Thanks." Conner smiled and shook hands. "Believe me, it's good to be up and around."

Jim chuckled. "I guess you had quite a scare, huh? We heard from your secretary about your . . . y'know, about the heart attack."

Conner patted his chest. "Double bypass. It certainly helps to put things in perspective."

"I guess so." Jim scratched his head. "I'm not sure if you remember, but we were in that same day. Of your heart attack, I mean. Annie and me. We met with you earlier that afternoon."

"Yeah, I remember. I was trying to convince you to move forward with that malpractice lawsuit. As I recall, you had decided to go home and pray about it over the weekend."

"Yeah, well, you could say we were asking God to show us a sign. We were real confused and weren't sure if we should go ahead with it."

Conner raised an eyebrow. "A sign, huh?"

Jim shrugged sheepishly. "Well, we didn't ask specifically for Him to give you a heart attack or anything, but when we heard about it on Monday . . . well, we kinda figured maybe God was trying to tell us something."

Conner found himself chuckling at that thought. "Do me a favor. Next time ask for something a little less dramatic, will you?"

Jim laughed.

Conner nodded back toward the building. "So, what brings you here? Are you visiting someone too?"

"Yeah, uh . . ." Jim looked up at the facility. "To tell you the truth, I'm not sure exactly what I'm doing here. Just trying to make a connection with one of the kids, I guess."

"Me too," Conner said. "Just an acquaintance really, some kid who got in with the wrong crowd, I think. I thought maybe I could be of some help, but unfortunately, I think I may have just made things worse. I don't think I'm cut out for this kind of stuff."

"Yeah." Jim looked down and sighed. "Yeah, I know what you mean."

They both fell into an awkward silence for a moment. Conner didn't really know the guy well enough to make further small talk, and frankly he was going to be late getting to the office as it was.

He turned to leave. "Well anyway, nice to see you again. I hope you have better luck than I did. Take care."

VALLEY OF THE SHADOW

MITCH GAZED DEEPER into the stranger's window of liquid light. He could see the images more clearly now.

"There's . . . like, another room back there," Mitch said. "Some kind of room."

Nathan stood still. "Good. See anything else? any details? What kind of room?"

Mitch squinted, pushed the dark glasses tighter against his face. "Umm . . . I see something. A bed, I think. And some other stuff . . ." Then he straightened up. "It's a hospital room."

Nathan moved closer. "Can you see the bed?"

"Yeah . . ." The surface seemed to grow calm, and the entire room came into focus. Someone was lying on the bed. Mitch could see a network of tubes, lines, and monitors behind it. He couldn't quite see the person's face. It was wrapped in gauze. The person was big—too big to be a woman or a child. It was definitely a man.

There was some kind of picture on the patient's arm. A tattoo. In fact there were multiple tattoos, the biggest one resembling a snake coiled around the upper arm. Though not exactly a snake . . . more like a dragon. A Chinese dragon wrapping around his arm, jaws open wide, fangs bared, horns curling up from its head . . .

It looked like . . . exactly like Mitch's tattoo. On his arm!

Mitch lurched away from the window. "This is some kind of trick," he said. "Just another hallucination."

Nathan grabbed Mitch's arm. "It's no trick. Look again!"

Mitch saw movement through the portal. Someone had just come into the room. It looked like a doctor. He leaned over the bedside and touched Mitch's head.

Mitch frowned. "Who's that?"

"Listen," Nathan hushed him again.

Mitch could hear another voice, echoing softly, as if far off in a vast canyon.

"Mitch."

The doctor took a clipboard off the foot of the bed and began reading. Mitch instinctively moved sideways for a better view, and the entire scene inside the window rotated along with him. Almost as if Mitch was able to turn and get a three-dimensional view of the room through the portal. Mitch had a clear view of the doctor's face now. He gasped.

"Conner?"

Mitch hadn't seen the guy in five years, but he was sure

that was Conner Hayden. Why was he dressed like a doctor? Mitch reeled. He watched Conner replace the clipboard and lean down again. Mitch could hear his voice better now. More distinct.

"I'm not going to let you die."

Mitch pounded the wall with his fist. "Conner!"

Suddenly the image went black.

Mitch backed away and pulled off his glasses. The hole in the wall now revealed only some wiring and part of a wooden stud behind it. The light and the watery surface were gone. It looked like just an ordinary hole in an ordinary wall. His brows curled down, and he turned to Nathan. "Where did it go?"

"These windows only last a few minutes." Nathan removed his glasses and shook his head. "Think what you want to think, but I'm telling you it's the truth."

Mitch inspected the hole. There was no sign of water or any electronic devices. Nothing to explain what he'd just seen. "I don't believe you. Give me one good reason why I should believe you."

"What's the last thing you remember? I mean . . . all those years ago, before everything started going crazy. Do you remember?"

Mitch tried to think back. He ran a hand through his hair. "I . . . uh . . . I was going to pick up Linda. My girlfriend. I was going to pick her up from work. I was going to propose. Had a ring and everything."

"It was a big night."

"I had my bike. I just got my Harley running. I wanted to surprise her."

"And then?"

Mitch paused. It was all hazy after so many years. He

had ridden north and then . . . He shrugged. "Then I saw the storm."

"You never made it to see your girlfriend," Nathan said.

"Because of the storm."

"No, because a Dodge pickup truck crossed into your lane and sent you flying into a ditch."

Mitch's lips tightened. "No, it didn't."

"You broke three ribs, fractured your pelvis, and sustained severe head injuries. Someone called an ambulance."

"Shut up!"

"They brought you to the hospital, but you had lost a lot of blood. They put you on a ventilator. They've been monitoring your brain scans, looking for the slightest glimmer of hope. Any sign that you might still be in there."

"I said shut up!"

Nathan grabbed Mitch by the collar. "That was two months ago! You've been here only two months!"

Mitch shook himself free and shoved Nathan aside. He stumbled to the front of the store, his chest heaving. The room seemed to sway beneath him. This was crazy. He couldn't listen to any more of this nonsense. He wouldn't.

Nathan drew up beside him. "This place . . . this isn't Indiana. It's like a movie set. It's all just a facade. Your body is lying in a hospital room in Illinois. In a coma. But your soul has gotten trapped here. In this place."

"I can't believe it."

Nathan continued. "Think about it. All the weird stuff you've seen here? This place does that to you. You see what you want to see. It even shows you stuff you don't want to see. Old memories. Dreams, nightmares. All of that can take on what seems like real form."

"Are you saying I'm dead?"

"No. Not yet. This place is just like a doorway. When someone dies, they usually pass right through to the other side. But
sometimes people get stuck in between. Trapped here. Not
dead but not really alive, either." He pointed at the hole in the
wall. "You're being kept alive—barely. But there's still some
hope. That's why you need to get back into your body. The
longer you stay here, the harder that's going to be. The less
chance you'll have of surviving at all."

Mitch turned away. This conversation was beyond bizarre.
He had been here for five years. He could remember every day.
Every book he'd read. How was that possible? "There's no way
it's only been two months."

Nathan's voice softened. "Time doesn't have any meaning
in this place. Not like it does in the material world. I know you
think it's been years, but it's only been two months since your
accident."

"How do you know all this?"

Nathan paused. "I've been sent to help you. To help you
find your way back."

"Sent by who?"

"God."

Mitch laughed. "Dude, God doesn't care what happens
to me."

"Yeah, I know that line. I've heard it all before. The fact is
He does care, Mitch. More than you know. I've got to help you
get out before it's too late."

"Too late for what?"

"Survival," Nathan said. "The longer a spirit remains
separated from its body, the less chance there is for the body
to heal. You've suffered major injuries, but there's still some
hope you might recover. That's why you have to leave that
farm. And we have to get going as soon as possible."

Mitch rubbed his eyes. His head was throbbing. "I can't take this anymore. Why should I trust you anyway? Howard hasn't done anything to hurt me. Other than being a little quirky and a terrible cribbage player, he's not all that bad. And we've managed to keep the aliens away. Give me one good reason why I should trust you."

At that point, the milk truck rumbled up in front of the store and its horn blared. Mitch moved to the window and peered out.

Howard waved at him. "C'mon, Hoss. The day's a-wastin'."

Mitch nodded and waved. "So," he grunted and turned back to Nathan, "give me one good reas—"

But the store was empty. Nathan—whoever he was—had vanished.

8

Jim Malone signed in at the main desk and made his way through the security gauntlet of the corrections facility. He produced a letter and some additional paperwork from his pocket, along with two forms of ID, and slid them to the woman behind the counter inside the first set of locked doors.

She was black, stout, and gruff looking. A mop of glistening dark curls hung low, just over her eyes. She squeezed the last bit of a cream cheese–laden bagel into her mouth and scanned the papers for several seconds. Then she curled an eyebrow at Jim.

Jim shrugged. "His . . . uh, his

probation officer said it was okay. Just to talk for a few minutes. He said to bring you this letter, and he said you could call him if you needed to."

"Popular kid," the woman grunted through a mouthful of bagel and pressed a button beneath the desk. The door to Jim's left buzzed. "C'mon through."

Jim pushed the door, left his keys and wallet inside a basket at the desk, and followed another guard to an elevator. They rode this up to the third floor and walked another hall to a cramped room divided in two by a counter with a thick glass window. Gray walls, beige tiles, smelling of a nauseating mixture of body odor, bleach, and floor wax.

"Wait here." The guard motioned for Jim to take a seat at the counter. Chrome, gooseneck microphones and plastic speakers were mounted on each side of the glass. The guard took the paperwork and left the room.

Jim was alone and felt a sudden wave of emotion wash over him. The walls seemed to draw close around him, like a trash compactor. The place felt cramped, stuffy, and dismal. A sterile, white clock clicked softly on the wall behind him. Several minutes went by. Jim kept an eye on the metal door on the other side of the room. His claustrophobic sense grew stronger and he found himself almost short of breath.

Another minute creaked by. Still no one came through the door. Jim could hear muffled sounds coming from beyond the walls. Coarse laughter mixed with angry, high-pitched rants and deep, barked orders. All probably quite normal for this place, but still it gave Jim a growing sense of despair. What would it be like to live in this place? Even for a few days?

Three more minutes passed, and at last the gray door across the room opened. A lanky youth stood in the doorway with a brawny figure looming behind him. The guard gave the kid a slight shove into the room, then pulled the door shut again, leaving the kid alone.

Jim vaguely recognized the boy's face. He'd gotten his name from the newspaper and had made initial contact with the probation officer.

Devon Marshall. Sixteen years old. Mother was an alcoholic. Father deceased. Devon had been arrested twice, once for possession of a controlled substance and the second time for selling it.

Devon stared straight ahead, not making eye contact and looking dazed or maybe drugged or something. He stood by the door for several seconds, then shuffled over and slouched into the chair across from Jim.

Was this one-way glass? The kid was acting like he couldn't even see him. Jim leaned toward the microphone. "Uh . . . can you . . . can you hear me?"

Devon stared at the glass. Not through it at Jim, just at the glass itself. Maybe at his own reflection. Jim frowned. What had they done to him?

"Are you okay?"

Devon didn't say a word.

"My name is Jim. Uh . . . Jim Malone. You don't know me, but I . . ." Jim suddenly found himself at a loss for words. It was an awkward enough situation, but now even more so with Devon's bizarre behavior. "I found you. Two months ago, when you were shot. I happened to be walking by and I saw you. You and your friend inside the car. I called 911. And I . . ."

Devon's face was a mask of indifference.

Jim went on. "You weren't breathing, and I performed CPR on you until the cops came."

Still no response.

Jim sat back a moment. This wasn't right. Maybe he'd

had some kind of brain damage. This wasn't normal behavior. "Look, I don't want anything from you. I just . . . I just wanted to talk to you. Just once."

He paused again and swallowed. His mouth was dry. "I wanted to say that I'm sorry about your friend. I was all alone. I couldn't save both of you. I got you out of the car and tried to help you. I called for help, but nobody else was around. . . ."

Devon's gaze flickered slightly. Up into the glass, as if searching for something.

Jim saw the reaction and leaned closer. "I'm sorry about your friend. I really am. I could only help one of you. By the time the cops came, he was already . . . It . . . it was too late."

Devon's gaze drifted across the glass, finally locking onto Jim's face. He peered through the glass into Jim's eyes.

Jim felt a chill crawl down his spine. It wasn't a friendly look. He tried again. "I had to choose. I don't know why I went over to your side of the car, to pull you out."

Devon's lips parted. A soft voice whispered, "You let him die."

Jim blinked and stared for a moment. "I—I couldn't help you both. I'm sorry. I really am. I could only help one of you."

The sight of the other kid's body lying beneath the blue sheet had haunted Jim's dreams nearly every night. The whole scene played itself out in his sleep. Over and over.

Devon stood up and leaned forward, pressing his hand to the window. The glass creaked and turned white as crystals of frost appeared at his fingertips. "You let him die." Another patch of frost appeared where his breath wafted onto the glass. It spread outward from his hands, creeping up to the ceiling and down to the countertop.

Jim slid his chair away, staring at Devon, now half-hidden

behind a thin veil of ice. A blast of cold air hit Jim's face, as though the AC had suddenly kicked on full throttle. Or more like he'd just stepped into a walk-in refrigerator. He could see the steamy tendrils of his own breath curling up in front of him now.

He caught one last glimpse of Devon's face. Eyes completely white, lips peeled back. Saliva foamed between his clenched teeth and dripped down his chin. His head began to jitter. Then his entire body shook.

Then he fell backward onto the floor.

"Help!" Jim found his voice again. He jumped up and pounded against the glass. "Somebody help him!"

VALLEY OF THE SHADOW

9

MITCH STARED OUT THE WINDOW,
watching the empty fields roll past.
Mile after mile of gray, lifeless countryside stretched out, it seemed, forever.
Howard was whistling again. They
were taking a different route back to
the farm so they could stop at the gas
station for oil and whatever food they
could scrounge up.

But Mitch's thoughts were wrapped
around the stranger he had seen in the
bookstore. And the bizarre scene he'd
witnessed through the hole in the wall.

He hadn't mentioned anything to
Howard. Nathan had said Howard was
not to be trusted, but Mitch wasn't
completely convinced Nathan could be

either. The guy seemed to know quite a bit about what was happening. But it could have all been a trick. Mitch had seen that kind of tactic before numerous times. For all he knew, this Nathan guy was just another of the aliens' attempts to get him to leave the farm.

Still . . .

"So, uh . . . so I was thinking," he said as nonchalantly as he could. "It'd be nice to get away for a day or two. Maybe take a little vacation or something."

Howard choked off his tune. His weedy gray eyebrows scrunched together as he threw Mitch a sideways glance. "Vacation? Are you tryin' to be funny?"

Mitch shrugged. "What's so funny about that? Nothing real long. Just a day or so. Just to get away for a bit. Y'know, go for a ride."

Howard laughed and shook his head. "This ain't no pleasure cruise you're on, Hoss. Those aliens mean business. They're everywhere. Whutch you gonna do at night? Fend 'em off with a flashlight?"

Mitch turned back to the window. "Don't know. I'll think of something. I'm just getting cabin fever, y'know?"

"Plus we ain't exactly in no position to go wasting gas willy-nilly like that. Just drivin' around for the fun of it."

"It'd be a good way to scout around. Who knows. Maybe there are other people out there like us. Holed up in compounds, thinking they're the only ones left."

Howard was still shaking his head. "That's awful risky, goin' off on your own like that. If you want a change of scenery, what say we load up the milk truck, bring along a couple generators and some lights. At least be smart about it."

"Yeah . . ." Mitch felt his jaw tensing. "See, I was thinking it'd be nice to get away on my own."

"On your own? It's not like we're fightin' off crowds here, son. It's just the two of us."

"Yeah, well . . ." Mitch's voiced softened. "Sometimes it's nice to just get away by yourself. Don't you ever feel that way?"

"Mmmm . . . not really, no. I've had enough bein' alone." Howard's fingers drummed the steering wheel lightly. "You . . . uh, you ain't mad at me or anything, are you? Did I do something to offend you?"

"No, I'm not mad." Mitch sighed, thinking he'd better drop the subject for now. "I guess I just saw those Harleys back there and . . . y'know, got the itch to ride again. Forget I brought it up."

"'Cuz if I did anything to get you mad . . ."

"Dude, I'm not mad."

"I know I can be a little obnoxious sometimes. Least that's what my wife used to say."

"Look, just forget I brought it up."

They turned into the quick mart, and Mitch took the flashlight and made his way inside. They had already picked the shelves pretty clean of food over the last year or so, but there were still plenty of auto supplies left: antifreeze, windshield cleaner, and several cases of Valvoline far back in the stockroom. Mitch slid the cases off the shelf and spotted another box shoved into the corner. An unopened box of ranch-flavored corn nuts. Twenty bags.

"Corn nuts." He grinned. "Jackpot."

He was reaching for the box when a deep moan rattled through the store as if a gust of wind had blown past the building. The stockroom door slammed shut, cutting off all the daylight from the store. Darkness fell around Mitch like a blanket, but he could sense someone . . . something else in the room with him. A soft rustling like a flutter of movement.

A chill rushed down his spine. A sensation he hadn't felt in a while. A long while. It was the feeling he'd had during his hallucinations—the creepy visions he'd had when this whole nightmare had first begun nearly five years ago. But they had occurred with less frequency after Helen and Conner disappeared. And eventually, as he had settled into his dismal routine on the farm, they had ceased altogether.

Mitch dropped the cases of oil and reached for his flashlight. This couldn't be happening again. Not again.

He snapped the light on and aimed it toward the doorway. And gasped.

The light fell onto the pale, gaunt face of a graying man. Mitch knew this face.

His mouth went dry. His throat felt like sandpaper as he tried to speak.

"Dad?"

IT WAS NINE THIRTY when Conner arrived at his office. His calendar displayed a relatively light schedule for the day, as it had for the last few weeks. Nancy had made a concerted effort to ease him into a full workload since he'd been back. Furthermore, her sarcasm and lawyer jokes had completely ceased. And she had gone out of her way to make sure he always had everything he needed, even before he knew he needed it. Files, faxes, phone numbers—it was uncanny and a little unnerving. But he wasn't ready to complain just yet. He rather liked this new Nancy.

Conner poured a cup of coffee from

the espresso machine in the lounge, then stopped by Gus Brady's office to say good morning. Gus was one of those guys whose clothes never fit quite right and who always looked just a little too tall for ordinary furniture. He sat hunched at his desk, typing furiously.

He glanced up from his laptop and flashed a quick smile when Conner knocked on the door. "Hey, Connie."

They had been friends since law school. In fact, it was Gus's influence that had gotten Conner his chance to join the firm twelve years earlier.

Conner leaned against the doorjamb. "You'll never guess who I saw this morning."

Gus stared at him for a moment, his eyes shifting across the room. He shook his head.

"Jim Malone," Conner said. "Remember the Malones?"

Gus's forehead puckered, then released. "Oh yeah, the malpractice." Then it puckered again. "They prayed themselves out of a fortune, as I recall. Us too."

Conner chuckled. "I guess that's one way to look at it."

"Well . . ." Gus snorted and went back to his computer. "That's how I look at it."

Conner hesitated a moment, pondering whether or not to press a little further. "You know, there was a time I might have looked at it that way too. But these days, I'm tending to be a little more open-minded."

Gus raised an eyebrow but didn't look up. "Open-minded?"

"You know . . . about them praying about their decision. I guess I'm putting a little more stock in that sort of stuff these days."

Gus didn't answer and still wasn't looking up. Conner could see a flush of red rising up his neck and across his cheeks. He ventured a little further. "I mean . . . you gotta admire that kind of faith, right?"

"Oh, man!" Gus glanced at his watch and swore under his breath. "Y'know . . . I forgot I have to jump on a conference call." He reached for his phone. "Sorry, Connie, I totally forgot about it."

"No problem."

Conner nodded and backed out of Gus's doorway, pulling the door shut. That seemed to be the way every conversation with Gus had gone since Conner had returned to work. Whenever Conner tried to steer their conversation toward his heart attack, or any religious topic for that matter, Gus would always manage to cut him off with some suddenly remembered meeting or call. It had gotten to the point where he wasn't even trying to be creative anymore.

Though it wasn't just Gus. Nearly everyone at the firm seemed to treat him differently since he'd been back. Conversations would fade the moment he turned a corner or walked into a room. People would gain a sudden interest in whatever folder or notepad they happened to be holding at the moment. Most would make furtive but hasty exits.

At first Conner thought he was just being paranoid, but lately he could sense genuine discomfort around him, as if no one knew quite how to treat him anymore. No one seemed to want to talk about the fact that he had nearly died. Maybe he'd been a little too forward about the whole thing. Or maybe he was just an unwelcome reminder of their mortality.

Conner had managed to share his story with nearly everyone at the firm over the last three weeks, though he hadn't given them all the details. Only what he had already shared with Marta. And while he didn't want to come across as macabre, it seemed to be the perfect opportunity to share his newfound faith as well. After all, wasn't that what he was supposed to be doing? At least he assumed that was one of the reasons he'd been spared.

It was serious business after all. Eternity. Conner was surprised—and saddened—at how little thought most people seemed to give the topic. Death was the one thing they could be certain of, yet they acted as though ignorance would make them live forever.

And he had been the same way. But no longer. He had witnessed the darkness firsthand. He had stood on the brink of eternity and gazed deep into the abyss. His pride and self-sufficiency were gone, and he desperately wanted his friends to know how his stoic agnosticism had finally melted away to faith.

Though not a blind faith. To his surprise, Conner had discovered plenty of evidence for this carpenter who had risen from the dead. It was there for anyone willing to examine it with an open mind. Yet for all his efforts, no one ever seemed very interested. No one responded with anything more than a polite smile and nod. And then an excuse to make a quick getaway.

It seemed the harder he tried, the more they avoided him.

It was just after ten o'clock when Henry Brandt called Conner into his office. Henry was the senior partner at the firm and a longtime mentor since college. He was semiretired, in the office three days a week. Though in his seventies, Henry still carried a lean, athletic build. He had just returned from a trip to Maui, and against his tanned skin, his neatly cropped white hair looked positively angelic.

Conner had always admired the man. Henry's agnosticism had been deeply influential during Conner's college years. Because of this, Henry Brandt was the one person with whom

Conner had been too intimidated to discuss his faith. Not that he regretted his decision, but he couldn't shake the feeling that somehow he had let the man down.

Henry leaned back from his wide mahogany desk as Conner flopped into the leather armchair with a snort of exasperation. "How are you doing, Connie?"

"Fine." Conner took a breath and held it a moment, not sure how to proceed. Then he puffed out his cheeks in a sigh. "Actually, I've never felt better."

Henry nodded. "Well, I'm glad to hear that. But I didn't ask how you were feeling; I asked how you were doing."

This was typical Henry Brandt sophistry. *Feeling. Doing.* What was the difference? At length, Conner shrugged. "In that case, maybe not so good."

Henry only smiled. "Having trouble getting back into the swing of things?"

"In a manner of speaking. Nancy's turned into a Stepford secretary—not that I'm complaining, mind you. But I can't help feeling that some people here are avoiding me."

Henry gazed into the distance for a moment. Then he drew a breath. "Look, I'll be frank with you."

"Please."

"I think you're making some folks here a little . . . uncomfortable."

"Uncomfortable? What do you mean?"

"Well . . ." Henry rubbed his jaw. Conner could see he was trying to choose his words carefully. "Some of them think you're becoming a bit of a . . . well, a zealot."

Conner blinked, then chuckled. "A zealot? C'mon, Henry . . ."

"Connie, you've gone from being a hard-core skeptic to the apostle Paul in a matter of weeks. Didn't you think that might be a little disconcerting to some of your friends?"

"Look, maybe I've been a little overeager," Conner said. "But I'm not trying to preach at anyone. I just want to share what I experienced that night. I almost died, Henry. It had a profound effect on me and my outlook on life. I think it's a pretty important subject. I mean, we're all going to die sooner or—"

"See . . ." Henry held up a hand. "That's the thing. People don't like to talk about death all the time."

"I don't talk about it all the time."

"Well, they say you're sounding obsessed."

Conner frowned. "You've had complaints?"

Henry shook his head. "Just overheard bits of conversations."

Conner sat back and folded his arms. "Well, I wouldn't describe it as obsessed. I just think in general we should be more aware of the fact that none of us knows how much time we have."

"We're all aware of that, Connie. Most of us just try not to dwell on it so much. It's a depressing subject."

"*Depressing* isn't quite how I would describe it. More like *terrifying*."

Henry sighed. "These so-called near-death experiences are actually quite common for people in your situation. And easily explained . . ."

"Not mine."

"Look, I'm not trying to repress your need to talk about what was obviously a very traumatic experience."

"Henry . . ." Conner leaned forward. It was time to lay his cards on the table. "You don't know the whole story. I mean of what I went through. This wasn't some hallucination or a bunch of random brain synapses. And I can prove it."

Henry blinked. Then frowned. "How?"

"When I was dying, this place where I found myself . . .
I wasn't alone there. I met five other people who were all
dying too. All at the same time."

"What people?"

"I had Nancy look them up. After the heart attack, I called
from the hospital and gave her a list of names: Helen Krause,
Mitch Kent, Devon Marshall, Ray Cahill, and Howard Bristol.
These people are real. I had never met them before. Had no
knowledge of them. But they were all dying too, at the exact
time I was having my heart attack. And we all crossed paths in
that . . . that place."

"What are you talking about?"

Conner hesitated. It had been hard enough to share the
details of his experience with Marta; how could he possibly
let Henry know? For two months, he'd kept it secret. Bottled
up. Afraid of what people might think. But maybe that was the
point. Maybe God was wanting him to share it. No matter how
crazy it made him look.

He took a breath . . . and a leap of faith. Then, starting
from the beginning, he relayed all the details of his experience. The storm, the creatures, the seizures, the mysterious
boy who had saved him. Everything. Henry listened without
interruption. Almost without expression. He just sat there and
stared at Conner.

When Conner had finished, Henry said nothing. His gaze
lowered.

After a moment, Conner said, "Well? What do you think?"

Henry took a deep breath and shook his head. "I think I'd
like you to take some more time off."

Conner narrowed his eyes. "You don't believe me? Check
with Nancy. I'll give you the list. Check for yourself—"

"We can handle things here. I'll put in a few more hours if I have to."

Conner sat back and laughed. "Henry, I have evidence. Just check out the names. These people actually existed. You don't hallucinate that type of stuff."

"And I want you to see someone. A professional. Get some help, Connie."

Conner's jaw tightened. "I'm not crazy, Henry."

"I'm not saying you are. But there's obviously something seriously wrong. And as your friend, I'm asking you to get help."

"What are you afraid of? That it might all be true?"

"This isn't about me, Connie. This is about you. I want you to get some counseling."

Conner now saw an older version of his former self in Henry Brandt. Denying the possibility that something might exist for which there was no scientific explanation. Not even willing to examine the evidence. For all his intellect, Henry really wasn't open-minded at all.

Conner clenched the armrests of his chair. "Y'know, Henry, you're going to be dead a lot longer than you've been alive. I just think you should know what you're getting into."

Henry fell silent again. This time he stared directly at Conner. So long, in fact, that Conner began to squirm. He lowered his gaze, feeling like an upstart wolf pup in the presence of the pack's alpha male.

At length, Henry spoke. "This is obviously interfering with your ability to perform your job."

"Henry, I don't need—"

"Connie." Henry Brandt wasn't smiling. "As your boss, I'm telling you. Take another week. In fact, make it two. Give your-self some time to get your head right."

MITCH STARED AT HIS FATHER in the darkness of the stockroom.

Walter Kent gazed back at him. His face was pale but darkened around his eyes. His lips seemed to tremble at the sight of Mitch.

Mitch backed away, the flashlight shaking in his hands. But his fear was slowly surrendering to anger. What did the man want after all these years? Why had he invaded Mitch's oasis? In some ways, Mitch had found a measure of peace in this dismal Indiana solitude. For while part of him hated the farm, still he found himself clinging to it like a tattered life preserver on the open ocean. He knew it wouldn't keep him afloat forever, yet he didn't dare think of letting go.

Mitch clenched his teeth. "What do you want?"

His father's brow furrowed. He took a step toward Mitch, his eyes glaring. "Why did you do it?"

"What are you talking about?"

"You killed her, Mitch. Why did you do it?"

An image flashed into Mitch's memory like the muzzle flare of a gunshot. The sight of his mother—thin arms flailing, struggling to breathe—and Mitch as a fourteen-year-old boy, standing over her. Sobbing. Forcing the pillow over her face.

Mitch pressed himself against the wall of the stockroom. "Leave me alone!"

His father took another step. "She was your mother!"

Mitch straightened up. "She was already dead!"

"She gave birth to you! She loved you!"

"She was suffering. You couldn't see that? How much pain she was in? No, you were too busy to notice! I put her out of her misery."

His father's eyes widened, then narrowed. His lips parted and he hissed, "That wasn't your choice to make. You played God."

"Somebody had to!"

In the beam of the flashlight, Mitch spotted a metal can on the shelf beside him. He grabbed it and hurled it at the image of his father, but it crashed against the door. Mitch swept the light across the room. His father—or whatever it was—was gone.

Mitch sank against the wall. His eyes stung as he fought his tears. He wouldn't cry. Whatever these aliens were doing, he wasn't going to give them the satisfaction. He wouldn't let them manipulate him like this.

After a minute, his breathing slowed. He got to his feet, picked up the cases of oil, and brought them out to the truck.

Howard was sitting in the cab, staring straight ahead. Fingers drumming on the wheel.

"Sorry," Mitch mumbled as he climbed into the truck. "I had to . . . It took a little longer than I thought."

They pulled onto the highway and headed back to the farm in silence. Mitch struggled to push the images of these most recent hallucinations out of his mind. First this Nathan character and now his father. But more than anything else, what Mitch found troubling was how long it'd been since something like this had haunted him. Why now? Why after all this time had he started to see things again? Was something happening to him? Were the aliens trying a different tack?

He sighed and rubbed his eyes, pondering whether he should share these events with Howard. He glanced at the old farmer. But Howard had stopped whistling and was staring, blank-faced, at the road ahead.

Mitch could sense that he'd somehow offended the old man with his talk of a vacation. He sighed again and scratched the back of his neck. "Look . . . dude. Really, it wasn't anything personal. It's no big deal. I don't need a vacation. I just got the itch . . ."

Mitch stopped and frowned. He could see Howard wasn't paying attention. Rather, the old man was now squinting at the road in front of them. A light afternoon fog had begun to settle and was starting to cramp visibility. Mitch peered into the mist and could see a vehicle up ahead, pulled off to the side of the road.

A lone figure stood next to it, waving to them.

VALLEY OF THE SHADOW

JIM MALONE FOUND HIMSELF sitting in the office of the corrections facility's assistant director, waiting for the man to arrive. At least he assumed it was a man. The name on the door read *D. Curtis* in black letters on the opaque glass. Steel file cabinets loaded with books and periodicals lined the walls on either side of the small room. Piles of manila folders were stacked precariously at the edges of the bulky metal desk. And amid the desktop clutter were a pair of wire baskets, also crammed with paperwork, and an old-style black rotary telephone.

Jim felt as if he'd been catapulted back in time to the seventies.

Then the door opened and the assistant director entered: an enormous black man, built more like a pro football player than an administrator. He stood well over six feet with beefy shoulders and chest and an ample stomach. His white pin-striped shirt was tight around his girth and only partially tucked into his belt. His head was shaved and he sported a thick salt-and-pepper goatee. He was perusing a folder through rectangular, black-rimmed reading glasses perched at the edge of his nose. Jim guessed it was Devon's file.

He sidled past Jim, squeezed around behind his desk, and sat down, looking almost comical, as if sitting in a child-size school desk. At first he ignored Jim, his eyes fixed on the folder in front of him. Then he sighed and looked up at Jim over his glasses.

"Mr. Malone, I'm Darnell Curtis." His voice was about as deep as Jim would've expected from a man that size. He reached a large, meaty hand across the desk. "Thanks for sticking around to talk to me."

"No problem." Jim shook his hand. "I told them every-thing I know. Devon was acting strange from the moment he entered. Like he was in a daze. I thought he might've been drugged or something."

"Devon was not medicated," Darnell said, glancing at the folder. He rubbed the top of his clean-shaven head. "You mind explaining exactly how you know this young man?"

"Well . . ." Jim hesitated a moment. "I don't really know him. I was the one who called 911 when he was shot a couple months back."

"But you didn't see who shot him?"

"I spoke to the police several times. I told them everything I knew. I just saw a black sedan drive away. I didn't see the plates or anything."

"So why the visit today?"

"Well . . . ," Jim began with some hesitation. He could see how this might look a bit suspicious. "I got permission from his probation officer. I know Devon's had it kind of rough lately, and I was just trying to help. I don't want anything from him. I just thought he could use some company. Y'know, a friend."

"That's nice of you," Darnell said, his eyes still on the folder. "We always appreciate it when the community— churches and that—get involved to help these kids. That's a good thing."

Jim shrugged. "Like I said, I wasn't expecting anything from him. I just wanted to touch base. I wanted to tell him I was sorry about his friend."

Darnell looked up. "His friend?"

"Yeah. See, that night he was shot, there were two kids in the car. I pulled Devon out and did CPR until the cops came, but I couldn't save his friend. I could only help one of them. And by the time the paramedics arrived, his friend was already gone. They couldn't save him."

"I understand."

Jim went on. "And it's been bothering me. I mean, I made a choice that night—I didn't think about it at the time, but I realized later that I had chosen which one of those boys lived and which one died." He looked down. "It's been a little hard dealing with that. I just wanted to let him know I was sorry . . . about his friend."

"Mm-hmm." Darnell leaned back and nodded to himself. He was quiet for several more seconds, rubbing his jaw. "So did you see Devon ingest anything while he was with you this morning?"

"No. I told the guard, I didn't see him put anything in his mouth."

Darnell sat up, closed the folder, and tapped his fingers on it. "What about all the water on the window?"

"The window?" Jim recalled the frost that had appeared on the glass out of nowhere and the sharp chill he had felt just before Devon's seizure. It was creepy and he had no explanation for it. At least nothing that made much sense. "I . . . I don't really know. It was like condensation, I think."

Darnell's frown deepened. "Condensation?"

"Well, I didn't mention it earlier, but for a few seconds it got real cold in there. Like the AC suddenly kicked in super high or something."

"The air-conditioning?"

"Just for a few seconds. The glass looked like it frosted up."

Darnell rubbed his scalp again, then slid his hand down to his jaw. "Frosted up, huh? No, you didn't mention that."

Jim looked down. "Well, it just seemed so weird, I didn't think anyone would believe me."

"Hmm," Darnell grunted and stared at Jim for several seconds longer. "So did Devon mention anything about the lawyer he met with earlier?"

"Lawyer? No. Like I said, he didn't really say anything." Then his eyebrows went up. "Wait . . . you mean Conner Hayden?" Had they both come to see the same kid?

"So you do know him."

Jim gave a nervous laugh. "No . . . not really. It's just that we—my wife and I—had met with him a couple months ago to discuss some legal issues. Then I happened to run into him on my way in this morning. Just by total coincidence, really. He said he had come to talk to one of the kids. I didn't even think to ask who. I just assumed . . ."

Darnell leaned forward. "Did he say anything? give you

any details? Because apparently Devon took one look at him and just freaked out. He didn't even want to meet the guy."

Jim shook his head. "I . . . I'm sorry. I don't know how they know each other."

Suddenly the old telephone rang and Darnell picked it up. "Darnell." He listened for a moment. "When?" His lips tightened and he spun his chair to face the wall. "Did anyone get hurt? . . . Okay, I'll be right down."

He hung up the phone and stood. "Mr. Malone, would you be available if we need to contact you with further questions?"

"Sure," Jim said, sliding his chair over to give the big man room to get around him. "Why? What's wrong?"

Darnell paused in the doorway. "It seems our friend Mr. Marshall isn't quite as sick as we thought. And maybe a little smarter too."

"What happened?"

"That was the nurse from our infirmary. She had called an ambulance to transfer Devon to the hospital. And when they arrived at the hospital, he miraculously revived and managed to escape."

VALLEY OF THE SHADOW

13

HOWARD ROLLED TO A STOP on the highway in front of the solitary figure.

He was young, Mitch guessed. Probably in his early twenties, with short dark hair, thick eyebrows, not terribly tall but with an athletic build. His face seemed to light up as he studied Mitch and Howard. He was talking up a storm even before they had gotten out of the truck.

"Man, am I glad to see you guys!" He came around to Mitch and stuck out a hand. "I've been on the run for two days now. D'you know what's going on? It's like an invasion or something, right?"

He shook Mitch's hand firmly. And repeatedly. Like a jackhammer.

Mitch shrugged, casting a glance at Howard. "Well, some-thing like that . . ."

"Name's Jason Devina. St. Louis."

"Uhh, yeah . . ." Mitch pulled his hand free. "I'm Mitch."

Howard waved. "Bristol. Howard Bristol."

Jason stood back, shaking his head. "I can't tell you how glad I am to see you guys. I thought I was like the last man on earth, y'know?"

"Well, I can assure you that ain't the case," Howard said.

"So, you guys heard anything? any news? What's going on?"

Mitch scratched his head. "Actually . . . we don't know a whole lot more than you do at this point. You say you're from St. Louis?"

Jason nodded, smiling. Still breathing heavy from relief. "Yeah, boy. I was driving home from work a couple nights ago. Well, I had stopped off at a bar first. But I'm driving down this empty highway when I see this cloud up ahead. Coming right toward me! Some kind of lights inside it. Like a UFO, y'know?"

"Sounds familiar," Howard said, looking sideways at Mitch.

Then Jason grew serious. He lowered his voice. "Have you guys seen any . . . you know, any . . ."

"Aliens?" Mitch was nodding. "Yeah. We've seen them."

Jason thrust his palms onto his forehead. "Oh man, I thought I was going nuts or something. Creepy-looking things. I mean . . . real creepy!"

Howard gestured toward Jason's car. A black Porsche. "You run outta gas?"

"Yeah . . . and there's no power around here. I couldn't find any gas for miles."

"Well . . ." Howard stuck a thumb over his shoulder. "I got

a place up the road a ways. It ain't much, but we got food and shelter. You're welcome to join us if you'd like."

Jason was already pulling a duffel bag out of the Porsche. "Thanks, man!"

The three of them climbed into the milk truck, with Jason squeezed in the middle. He prattled on, recounting the details of the previous two days.

Mitch didn't say much. He had learned over the years not to provide too much information to strangers all at once. The whole time-paradox thing was often too much for people to handle. How Mitch and Howard had been living here for years while to the newcomers, it was almost always a brand-new experience.

According to Jason's recollection of events, the date he'd encountered the mysterious storm was only a couple of months after Mitch had . . . nearly five years ago. But that general timeline was consistent for everyone they'd met so far. No one seemed aware that so much time had actually passed.

All Mitch could figure was that the aliens had abducted vast numbers of people within a few months of each other but were holding them in some sort of suspended animation and then releasing them at different times—maybe just to see how they would react or interact with other people who'd been released earlier.

Nothing else seemed to make sense. The whole thing was way beyond weird, with no logical explanation. But he had come to accept it by now. Logic had long since abandoned him. This was just the way things were.

Jason talked the whole way back to the farm. In many ways, his story was very similar to Mitch's. Jason had a serious girlfriend whom he'd hoped to marry. Now she was gone like everyone else. He was being watched and followed by the gray creatures wherever he went. He had come up with the plan to head east, just as Mitch had done five years ago. He'd driven through the night and run out of gas on this stretch of highway.

Jason seemed to bounce when he talked, bobbing his head and gesturing with his hands. He was short and jittery. A tightly packed bundle of electrified caffeine. Like the hyperactive little mutt that followed the big bulldog around in those old cartoons.

But Mitch liked him anyway. He was a refreshing change to the parade of senior citizens they'd been having over the years.

They arrived at the farm and Jason jumped out of the truck.

"Whoa." He stood with his hands on his hips, staring at the compound. Mitch could see he was beginning to put two and two together. After a moment, he turned around. "How'd you guys get this all together so quick?"

Mitch and Howard exchanged glances. Howard put his hand on Jason's shoulder. "Son . . . I know it feels like this all started for you just a couple days ago. But truth is, we've been here for . . . well, for quite some time."

Jason shook his head. "Whaddya mean? How long?"

Mitch shrugged. "I've been here for almost five years. Although it's hard to keep track of exactly how long. And Howard was here long before me."

"Five *years*?" Jason turned and gazed at the compound again. Then he looked back at Mitch and Howard. "How . . . ? I—I don't get it."

"Dude," Mitch said, "you'll go crazy trying to figure it out. We don't have all the answers. What we do know is that these creatures have been here for a long time and they can manipulate our senses. Make us see and hear and touch things that aren't there."

Jason stared at them, openmouthed. For the first time since they'd met him, he was speechless.

"Listen . . ." Mitch put a finger to his temple. "They know how to get inside your head. Read your thoughts and memories. For all you know, your whole life might have been an illusion. Or maybe this all is. I don't know anymore."

Howard patted Jason's shoulder. "I know it's a lot to handle all at once. To suddenly realize your whole world might not be what you thought it was."

"No!" Jason pulled away. "Maybe you guys are the illusion. How do I know I can trust you? How do I know you're telling the truth?"

"You don't." Mitch headed toward the house. "So you need to decide if you're going to stay here with us or move on alone." He pointed over his shoulder. "But whatever you do, I'd stay away from those woods if I were you."

VALLEY OF THE SHADOW

CONNER SAT IN HIS MERCEDES,
drumming his fingers on the steering
wheel and staring at the enormous
stone house nestled among the trees.
Walter Kent's brooding mansion was
set back a hundred feet off the street,
half-hidden behind a pair of large oaks
in the massive front yard. A six- or
seven-foot hedge encompassed the
entire yard.

Conner's mind was still bristling
from his conversation with Henry
Brandt. He'd never known the man to
be that closed-minded before. Or that
quick to pass judgment. Henry didn't
care about the proof Conner could have
provided for his experience. Instead,

he'd simply predetermined that Conner was mentally unstable, perhaps due to the lack of oxygen during his heart attack. *"Get your head right,"* indeed!

Conner had collected his things and made a quick exit, not even giving an explanation to Nancy, who had just gotten him a fresh mug of coffee. Let her talk to Henry if she wanted to know details.

Conner sighed and rolled his neck. He knew he couldn't afford to get too worked up about this. If they wanted to peg him as a fanatic—what was the term Henry had used? *Zealot*—then so be it. He'd take the two weeks. And maybe find another job.

But he didn't want to go home just yet. Marta was still at work, and the last thing he wanted to do was dodder around the house like an old retiree.

So he found himself loitering in Walter Kent's neighborhood. Again. He'd done so on several occasions during the past two months. He had tried to make phone contact initially but was quickly turned away by Kent's assistant. Apparently the former congressman was fighting his own battle with cancer and couldn't be bothered with lawyers.

Mitch had neglected to share that bit of information with him—that his father had cancer. It explained a lot, though. It was probably what had prompted Kent to call Mitch that night. To make amends, patch things up.

Conner shook his head. What must have been going through Mitch's mind? Hating your father for so long, only to have him call to tell you he has cancer?

It also explained why Mitch was as surly as he was. Probably the guy was normally happy and fun-loving. But he'd been dealing with all these other issues.

All the more reason to make contact with Kent. This had

to be the reason God had brought Conner back. To help bridge the gap between Mitch and his father. To convince Walter Kent not to give up hope. And to save Mitch's life.

Conner took a breath and pulled up the winding driveway. It wove between a few trees and circled a fountain at the front entrance. Conner got out and stared up at the imposing stone archway. He went to the front doors and rang the bell. He could hear a chime ringing inside.

After several seconds, an attractive woman opened the door. She looked to be in her thirties and was very business-like in a black, knee-length skirt and white blouse, hair up in a bun, and black-framed glasses.

Conner was caught momentarily off guard. If this was the assistant he'd spoken with—argued with—over the phone these past weeks, she was younger than he'd expected. "Uh . . . yes, I was wondering if I could see Mr. Kent. Just very briefly. It's extremely important."

The woman wrinkled her nose, as if smelling an unpleasant odor. "Umm . . . A, no one can see the congressman without an appointment, and B, we're not making any appointments at this time."

Conner smiled, trying to seem personal and professional at the same time. "I completely understand, and I would have gone through the normal procedures to see Congressman Kent, but this is a personal matter concerning his son, Mitch."

She sighed deeply and pursed her lips. "Are you that lawyer? I told you Mr. Kent does not wish to discuss his son's condition with you."

Conner nodded. "Yeah, see, I think there's been a misunderstanding. I don't wish to discuss any legal issues. I'm not here on business. As I mentioned, I know Mitch personally and wanted to speak with his father. I talked to Mitch on the night of his accident. I know they've had personal issues and I just want to try to help."

"Mr . . . Hagmen, is it?"

"Hayden."

"Mr. Hayden, the congressman is very ill and unable to speak with anyone right now."

"Well, can you give him a message? I'm just trying to find out if he's made any decision on disconnecting Mitch from life support. I just—see, Mitch isn't dead and I wanted to let him know there's still hope."

The young woman sighed again. "Mr. Hayden, I don't know what your angle is, but this is an extremely personal matter—"

"Yes, yes, I understand that. That's why I need to speak with Mr. Kent. Just for a few minutes. As I said, it's extremely urgent."

"And as *I* said, he is too sick to speak with you."

"I just want to implore him not to disconnect his son. Please! He's not dead. I firmly believe he can be saved." Conner started crowding the door, trying to catch a glimpse of Walter somewhere inside. If he could just get the congressman's attention. All he needed was a minute.

The woman placed her hand firmly against Conner's chest. "Sir, I'm going to have to ask you to leave. And if—"

"I will, I promise; I just need a minute—"

"And if you don't, I will have you removed from the premises. Is that understood?"

"Please give him that message then, won't you? Please tell him not to disconnect Mitch."

"Mr. Kent has already made final arrangements for his son."

"Final arrangements? What do you mean? What arrangements?"

"I'm afraid that's none of your business."

"He's going to disconnect him? Is that it? Please just tell me."

She turned and called to someone inside. "Eric, can you come and escort Mr. Hayden off the premises?"

Conner threw his hands up in frustration. "I don't need anyone to escort me. Just promise me you'll give Mr. Kent that message. Please? I'm begging you."

The woman stepped aside as a tall, block-shouldered guy in a suit emerged. He appeared in no mood to talk but grabbed Conner's arm and started to lead him back to his car.

Conner called over his shoulder, "Don't you understand? I'm his friend! I'm trying to save his life!"

VALLEY OF THE SHADOW

15

THERE WAS NOTHING like the feeling of a shave and a hot shower in the morning. Howard stood in a white T-shirt, peering into the upstairs bathroom mirror. He rubbed his cheek, inspecting his leathery though freshly shaved skin, and ran a comb through his hair one last time. Then he slipped on one of his plaid shirts and buttoned it to his chin.

It was just after eight o'clock and noises drifted up from outside—voices and shuffling feet. Howard went to the bathroom window overlooking the farm compound and the forest beyond. Mitch and Jason had started another game of basketball on the makeshift court they'd constructed. Jason had been with them for nearly a week now, and he and Mitch had become fast friends. Earlier in the week, they'd raided a sporting goods store for the hoop and backboard and mounted it over the entrance of the maintenance shed, where there was a concrete apron just big enough for half-court games.

Howard rubbed his jaw as he watched them play. Mitch clearly had the benefit of size and strength, but Jason was quicker and more agile. They had played numerous games over the previous few days. Mitch had admitted he wasn't very good, but he said he needed to have something to do other than sit on the porch or play cribbage. Howard missed the cribbage games, but as long as this helped to keep Mitch's mind off taking a vacation, he was all for it.

As Howard stood watching, a gust of wind moaned through the rafters and rattled the window. A moment later a soft voice came from behind him. Deep and airy—almost as if out of a dream.

"Beloved."

It made the hairs on his neck stand up.

He had heard it before. Countless times. His stomach tightened. Resisting the impulse to turn around, Howard kept his eyes forward, out the window. He nodded down toward Mitch and said, "He hasn't talked any more about leaving. Not since this Jason kid showed up."

"He must not leave," the voice replied.

"It's been a long time," Howard said. "He's getting restless."

"We can't let him go, beloved."

"What about this Jason? He ain't going to be around forever. And once he's gone, Mitch's urge to leave will be even stronger. What then?"

Howard turned, but the bathroom was empty. He looked

in the mirror again. His reflection gazed back at him, eyes white and soulless. Then the image spoke. "He has so much anger, this one. Deep inside. So much hate. We love it. We cannot let him go."

Howard turned away, his jaw clenched. They used to long for his fellowship alone. They used to be content with him. Jealousy began to roil inside him. "And what about me? I've always been faithful to you. Haven't I always been faithful?"

"You have, beloved. Ever faithful." The voice grew tender. "But are we not always hungry? Do we not always seek more?"

"Yes," Howard grunted. "You never have enough."

VALLEY OF THE SHADOW

16

DEVON MADE HIS WAY on foot through a maze of alleys and side streets. His mind was a fog of hate, fear, and desperation. Hate for the people trying to lock him away. Fear of what was happening to him now and the cold, dark force that seemed to be controlling him. And desperation to find answers.

Devon wasn't sure exactly where he was headed and only half recalled the most recent events that had brought him into the streets. He had managed to overpower the paramedics as they were wheeling him into the hospital. They didn't put up much of a fight. After all, it wasn't their job to guard him, just transport him. The only thing that seemed clear to him now was a pressing desire to get away.

But Devon felt exposed. He'd escaped with only his jeans, shoes, and white T-shirt. He needed to find a jacket. Sweatshirt. Anything.

His mind flashed with brief, terrifying images of his life over the last two months. Bizarre aliens constantly watching him—hunting him. Strangers with familiar faces. Friends he could no longer remember. Shreds of half memories, like a giant puzzle with its pieces in a continual state of flux. As if floating about in space, bumping into one another at random, but never congealing into a final picture.

And a voice inside him, like a distant rumble of thunder, never fully audible but never fading away.

Run!

His chest pounded as he jogged a zigzag course through the city, pausing behind Dumpsters, avoiding main thoroughfares. Always sticking to side streets and alleys. Unsure of his final destination, his only pressing thought was to keep moving.

North.

There was someplace he was supposed to be. Out of the city. There was something he was supposed to do. He had to find transportation.

He was jogging through a narrow alley when an arm flashed out from behind a Dumpster and clotheslined him squarely across the neck. Devon fell back onto the cracked asphalt, his head spinning.

He swore and sat up. A tall, thin man stood over him, glaring down. His skin was sickly pallid and his face so gaunt it was almost grotesque. Long black hair hung down over his eyes. He was clad in tattered, mismatched clothing: a brown wool overcoat with the elbows frayed, torn-up jeans, and gloves with the fingers missing. His eyes seemed to glow a pale yellow-white under the dark strands of hair hanging in his face.

Devon recognized him. The guy in the crowd. And from inside his mirror.

"What do you think you're doing?" the stranger hissed. His face was a mask of utter contempt. "I help you escape and you just take off? What are you going to do? Run around the whole city dressed like that until you get caught?"

Devon pointed a shaky finger at the man. "I . . . I seen you before. . . ."

The pale man grinned; his teeth were brown with decay. "So you remember me. Maybe you're not as stupid as you look."

"What do you want?"

"I have a job for you, chief."

"What are you talking about? What job?"

The pale man leaned close. "Just a little project. I'll tell you more when you need to know it." He reached down and plucked Devon off the ground, dusting him off. "There you go. First you need to get dressed. Follow me."

He clutched Devon's arm and herded him through the alley. His grip was like ice. They followed an erratic path along more side streets for several blocks. Soon Devon found himself back in what felt like a familiar neighborhood. Streets with rows of brick-faced apartment buildings and storefronts with wrought iron rails across the windows.

They emerged from an alley onto a side street where Devon finally spotted several faces he recognized. A group of teens had congregated outside a drugstore to smoke. Hoods up, heads down, hands in pockets.

Pale Man pointed to the group. "I think you know one of them. Go get his jacket."

One of the kids spotted Devon and pulled away from the rest. He wore an oversize black hooded jacket. He took a few steps toward Devon, eyes narrowed. Then his face brightened. "Yo, Devon. What up? Whutch you doin' here?"

Devon drew close and studied the boy's face. He knew this kid. They had been friends once. . . .

Pale Man leaned into Devon's ear. "His name is Travis."

"Hey, Trav," Devon said in almost a whisper.

Travis grinned. "What up, brah? You get out? When'd you get out?"

"Don't chat; just get his jacket," Pale Man whispered.

"Jacket," Devon heard himself saying. "I need your jacket."

"Dude." Travis snorted. "I ain't giving you my jacket."

Devon felt a sudden rush of anger well up inside him. Like a volcano, he could feel himself trembling, ready to explode. But cold. He was freezing cold. His throat grew tight. With a surge of power, he grabbed Travis by the neck and pulled him close. Devon felt like he was holding a rag doll in his grip. Like he could snap the kid's neck with one hand. The world seemed to turn red and his rage felt nearly uncontrollable. He heard a growl coming from his throat.

"I need your jacket!"

But it wasn't his voice. Deep and gravelly, it didn't even sound human.

Travis's eyes widened. He tried to speak but could only manage a gargled whisper with Devon's fingers around his neck. He fumbled with his jacket and let it drop to the sidewalk.

Pale Man closed his yellow eyes for a second and he breathed in deeply. "Mmm, that feels good." He stepped back and curled up the corner of his mouth. "That's what we like to see, chief. A little fire in the belly."

Devon released his grip on Travis, picked up the jacket, and slipped it on, pulling the hood up over his head, low across his face. He cast a quick glance at Travis, crumpled on the sidewalk, gasping for air. Then he turned away and disappeared back into the shadows of the alley.

VALLEY OF THE SHADOW

MITCH COLLAPSED on the porch steps. His jeans, T-shirt, and long, sandy hair were drenched with sweat. They had started basketball around eight that morning and played three games up to twenty. And now Mitch was beat.

Jason stretched out on the grass next to the steps, equally drenched. "Dude," he said between breaths, "I've never played that much in one day. I'm gonna be sore tomorrow."

Mitch grunted in agreement and guzzled a pitcher of water, letting it drip down his chin, neck, and chest.

In the week since Jason had first shown up, they'd started playing a game or two every day. Jason seemed to be all about sports. More to the point, Mitch decided, he was all about sports *bars*. His interest seemed primarily an excuse to hang out with his buddies for drinks after the games. He played softball in the summer and basketball during the fall and winter months. And what he may have lacked in height, he claimed to more than make up for with talent. Though Mitch was finding that it was more energy and bluster than actual physical prowess.

Initially Mitch wasn't much of a challenge, but over the last few days, he'd developed better ball handling and shooting techniques and was starting to become a serious threat. Every day he got a little better. And every day drew them into fiercer competition.

Jason sat up and ran his hands through his hair. He stared out at the court for a moment, then sighed. "Me and my brothers used to play two-on-two every day during the summer back home. My dad put in a full court slab for us in our backyard."

"Sounds like he got his money's worth out of it," Mitch said.

Jason nodded. "Yeah, he played in college and coached our high school team, so you can imagine basketball was a big part of my life growing up."

"Did you play in college?"

"Me? Nah. I did okay in high school but never was big enough to get noticed by any college scouts." He shrugged. "Which is okay. My game was always baseball. I just never had the heart to tell my dad."

Mitch was silent for a moment. "Did you get along with your old man?"

"Yeah, he was cool. I guess his father was kind of abusive—y'know, a drinker. So my dad really went out of his way to avoid making the same mistakes with us."

"Good for him."

Jason glanced up at Mitch. "Why, was your dad a jerk?"

"Worse," Mitch snorted. "Politician. He was never around very much and never had much time for me when he was."

"Politician, huh? What, state or local?"

"Congress. He spent most of his time in Washington."

"Cool. You ever get to visit? Y'know, did he ever take you around? meet the president or anything?"

"I went a couple times when I was younger. Then my mom got sick and we stayed home after that. Never met the president. But I think my old man probably did."

The screen door opened and Howard stepped out onto the porch. He shook his head. "Don't go wearin' yourself out playing basketball. We gotta make a gas run in a couple of days."

"Gas run?" Jason sat up. "Where to?"

Mitch held up a hand. "Dude, we've been siphoning every drop we could find from every town in a thirty-mile radius. Trust me, it ain't fun."

Jason got to his feet and grabbed the basketball. "Hey, man, it's all in how you look at it."

Mitch waved him off.

Jason returned to the court and took a few more shots. One of them missed completely and bounced into the open maintenance shed. He went to retrieve the ball and suddenly doubled over in the entrance, holding his stomach and groaning.

Mitch jumped up and ran to the court but stopped at the edge of the concrete. Jason turned and lifted his T-shirt. His abdomen was covered by a purple rash. It looked like an enormous bruise. Mitch froze, staring at the discoloration.

Jason examined it. Then looked up. His face was drained of color. "W-what is it?" he stammered. "What's going on?"

Mitch just shook his head, unable to speak. He had seen this before. Too many times. The purple rash that crept across a visitor's body. Usually right before . . .

"Dude, get in the house!"

"What?" Jason held his stomach and winced again.

Something moved in the shadows of the maintenance shed. Mitch gasped and stepped back. Jason apparently noticed Mitch's expression and turned in time to see two gray creatures emerge from the shadows, just within the entrance of the shed. A pair of long gray arms lurched out and wrapped around Jason's torso. Multiple spiderlike fingers fanned out and dug into his flesh. Mitch could see the discoloration spreading over the rest of Jason's body. His arms, calves, and the back of his neck.

The creatures yanked him into the darkened shed like a rag doll. Jason screamed. A terrified, high-pitched cry for help.

Mitch snapped out of his shock and lunged across the court. But the second creature emerged from the shed, looming in front of Mitch, shoulders drawn back, head forward. Its vacant white eyes glared at him. The gray skin of its mouth peeled open to expose rows of black teeth. It stood there, poised and threatening, blocking Mitch's path.

Mitch skidded to a halt and fell backward onto the cement. Jason's screams still echoed from inside the shed. Then the door on the far side of the shed burst open and Mitch could see the shadowy silhouette of the first creature dragging Jason through the doorway and out across the field toward the . . .

Toward the forest!

Jason was still struggling, flailing his limbs.

"Mitch!" His voice echoed, growing more distant. "Help me!"

But terror seized Mitch again. A sharp, paralyzing fear. Part of him screamed to get up, to go and save his friend. But another part screamed to save himself.

Mitch stared up at the creature looming over him. It glared at him—at least as much as its alien features could resemble a glare. Then, Mitch made his choice. He scrambled back away from the entrance to the shed. Back, off the basketball court . . .

And back into the house.

VALLEY OF THE SHADOW

18

JIM MALONE GOT HOME shortly
after noon, full of anxiety. He couldn't
help but feel a sense of responsi-
bility for Devon's escape from the
detention facility that morning. His
seizure had occurred only after Jim
had started talking, trying to explain
things.

The house was empty when he
arrived. His two oldest children were in
school and Annie had gone shopping
with the other two.

Jim also couldn't get over the
coincidence that both he and Conner
Hayden had come to visit the same kid
within minutes of each other. It was
weird enough just running into the guy,

but the fact that they had both come to see the same kid? That was more than a little bizarre.

Then there was Devon's strange behavior toward Hayden. What had the facility director said? That Devon had freaked out the moment he first saw the lawyer. But why? What connection did they have?

Jim shook his head. Part of him wanted to forget about the entire ordeal. He'd tried to help Devon, but now it no longer concerned him. He barely knew Hayden and he didn't know Devon at all. Yet something his wife always said came back to him: "Nothing ever really happens by accident."

Jim dug through the drawers in the kitchen desk and finally plucked out Hayden's business card. He stared at it for a minute, still debating whether or not to contact the lawyer again. It really wasn't any of his business, but something told him that maybe Annie was right.

Jim dialed the office number on the card. After three rings, a woman answered. Jim asked to speak with Conner.

The woman hesitated for a moment. "Mr. Hayden is not in the office today. But I can transfer you to Jeff Hildebrandt; he's handling—"

"No thanks," Jim answered quickly. "Will he be in tomorrow? Can I leave a message?"

There was another pause. "Actually, Mr. Hayden has taken a leave of absence. I'm afraid he won't be available for a couple weeks."

"A couple weeks?" Jim frowned. Maybe he was still taking medical leave. "Do you have his home phone number? I just need to ask—"

"I'm sorry, sir; we can't give out that information. But I can try to get a message to him that you called."

Jim left his name and number, just in case, then hung

up and rubbed his eyes. This whole thing was wearing on his nerves. He could get on the Internet and try to locate Hayden's home phone number. But that felt too much like prying. Jim drummed his fingers on the desk, trying to work up the nerve to go further.

Suddenly the phone rang, shaking Jim from his thoughts. He answered.

"Hello?"

"Mr. Malone?" The voice sounded familiar.

"Yes."

"Mr. Malone, this is Darnell Curtis, from the juvenile detention center. Do you have a moment?"

"Sure, what can I do for you?"

"I was wondering if I could ask you a few questions about Mr. Hayden, the man who came to see Devon earlier this morning."

"Um, yeah. I don't really know him very well."

"I understand," Darnell went on. "But I'm having some trouble getting in contact with him. I'm trying to figure out what connection he might have with Devon."

"I just assumed he was representing him. Or maybe trying to give him legal advice."

"I've been reviewing the tape of their meeting, and I have to say, their conversation was pretty bizarre."

"What do you mean?"

"Well, I can't go into details at the moment, but Hayden kept referring to the night Devon was shot. He said something about having a heart attack that same night. He seemed to be trying to convince Devon that it was real. Their experience was real. That it really happened."

Jim nearly dropped the phone. "Whoa—whoa, wait a minute . . . He's right."

"You know what he was talking about?"

"Yeah . . . he's right," Jim said. Things were starting to come into focus. "He did have a heart attack that night."

"How do you know this?"

"Well, we had met with him earlier that same afternoon— my wife and I. We had a meeting to talk about a malpractice lawsuit. But we wanted to think about it more over the weekend. And then on Monday, we heard from his office that he was in the hospital. He'd had a heart attack and was having surgery."

"Are you sure they said he had the heart attack Friday night?"

"Yeah, I'm sure," Jim said. "But . . . what does that mean?"

"Are you a religious man, Mr. Malone?"

"What? Yeah . . . I guess so. Why?"

"Because Hayden was telling Devon that they had both had the same experience. I think he was referring to their near-death experience. They were both dying at the same time and somehow had experienced the same event. They'd somehow met each other."

Jim laughed nervously. "Look, I believe in life after death. I mean . . . I'm a Christian and all, but that . . . that sounds a little crazy, don't you think? What if he was just trying to trick Devon or something?"

There was a pause. "Normally I'd agree with you. But judging from Devon's reaction to seeing Mr. Hayden again— or really for the first time . . . He was shocked. I mean, almost terrified. It was like Devon recognized him. I guess I'm tempted to give the story the benefit of the doubt."

"So what experience did they have? Did he describe any of it?"

"No," Darnell said. "But he did mention two other

people. A Helen and Mitch. Do either of those names ring a
bell with you?"

"Helen and Mitch? No . . . I'm sorry, they don't sound
familiar."

"Hayden said that Mitch was in a coma. In a hospital up
in Winthrop Harbor."

"Winthrop Harbor?" Jim frowned. "Well, we should try to
find out if—"

"Way ahead of you, man. I called in a few favors and did
some checking. There's a Mitch Kent currently in ICU at Good
Samaritan. He's in a coma from injuries received in a motorcycle
accident two months ago. And get this . . . it was the same night
Devon was shot and Hayden was having his heart attack."

Jim felt chills pour down his back. "You're kidding me."

"Now all that brings me to your experience with Devon.
And how he was acting."

"You mean his being out of it? Like drugged or something?"

"Yeah, disorientation and the seizure. But there was one
other thing. . . ."

"What's that?"

"The cold. You said for a moment before his seizure it got
real cold in the room. The window frosted up, you said."

"Yeah." Jim was nodding at the phone. "Yeah, like the AC
had kicked in or something. I could actually see my breath."

"Right. Only there is no AC in that room."

"So . . . what are you saying?"

Darnell gave what sounded like a nervous chuckle. "Well,
officially, I'm not saying anything. Officially, my office is working diligently with the police to find Devon and bring him back.
But unofficially . . ." He paused a moment. "Unofficially, I think
there's something very weird—spiritual or paranormal or whatever you want to call it—going on."

Jim sat with his mouth open. He suddenly felt detached, like he was watching himself in a movie. A bizarre, low-budget horror flick about demon-crazed zombies running amok. He shook his head. This was crazy.

"Mr. Malone?" Darnell's voice drew Jim out of his daze.

He blinked. "Uhh . . . yeah. So . . . what does that all mean? I mean . . . what can we do about it?"

"Again, officially, nothing. We let the police handle it. But it sounds to me like Devon is in more trouble than just being chased by the police. A lot more."

"Well, Conner, I've been wondering when we'd get the chance to talk."

Norman Lewis—Pastor Norman Lewis—closed the door to his study and sat down in the chair across from Conner. Lewis was sixtysomething and grandfatherly, his brown hair trimmed with gray and neatly combed. In fact, a little too neatly, Conner thought. Not a hair out of place.

Conner also took note that the guy didn't sit at his desk, which might've suggested a position of authority. Instead, he seemed to treat Conner like a friend. An equal.

Then again, maybe that was the impression he was trying to give—that they were friends. Like some pre-scripted psychological trick from Pastoring Techniques 101: *How to Elicit Trust from Your Minions While Pretending to Be Their Equal.*

Conner had called Lewis shortly after lunch—upon arriving home from his encounter at Walter Kent's house. He was frustrated and found himself getting angry with God again. Why would God bring him back to life and make it so difficult to accomplish the task that He'd brought him back to do? And to make matters worse, Conner was now fighting against the clock as well. If Kent had made "final arrangements" for his son, that could only mean he was having Mitch disconnected from life support. And probably soon.

So with reservations—but nowhere else to turn—Conner had looked up the pastor's number and given him a call. Marta was still at work, but Conner wasn't sure he wanted her along anyway.

Conner tapped his fingers on the leather armrest, unsure of how to begin the conversation.

But Lewis smiled. "So Marta shared with me a bit of your . . . well, your story and how you came to faith. I don't think I know anyone with that dramatic a testimony."

"Mmm." Conner nodded. "Road to Damascus."

"Well, I'm eager to hear more about it. That is, whenever you feel comfortable enough to share it."

"Actually, not even Marta knew the whole story—at least not until this morning. I finally told her everything."

"So what took you this long to share it all with her?"

Conner shrugged. "I guess I was afraid she'd think I was . . ."

"Crazy?"

Conner peered at the pastor with a raised eyebrow.

Lewis gave a sheepish smile. "Yeah, she called this morning to ask for prayer. She didn't share any details. But she said you had told her an incredible story."

"She did, eh?"

Lewis held up a hand. "Now she loves you very much and has a great deal of respect for you. She didn't seem to think you were crazy. She's been praying desperately for you, over four years now. You may not know it, but we all have."

"Praying?"

"For your soul. Your salvation."

This was a new thought for Conner. He knew Marta loved him, but it never dawned on him that she had actually been praying for him. And what was more, had even gotten her whole church involved. He felt a brief flash of annoyance at the idea of all these strangers imposing on his private life this whole time. Knowing personal details about him. Praying for him without his permission.

But then another thought struck him. The story of the Prodigal Son that he'd read recently. How the father had longed for his child and yearned for him all the while he was gone. Watching for him, praying for him, even while he was off living the high life. Before he'd even repented. That wasn't imposition. It was just . . . love.

Lewis cleared his throat. "You know, Conner, I was once an agnostic myself."

"You were?"

Lewis nodded. "I taught philosophy at Notre Dame. Like you, I didn't become a Christian until later in life. I was thirty-six."

"So what happened?"

"My conversion wasn't nearly as dramatic as yours— although I did nearly die in a car accident. That's what helped me turn the corner, so to speak. But really, my conversion was the product of pure grace." His smile broadened. "And thirty-six years of a faithful mother's prayers."

"That's perseverance."

"You have no idea." Lewis chuckled. "So you and I are pretty similar. Both former agnostics. Both of us prayed into heaven by the women who loved us."

Conner's lips curled up slightly. Then he grew serious again. "So when you had your accident . . . did you . . . experience anything? see or hear anything?"

"No. My heart never stopped. I never lost consciousness. But as I was pinned inside that car waiting for someone to come along and find me, I felt a sense of fear. I mean an overwhelming feeling of pure dread. Like someone had dropped a huge blanket over me. Just covering me in complete darkness. Smothering darkness."

Conner swallowed. A chill skittered down his back for a moment as he recalled standing at the edge of the abyss, gazing into that vast, unending darkness. A darkness that could almost be felt. More than just an absence of light, as though it were a physical thing. He shuddered.

Lewis went on. "It was like getting a peek into a place where you were completely alone. A place void of even the presence of God." He breathed a deep sigh. "I knew then and there that I needed to get serious about my agnosticism."

Conner looked up. "What do you mean?"

"I realized I'd been a lazy agnostic. I had convinced myself it was impossible to know God without making sure it really was impossible."

Conner nodded. "You can never be sure you can't know something."

Lewis chuckled. "Exactly. I came to the realization that all my arguments against God's existence were purely . . ." He seemed to search for a word. "Purely operational. I saw all the evil and tragedy going on around me and thought that if God existed, He wouldn't allow any of this to occur. And since it was occurring, He couldn't be real."

"That was me, too," Conner said. "That's exactly where I was."

"My entire argument was based on an emotional reaction to what I saw happening. I didn't like the way God operated, so I decided He must not exist. But I was imposing my own values onto God, thinking that God had to behave like I would—according to my logic and values. I wasn't open to the possibility that maybe God might allow evil to succeed for a time in order to fulfill a greater goal. He can allow tragedy to occur because He has a higher purpose. One I couldn't see because I'm a finite human being."

This was getting a little too close to home. This pastor was no longer describing his own feelings but Conner's as well. "But why doesn't He just let us in on it? Why does everything have to be such a secret?"

"His mysterious ways?" Lewis shrugged. "Maybe in part to build our faith. To teach us to trust Him. Like a parent forcing a child to learn how to swim. It's scary and unpleasant for the child at the time, but in the end it's better for that child to know how to swim than to . . ." He stopped midsentence. His face went white. "I'm . . . I'm sorry, Conner. I wasn't thinking. That was a terrible analogy."

Conner found his hands clenching the armrests. His jaw had tightened, and his chest. He took a breath. An image flashed in his head—Matthew's face beneath the water, his eyes vacant and dead . . .

"No," Conner said softly. "It's all right."

"I just wasn't thinking. . . ."

"Actually it's a perfect analogy. God allows these things

ultimately for our own good. We just don't always understand it at the time."

"Or maybe for someone else's good," Lewis added. "Or sometimes just for His own glory. You remember the story of Job? God allowed terrible suffering into a faithful man's life, all to prove a point to Satan. And He never once explained to Job why He allowed it. Job accepted it initially, but soon he began to plead for an answer. Then he ended up demanding one.

"And when God finally responded . . . it wasn't a gentle answer. He didn't speak in a still, small voice or in a soft, motherly tone. He spoke with power. Out of a storm. He invoked His sovereign prerogative: He is God and He will do as He pleases. He may choose to let us know the reasons . . . or He may not."

Conner shook his head. "That won't win Him any popularity contests. Not these days."

"You're right. It's definitely easier to talk about His kindness and love. But the subtle danger there is that before you know it, if that's all we focus on, we start to think that maybe, in some way, we must be kind of lovable. That maybe there's something good in us and maybe we deserve His love."

Conner rubbed his jaw. He hadn't thought of that before.

Lewis went on. "Now in the end, God did show His love to Job. He restored everything twofold. But not until Job came to a place where He recognized God's rightful authority and bowed down in humility and repentance. We can never fully appreciate God's love until we understand how completely undeserving we are of being loved."

They both fell silent for a moment as that thought sank into Conner. Was he demanding answers from God as well? or some kind of explanation? And was he expecting God to

respond on Conner's timetable? What right did he have to
demand anything from the Almighty?

Conner shook his head. It was an easy trap to fall into.
Perhaps he could use a little humility. At length, he spoke up.
"So let me tell you what happened during my heart attack."

VALLEY OF THE SHADOW

20

MITCH SPENT THE NEXT TWO DAYS
inside the farmhouse, refusing to talk
or to even go outside. He barely ate and
stopped playing cribbage altogether.
Instead, he spent most of the time just
sitting in the living room, staring out
the front window.

He felt numb inside, like his brain
was shutting down. He had seen dozens of people get dragged away by
the aliens before, just like Jason had
been. And he had never gotten used to
it. They were always violent, terrifying
events that paralyzed him with fear.
Frozen and unable to help, and feeling
strangely detached as if he were in a
dream, trying desperately to flee only

to find he couldn't move his legs. He couldn't run. Couldn't walk. He could barely even crawl.

It was like that every time. In fact, he had come to dread the sight of any visitors because he knew invariably they would meet a gruesome end. One way or another. And so Mitch had stopped being friendly to them at all. He refused to allow himself the risk of becoming even slightly attached. It was bad enough watching this happen to strangers; he couldn't bear to watch it happen to a friend. So he simply determined not to let anyone become a friend.

Until now.

Somehow Jason had wormed his way through Mitch's defenses. Maybe it was the experience of having someone around who was closer to his own age. Maybe it was the guy's incessant jabbering. Mitch wasn't sure. But somehow, without even realizing it, over the week Jason had been here, they had become friends.

Mitch grunted. Some friend. He hadn't even been able to muster the courage to help the kid. He had relived the event in his mind during the last two days. Over and over, he watched the creatures grab Jason and carry him off, arms flailing, screaming for help. And Mitch watched himself running to save him, only to freeze at the last minute. Just like a frightened child.

Like a coward.

Mitch ran his hand through his hair. He hadn't slept more than a few minutes at a time. His dreams were haunted by visions of Jason. And slowly a grim resolve began to grow inside him.

He had to leave.

The other image haunting his thoughts was that of the stranger he'd encountered the week before. This Nathan guy

who seemed to know Mitch. Who had warned him to leave the
farm. To get away from Howard.

At the time, Mitch was still doubtful. Still unsure. Maybe
still afraid to leave. But now? Now he was afraid to stay. It
was as if this farm were cursed. Anyone who came here disappeared one way or the other. Mitch knew these creatures
weren't going to leave them alone. They weren't going away.
And it was just a matter of time until they came for him.

Mitch went to the kitchen window and glanced outside.
It was only midmorning, and Howard was busy in the barn,
changing the oil in the generators. The milk truck was parked
next to the barn. It had been their main source of transportation over the last five years, but Howard also had a pickup in
the garage next to the house. He'd use it occasionally when
they needed supplies on a non-gas-run day.

Mitch went to his room and threw a few items into his
duffel bag. Then he grabbed the keys to the pickup from the
drawer and stole out the front door. He slipped into the garage
and carefully rolled up the main door, wincing at every loud
squeak and rattle. The noise seemed intensified against the
eerie stillness of the gray, overcast world around them.

Mitch peeked back at the barn but couldn't see any sign
of Howard. He didn't know why he was worried. It wasn't like
the guy would be much of a challenge in a fight. But still,
something urged him to be as quiet as possible.

He slipped the truck into neutral and pushed it out of the
garage. He recalled that the thing was in need of a new muffler
and thought he was better off not starting it up until he came
to the end of the long driveway.

Mitch pushed it slowly down the driveway and winced
again. The dry crunch of the tires on gravel seemed as loud
as gunshots. The driveway ran on a slight decline toward the

road, and Mitch hopped inside once the truck began rolling on its own.

He kept one eye on the rearview mirror until he reached the road. Then he took one last look at the farm. The old clapboard house and outbuildings stood like a dismal oasis against the gray skyline. Flat, brown fields stretched out in all directions, broken only by occasional patches of barren, skeletal trees.

Mitch turned the key and the engine chugged and sputtered. A chill swept over him. "C'mon," he whispered.

He tried again. The engine chugged to life, fired a moment, then died with a loud pop.

Mitch swore and tried it again. He glanced at the barn.

Howard was standing in the doorway. Hands on his hips. Staring at him.

The old truck sputtered to life and Mitch gunned the accelerator. The tires kicked up gravel as the pickup fishtailed out onto the road. Mitch took off south, toward Harris. Back to where he had met Nathan. He could get one of the Harleys, find the key, gas it up, and be gone again within minutes.

The truck rattled and squeaked as it barreled down the narrow county highway. Mitch kept a constant watch on the rearview mirror. No doubt, Howard would pursue him in the milk truck. Try to talk him out of leaving. Probably scold him for being so foolish.

Above the din of the engine, Mitch could hear a low rumble. Deep and sustained, it seemed to grow louder every second. The steering wheel began to vibrate.

As he approached an intersection, he spotted movement in his rearview mirror. Something was coming up behind him. He craned his neck to get a better view. Something big and black rumbled across the sky just overhead. It overtook him quickly. A huge, black mass—like a meteor—tumbled and rolled through the air, leaving a billowing trail of smoke in its wake. The whole truck rattled as it passed him with the roar of a jet. It was no more than a hundred feet in the air and descending quickly.

It smashed into the ground in the middle of the intersection, spraying chunks of asphalt and rock into the air. Thick, black smoke billowed around the crater. Mitch swore and slammed on the brakes. The pickup swerved sideways as it skidded to a stop.

Mitch could barely see the object itself amid all the smoke. But he glimpsed something that looked like a huge, charred mass of tangled branches and limbs—as if someone had uprooted an entire tree and rolled it into a ball, like crumpling up a piece of paper. Mitch peered at it, his heart pounding. Then his eyes widened.

Inside the smoke and debris, something moved.

VALLEY OF THE SHADOW

21

NORMAN LEWIS GAZED at Conner without expression as Conner finished recounting the details of his experience. The storm, the creatures, the seizures and visions. All of it. The guy might think he was crazy, or maybe just tell him to leave, but Conner didn't care anymore. He was desperate for help. In for a penny, he thought, in for a pound.

Lewis shook his head. "That is without a doubt the most incredible story I've ever heard."

"You don't believe me, do you."

"Of course I do. There've been plenty of hellish near-death experiences reported by people." Lewis shrugged. "But I've never heard anything this detailed before. It's pretty amazing. And your revival at the hospital sounded nothing short of miraculous."

"That's my thought exactly," Conner said. "So God obviously brought me back for a reason. I think He wants me to do something."

"You mean saving Mitch?"

"That's what I believe."

Lewis drew in a breath and leaned back in his chair. "Hmm . . ."

Conner spread his hands. "I'm just guessing here. I'm new to all this."

"Well, there may be many reasons He saved you. He's given you quite a story. Maybe He wants you to share it with others."

"But how do I know? I mean . . . how do you know what He wants you to do?"

Lewis laughed and rubbed his eyes. "Conner, that's the million-dollar question. Everyone struggles to understand what their ultimate purpose in life is."

"But what about the short term? Shouldn't I be concerned about Mitch? His life is hanging in the balance and I need to do something. I can't let him die. I can't let him go to hell."

Lewis's face grew serious. "You're right. You should be concerned. I think if all of us could get a glimpse of how terrible eternity without God is going to be, it'd give us a whole new perspective on life. And a greater sense of urgency."

"But everything I've tried so far has failed. It's like God keeps shutting the door in my face. I don't know what to do anymore. And now I hear that Mitch's father has already made 'final arrangements' for him."

"God doesn't hold you accountable for things outside your

control. If you've done everything in your power to help Mitch, you have to leave the rest to God."

"But that's just it. I keep wondering if I really have done everything in my power to help him. I feel like God keeps telling me Mitch needs my help, but I don't know what more I can do."

"Are you talking about your dreams? Is that how you think God is speaking to you?"

Conner thought a moment. He had described his recurring nightmares and his sense that God was somehow using them to urge him to action. "I guess so. Does that seem a little too weird?"

"Well, I generally view dreams and visions with a healthy dose of skepticism. I've seen way too much false teaching come through somebody's so-called personal revelation," Lewis said. "In your case, it might just be your mind's reaction to such a traumatic experience. On the other hand, there've been times when I've felt the distinct impression that God has placed a burden for someone in particular on my heart."

Conner slumped in his chair. "So you're saying maybe He is trying to tell me something or maybe He's not."

Lewis chuckled. "You're right, I'm not being much help. But consider this: what if it's not Mitch?"

"What do you mean?"

"What about Devon or . . . this Howard Bristol? What if God is trying to tell you something about one of them?"

Conner rubbed his jaw. "Well, I finally went to see Devon this morning. He was so freaked out, he didn't even want to talk to me."

"What about Howard?"

Conner stared at the pastor. He had to be kidding. Howard Bristol? The guy who had purposely deceived them?

who had led Conner into a trap? The man was probably demon-possessed—supposedly lying in a coma somewhere in Indiana. Conner just wanted to stay as far away from him as possible. "You're joking, right?"

Lewis smiled. "I know you said he was working with those creatures, but maybe that's the problem. Maybe he's trapped and God is moving you to help him. After all, your dreams have been centered on his farm, right?" He shrugged. "Maybe this isn't about Mitch at all."

MITCH SAT IN THE TRUCK, gaping at the smoldering object in the road. Black smoke billowed up in a thick column. Inside, the charred and twisted mass seemed to shudder. Then it began to uncurl slowly, as if unfolding from within itself. Long, gnarled limbs emerged, reaching up and stretching out to the sides. Still shrouded by smoke, the thing lurched and straightened up.

And up.

Mitch's eyes widened. The thing rose—as if on haunches—as tall as a tree. Like an enormous, contorted skeleton of some prehistoric beast. It was roughly bipedal, with a misshapen torso resting on a pair of what appeared to be legs. Two elongated, multijointed arms protruded from its upper body like black, gnarled branches.

It bent forward and stretched its massive jaws open with a roar. A deep and deafening bellow that rumbled into the distance. It was like no creature Mitch had ever seen. Like something out of a nightmare. It had no eyes or snout or ears, just immense jaws, bearing a tangle of black and twisted fangs that dripped with tarlike saliva. Multiple horns and protrusions curled up from its head and shoulders. It almost appeared to be more plant than animal.

But it moved like an animal. Stepping out of the smoke with a single, giant stride, it reached one of its arms toward the truck. Huge claws unfolded.

Mitch threw the truck into reverse and stomped on the accelerator. Tires screamed and the pickup lurched backward as the beast's claws crashed down, embedding themselves into the pavement.

Mitch squealed backward away from the intersection, then jerked the wheel hard and spun the truck around. He caught a glimpse of the creature in his mirror, struggling to loose its claws from the asphalt. Mitch slammed the truck into drive and tore off.

He glanced back and watched as the creature managed to free itself. It lurched after the truck with huge, awkward strides. Half upright, half on all fours—like a gorilla—the giant beast pounded after him. Mitch could feel the road shuddering beneath the truck. His hands tightened, white-knuckled, on the steering wheel. The creature roared a second time and Mitch looked back again.

It filled the entire rearview mirror.

Once more, the creature reached out and swiped at the

pickup. A massive clawed fist smashed onto the road, just missing the back of the truck. Mitch swerved, but the beast was too fast. It swung its arm again and knocked the truck's back end sideways. Mitch lost control and the pickup tipped on two wheels, then flipped and started rolling.

Mitch felt his head snap forward and smash into the windshield. Everything flashed red and he could feel himself tumbling in the cab. A dizzying blur of weeds, sky, and asphalt whipped past the windows. Glass shattered, metal crunched. And then everything stopped with a sickening thud.

Mitch found himself lying crumpled on the inside roof of the cab. Dirt and weeds filled one of the windows, but Mitch could see a strip of gravel and gray sky out the other side. The ditch. He still had the presence of mind to realize he'd landed in the ditch.

Mitch could hear the creature bellowing. It was somewhere close. And coming closer. The truck shuddered with its footsteps. Mitch's vision blurred, then began to fade. He could feel himself losing consciousness.

A shadow passed over the truck and something now blocked his view of the sky. The last thing he remembered was the sound of crunching metal as the whole truck shook.

Then everything went black.

VALLEY OF THE SHADOW

23

Just after two o'clock, Devon and Pale Man approached the apartment building on West Seventeenth Street. Now that Devon had gotten a jacket, Pale Man informed him that the next thing he needed was transportation.

They scanned the street in both directions. There would be police, no doubt, watching. Devon pulled the hood lower over his face, hurried into the building, and slipped up the back stairwell. It was graffiti-laced and littered with flattened plastic bottles, wrappers, and other trash collecting in the corners. They climbed to the third floor and moved down the hall. Stopping at one of the doors, Devon knocked twice.

Nearly a full minute later, he heard feet shuffling on the other side. Then a woman's voice, soft and hoarse, came from behind the door.

"Who is it?"

"Me." Devon pulled the hood back off his head and moved in front of the spy hole.

After several long seconds of silence, he heard the click of a dead bolt. The door cracked open as far as the security chain would allow. Puffy, bloodshot eyes peered at him from the darkness inside.

"What are you doing here? When did you get out?" The woman hissed.

"This morning."

"They let you out?"

"Not exactly."

The woman swore. Her tone grew harsh. "No! You gonna drag me into all your mess? Just go away."

Devon clenched his fists. He could feel the anger roiling inside of him. An uncontrollable rage. He leaned in toward the opening. "I need your car."

The woman laughed out loud. "Cops gonna pick you up before you get to the end of the block. I ain't giving you my car."

Pale Man was leaning against the wall. He sighed. "We don't have time for this, chief. Get the keys."

"Mom—" Devon placed his hand against the middle of the door—"I need the car."

He shoved the door open, tearing the security chain's bracket right out of the doorframe. The woman screamed and retreated down the hall.

Devon was inside in an instant, caught his mother by her neck and spun her around. She was frail and thin, her hair a tangled mass hanging over her eyes. She wore only a large T-shirt that draped down to her knees.

Clutching her by the throat, Devon forced her into the kitchen and up against the wall. She flailed wildly, knocking a pan off the stove. She clawed at his hand, cursing him in gargled rasps.

Pale Man followed close behind him. "Don't do anything stupid. Cops won't make you a high priority. So far you're just a street punk stealing a car from his crackhead mother. No big deal. But we don't need any corpses lying around." He chuckled softly. "Not yet."

Devon leaned close to his mother's face and hissed through his teeth, "Where are the keys!"

But it was not his voice.

His mother stopped struggling, her eyes wide. She pointed a trembling finger to the cupboard across the room.

Devon glanced over his shoulder, then let her drop to the floor. He opened the cupboard to find a key ring hanging from a nail inside. Snatching the keys, he turned and glared at her.

"If you call the police, I'll kill you."

His mother clutched her neck, sobbing and coughing in a crumpled heap.

Devon turned back down the hallway and a moment later was out the door.

VALLEY OF THE SHADOW

**24**

MITCH FELT HIS BODY FLOATING in darkness. He sucked in a breath and sat up straight. And winced. His temples throbbed. He ran his fingers across his forehead and felt the soft texture of a bandage around his head. His hands were scraped. His vision was blurred but he could see he was back in Howard's living room. Back on the farm.

It was growing dark outside. The gray daylight had faded into dusk and the room was lit only by a few candles. How long had he been out?

"Welcome back." Howard's voice startled him. It came from the shadows of the corner where Howard was sitting in the rocking chair.

Mitch's heart pounded as the memories of his encounter rushed back into his head. The creature. What was that thing? And how had he gotten back here? What had happened to the truck? Had it all been just another hallucination?

"Wh-what happened?"

Howard sniffed and clicked his tongue. "You tried to steal my truck."

"Did you see that thing? That . . . that . . . What was it?"

Howard shrugged. "I didn't see anything."

"How'd I get back here?"

"I brought you back."

"You did? How? That thing smashed your truck. I thought for sure it was going to kill me."

"Don't know what to tell you." Howard glanced out the window into the growing darkness. "I tried to follow you in the milk truck and found the pickup all smashed to pieces. You were inside, out cold. I figured you just lost control and went off into the ditch on your own."

Mitch rubbed his head. "I didn't. I saw this big black . . . monster. I mean it was definitely something we haven't seen before. It was huge. Big as a tree. It smashed your pickup and me along with it. All in broad daylight. I swear that's the truth."

"Well, I didn't see anything. Just you layin' in the ditch."

"You believe me, don't you?"

Howard rubbed his jaw. "Mitch, I opened my home to you. I've done my best to be welcoming and hospitable. And I don't mind you borrowing my truck from time to time if you need it. I'd just appreciate it if in the future you'd ask permission first."

"Dude. You have to believe me on this. There's something new out there. Something we haven't seen before. Something worse than those gray things. Man, a lot worse."

"It didn't kill you, did it? Didn't carry you off somewheres?"

"No. You're right. It must've just left me there. Like it was just trying to . . ." Mitch frowned. "Just trying to keep me from leaving."

Howard took a breath. "Well, either way, it's getting dark. I got to get them generators running."

Howard left and Mitch leaned his aching head back to consider this new development. He recalled Nathan's revelation and warnings from the week before, telling Mitch he was having some kind of out-of-body experience. Telling him that he needed to leave the farm. Well, Mitch had tried to leave the farm, and look what happened.

Mitch watched the floodlights come on across the compound. He could see Howard walking from the barn to the maintenance shed, checking cables and generators, whistling a cheerful tune.

He seemed to have already gotten over the incident and was now back to his former, chipper self. Mitch found it more than a little odd but decided he wouldn't make an issue of it. That was Howard, after all. He did, however, begin planning his second escape.

And this time, he knew exactly how and when he would do it.

VALLEY OF THE SHADOW

JIM MALONE WAS SITTING in his living room when Annie arrived home at three o'clock. She brought in groceries and was busy telling him about her day. But Jim's mind was wandering.

He'd been debating what to do about Devon. He kept telling himself to forget the whole thing. Forget Devon. Forget about Conner. None of this was any of his business anyway.

But also nagging at him was a soft inner voice, urging him to see it through. Or at least to dig further. To find out more. The phone call from Darnell had certainly revealed some compelling facts, and Jim couldn't help but feel he had some deeper role to play in the whole thing. Still, he had never been comfortable getting involved in other people's lives. He'd always been one to mind his own business.

Annie was in the kitchen, putting away the groceries while their two younger kids were scrapping over the Playmobil set in the living room. Miniature pirate figures, a ship, and a million accessories lay strewn across the carpet.

Jim sat in his chair by the window, oblivious to the din and the clutter. His mind was starting to shut down. It'd been nearly twenty-four hours since he'd had any sleep. He had gone to visit Devon that morning right after getting off work. Between Jim's third-shift job at the warehouse and Devon's schedule at the juvie center, it was the only visiting time slot Jim could swing without being a relative or from the probation office.

At least he'd have the weekend to rest. His workweek didn't start again until Sunday night. His brain had been running on adrenaline and coffee most of the day, but right now he was tired of thinking.

He looked up to see Annie in the kitchen doorway. Her red hair was pulled back and she was wiping her hands on a dish towel. "So how did it go with Devon this morning?"

Jim hesitated. "I'm not sure you're going to believe me."

Annie sat down on the couch across from him. "Why? What happened?"

Jim took a deep breath and began telling Annie about the day's events. His chance meeting with Conner Hayden, his bizarre encounter with Devon, and the eerie details he had learned from Darnell.

At first Annie looked like she thought he was kidding, and it took Jim several minutes to convince her that he was in fact telling the truth. Her face grew solemn. Jim couldn't tell if the expression was because she finally believed him or because she had just concluded he was crazy.

"You really think there's something supernatural involved?"

Jim shrugged. "I don't know. I've never experienced anything like this before."

"So did you call Conner?"

"I had his business card, but his secretary said he's going to be out of the office for a while."

"There's got to be a way to get his home number. On the Internet. Or I'm sure his office has it."

Jim shook his head. "I already tried; they don't give out that information."

"Did you tell them it was important?"

Jim grunted. "They said they could relay a message, but I didn't know what to tell them."

"You have to let him know what's going on. He obviously knows Devon. Maybe he'll know where to find him."

"I know," Jim said. "I left them our number. But in a way I'm hoping he won't call. Part of me doesn't want to get involved."

"But think about it," Annie said. "This isn't just a coincidence. There was a reason we were at his office that afternoon. And why you were there to save Devon that night. And there's a reason you're involved now."

Jim sighed. "I just wish God would let us know what it is."

Of the two of them, Annie had always had the stronger faith. She was the one who initiated bedtime devotions and prayers with the children. She was the one who had to remind him to say grace before the family meals. And she was the one who made sure everyone got up and ready on Sunday mornings in time for church.

Jim had never been very comfortable with all that himself. He'd always felt awkward somehow, talking about God in front of other people. Even his own kids. But then he'd never had a role model as a kid. He'd never even met his own father. Never learned how to actually be one.

After a moment Annie leaned forward. "Jim, we should pray."

"For what?"

"Help," Annie said. "Wisdom. Some kind of clue as to what to do about all this."

Jim rubbed his eyes and leaned his head back. "How about for the cops to find Devon before he does anything stupid."

"Well, yeah. That too. Have you called his probation officer?"

"No. But look, they're just going to tell me not to get involved. I mean, it really is a police matter."

Annie sat back. "I know, but if God brought you into both of their lives for a reason, maybe it's to help in a way the police aren't able to."

Jim nodded. It was like she was reading his mind. "I've been thinking that same thing all afternoon. And there's only one other person I can think of who might need our help right now."

26

OVER THE NEXT TWO DAYS, Mitch managed to stow several items in the back of the milk truck, out of sight. A few tools, a small hand pump and gas can, as well as his duffel bag. His plan was to sneak over to the Harley dealership in Harris during their next round of gas collection. He'd get himself a bike and make a quick getaway. Whatever that thing was that had attacked him, he figured he'd have a better chance of outrunning it on a motorcycle than in Howard's old pickup.

At the end of the week, they returned to Harris. This time they began in the northeast quadrant of town and worked their way toward the center. By midday they had collected enough gasoline, so Mitch made his usual excuse.

"I'm going to browse books over at the library," he said, trying to sound casual. Earlier, he'd managed to sneak his bags from the truck when Howard wasn't looking and stash them inside one of the storefronts.

"Big surprise there." Howard rolled his eyes. "I'll head over to that grocery store we passed on our way into town. We need to stock up on food."

"See you in an hour or so." Mitch waved him off. "Don't forget the Slim Jims."

After Howard had gone, Mitch retrieved his bags and jogged to the Harley shop. He forced his way in through the service entrance and then began to explore the showroom. There were several options to choose from. His initial impulse was to pick the sleeker, more maneuverable Night Rod, but he opted instead for one of the cruisers in the Touring series. At the front window was a beautiful Road King Classic. Mitch dusted it off, then stood back and eyed the side carriers. The extra storage would be more useful at this point. And the ride would definitely be more comfortable.

After five minutes of searching, he discovered all the keys in a drawer behind the counter. He quickly found the key to the Road King and began checking the oil, coolant, and brake fluids. They were all satisfactory, despite how long the bike had been sitting. There was a bit of gas in the tank, but Mitch knew he'd need more. Then he recalled a van parked out back that they hadn't siphoned yet. Mitch found several gallons still in the tank. He transferred five gallons into the Road King and prepared to get it running.

The battery was dead, so Mitch wound up struggling with the kick-starter. It took him another twenty minutes to get the bike running, but he finally stepped away, dripping with sweat as the V-twin roared to life.

Mitch packed his tools and other belongings into the side carriers and found a leather jacket on one of the sales racks. Then he backed the Road King out of the showroom, into the attached service garage, and out the rear bay door.

He took off down a side street opposite the direction Howard had gone. He checked his watch. It would be almost a half hour yet before Howard returned from the grocery store. He'd surely spend another ten or fifteen minutes searching for Mitch at the library and the bookstore. By then, Mitch would be long gone.

The wind tugged at Mitch's hair. He didn't know exactly where he was going, but he found himself smiling. It sure felt good to be on a bike again. It had been five years since he'd left his old Harley on the dock back in Illinois. That had been far too long.

Mitch gunned the accelerator but kept an eye on his rearview mirrors, scanning the sky behind him. He hoped he had a large enough head start.

With every mile he traveled, Mitch found himself becoming more and more alert. And he was becoming more aware of the sensation. As if he were slowly waking from a long sleep. He began calling up images, delving into dormant memories of his life before . . .

Before all of this happened.

He could picture Linda again. Vividly. Almost like he was looking at her photograph. His chest began to ache as a growing awareness washed over him. He realized how long it'd been since he had seen her or since they had spoken. And he was now keenly aware of how badly he missed her.

He recalled the night of the storm. The clouds rolling

across the sky, like billows of black smoke—lights flashing inside. A bright light blazed in his face just before he had blacked out.

His breathing quickened as the memory grew more vivid. Not a light. Two lights. Mitch's heart pounded. Two lights?

Headlights.

Coming right at him!

Mitch squeezed the brakes and the Road King skidded to a halt on the empty highway. Mitch just stared blankly ahead. His chest heaved. It was only a flash of a memory, like the flare of a gunshot. He could see the headlights swerve toward him. He'd seen them coming but hadn't been able to veer out of the way. His mind raced. It was a truck. It had swerved as if to avoid something and then crossed into his lane. It happened too fast to react. Almost too fast even to remember.

Mitch looked behind him. Then to the road ahead. But it was empty. Silent.

Nathan was right. Mitch could recall the flash of the head-lights. He had been hit. He looked at his hands, patted his chest and legs. He should be dead.

How was it he was able to recall things better now? Did it have something to do with his proximity to Howard? to the farm?

The farther away he got, the clearer his thinking was becoming.

He checked his watch. He'd been traveling for over half an hour. Howard would probably be pulling up to the library about now. He'd have only a few minutes before the old guy suspected anything.

Mitch snapped the bike in gear and tore off, faster now than before.

Mitch increased his speed. He was doing well over eighty

now, but the road jogged and curved. And still, miles of open farm fields surrounded him.

Should he find shelter? Should he just keep traveling? Doubts started peppering his mind.

He suddenly felt an overpowering sense of nakedness. Exposure. As if he were the only object moving across a vast stretch of desert. Nowhere to hide. Easily spotted from the sky.

A road sign indicated that he was approaching another town. New Castle. Four miles. Mitch decided he'd be better off finding some kind of shelter.

After a few more minutes, he came upon the town. He slowed and cruised past several houses. This town was smaller than Harris. Much smaller. It was little more than an intersection with a gas station on one corner and an old mom-and-pop grocery store across from it. Ten or twelve small houses were clustered along the side street, dingy and over-grown with weeds, paint peeling from the clapboards. There was nothing here that could provide any real shelter. But it was either this . . . or keep riding.

Mitch pulled into the gas station and circled around back. After a few attempts, he managed to kick in the rear mainte-nance door. The wooden jamb was soft with rot. Once inside, he opened the bay door, pulled the Road King into the service area, and closed everything up again.

He kept watch from inside, his heart was thudding in his chest. Several minutes crept by. Nothing moved outside.

Maybe the mysterious black creature wouldn't show up this time. Mitch really had no idea what it was or how it man-aged to find him during his previous escape. It had simply appeared out of nowhere. Mitch tried to formulate some kind of strategy. But his mind was bristling with too many memories and too much fear.

Ten more minutes passed and eventually Mitch's heart rate began to slow. He paced from window to window, keeping an eye on the road out front. He figured he'd wait five more minutes and then leave. He didn't feel any safer inside this place than he did on the road.

In fact, the farm had been the only place he'd felt safe.

Though not necessarily safe. Just numb. An absence of any feeling. Part of him longed to go back and slip into that numb state again. But something—like a small voice—urged him to stay the course he'd taken so far.

A low rumbling brought him up from his thoughts. Mitch peeked outside again. It was the sound of a car approaching. Though it sounded bigger than a car.

It sounded more like a truck.

CONNER PICKED AT HIS SUPPER,
thinking of ways to explain his day
to Marta and Rachel. He had freaked
Devon out with his unannounced visit
to the juvenile center, he had managed
to *almost* get himself fired from his job,
and then he had nearly been arrested
after acting like a nutcase at Walter
Kent's house.

And probably worse than all of
those things was the fact that he had
gone to visit their pastor. After all of
Marta's pestering to set up a meeting,
she'd probably be most upset that he'd
visited Lewis without taking her along.
But Conner couldn't wait for her to get
home. The sense of urgency he felt

was too strong. And while the talk with Pastor Lewis had been more helpful than he'd expected, in some ways it had only made those feelings worse.

Marta and Rachel exchanged the usual small talk about their days. And Conner did his best to appear casually interested. Normal. Or as normal as possible.

After several minutes, Marta turned to him. "So did they give you a caseload yet?"

"Mmm, not yet. But I'll get involved in something soon enough. I'm just enjoying the grunt work at the moment. You know, not all the pressure."

"Right." Marta apparently interpreted that as sarcasm. "So did you talk to Henry? Just tell him you're itching to get back in the game. Or haven't they gotten home from Maui yet?"

Conner swallowed. "No, he's . . . he's back. He flew in a few days ago."

"Well, talk to him. Tell him you're ready. He'll give you something."

"Yeah . . . I will. I'll mention something to him."

"You are ready, aren't you?"

"Sure. Yeah."

Conner knew he had to change the subject, and quick. He couldn't talk about work. Not now. He'd never be able to hide his frustration over what had happened. Or his discomfort. Marta would sniff that out in a heart—

"What's wrong?" Marta's eyes narrowed.

"What?" Conner looked up, tried his best to seem nonchalant. He cleared his throat. "Nothing's wrong."

Marta wasn't buying. "Connie, what happened?"

Conner caught Rachel's eyes darting back and forth like she was watching a tennis match. He forced a laugh. "What makes you think—?"

"Connie . . ."

"Nothing's wrong." Conner put down his fork and dabbed
his mouth with a napkin. He could feel Marta's gaze but did
his best to avert it . . . without looking like he was trying to
avert it.

After several tortuous moments of silence, Conner took
a breath. "Well, I did talk to Henry today. . . ."

"So what happened? Wait . . ." Marta leaned forward.
"You didn't tell him what you told me this morning, did you?"

Rachel glanced at Marta. "Tell him what?"

"Actually," Conner said, "he called me into his office."

"And you told him?" Marta gaped. "Everything?"

"Told him what?"

Conner hated when Marta wore him down like this. It
was like she was the lawyer and he was the hapless defen-
dant. "I didn't intend to at first. But he said people were
complaining that I was acting like a zealot, and—"

"A zealot? They said you were acting like a zealot? You've
only been back a couple weeks!"

"—so I had to defend myself. I had to tell him."

Rachel slapped her palm on the table. "Tell him what?"

Conner rubbed his eyes. He was tired and on edge at the
same time. Part of him badly wanted to sleep, but another
part felt like jumping up from the table and doing something.
Anything.

He looked at Rachel. "There was more to my . . . my heart
attack than I told you about."

"More?" Rachel blinked. "What do you mean?"

"I mean there was more to my experience . . . y'know,
when I was dying. More that I saw and did." Conner bit his lip.
"A lot more."

Rachel looked at Marta. "Did you know about this?"

Marta shrugged. "I just found out this morning."

Rachel's head swiveled back to Conner. "Well, what happened? Why didn't you tell us before?"

"Sweetie, it's all very bizarre and creepy. And frankly I was afraid I was going crazy."

"So is that why you went to see Pastor Lewis this afternoon?"

Marta straightened up. "What?"

"Wh-what?" Conner stammered. "Where'd you hear that?"

"Well . . . ," Rachel began with some hesitation. "When I got home from school, Mrs. Lewis called—must've been while you were on your way home. She said you had left your Bible there. I guess I forgot to tell you."

"Nice," Conner grunted.

Marta leaned forward. "You went to see Pastor Lewis without me?"

Conner found himself searching for words. Was this God keeping him honest? Or was it just His idea of a joke? "Look, I was a little frustrated with everything that happened, so I decided maybe it wouldn't hurt to just visit for a bit."

"Without me?"

Conner stood. He could feel his defensiveness giving way to anger. "Yes." His voice grew sharp and he leaned over the table. "Yes, I went without you. I wanted to talk to him. Man-to-man. Okay? And you know what? I told him everything too. I figured, why not let the whole world know I'm going crazy? Why not let them all think I'm nuts?"

He left the dining room, snatched his keys from the kitchen counter, and headed for the front door.

"Where are you going?" Marta called after him. "Don't get mad."

"I'm not mad," Conner huffed. "I just need to go out for a bit."

"Where are you going?"

"Out."

His anxiety was growing, like a pot coming to a boil. He found he couldn't sit still any longer. He felt as if he'd just taken an IV of pure caffeine. The sense of frustration that had been gnawing at him earlier was now overwhelming, and he couldn't keep it bottled up anymore. He was tired of just sitting around. Waiting for answers. Waiting for God. He had to get out of the house. He had to do something.

And he knew exactly what it was.

VALLEY OF THE SHADOW

28

MITCH'S SHOULDERS SLUMPED as he watched the milk truck roll to a squeaking halt at the intersection. Howard climbed out, tugged off his cap, and wiped his forehead with a bandanna from his pocket, a slight smirk on his face.

What was the old man doing here? How did he know which direction Mitch had gone?

"Mitch!" Howard called out, peering into the grocery store and then over at the garage.

Mitch instinctively ducked back from the window.

"I know you're here. What . . . you get one of them Harleys? You got the itch to ride again?"

Mitch inched forward so he could just glance through the window without being seen.

Howard kept on. "I don't think you've thought this through, Mitch. Whutch you gonna do come nightfall? Build a campfire? You think that's gonna keep you safe?"

Mitch remained still. Maybe the guy would get tired and go home. Maybe he just wanted to say his piece.

Howard's pleasant expression began to turn sour. His voice grew harsh. "I opened my home to you, boy. I saved you. Gave you shelter and food. And this is how you repay me? Where would you be without me, huh? Where would you be?"

Mitch could see Howard glaring at the gas station, his forehead gnarled up in a frown. He waited a moment longer, then turned back to the truck. "I can't be responsible for what happens to you now," he said as he climbed into the cab. "You keep on this path and you're on your own." He slammed the door and leaned his head out the window. "You hear me? You are on your own!"

The truck chugged to life. Gears ground as the vehicle lurched forward into the parking lot of the grocery store. Howard turned it around and pulled onto the road, back the way he had come.

The truck growled off into the distance and within seconds, silence returned. Inside the garage, Mitch breathed a sigh.

Obviously there was something wrong with Howard. Something Mitch hadn't seen before—or refused to see. Maybe he was still angry that Mitch had ruined his pickup. Maybe he was mad that he'd have to siphon gas by himself from now on. Or maybe . . .

Maybe he was just afraid to be alone.

A gust of wind rattled the big bay door of the garage with a soft moan. Almost like a whisper.

Someone was standing in the shadows of the garage. Mitch's hands were sweating. His heart pounded. "What do you want?"

A voice replied, "Do you have any idea what kind of embarrassment you are to me?"

The figure stepped out of the shadows, but Mitch had known who it was as soon as he'd heard the voice.

"Just leave me alone, Dad."

His father ignored him. "Why can't you act like a normal kid? Why does everything have to revolve around you?" He held out a piece of paper. He had that wild-eyed look. Lips all puckered, nostrils flared.

Mitch rolled his eyes. "What now?"

"Smoking marijuana?" His father's eyes were red but fierce. He rattled the paper in the air. "It's bad enough that you can't get along with anyone there, but now you're smoking pot? Do you have any idea what the press will do with this?"

Mitch frowned. He remembered this conversation. He was sixteen. His first year at St. Anthony's. He'd been kicked out of every other private school his father had stuck him in. Fighting with students. Disrespect for faculty. Mitch had hated the uniforms, the rules, and the snobbery.

So his old man had finally enrolled him in a Catholic school. And this was worse than all the others. Mitch hated the teachers, the nuns and priests. They creeped him out more than anything. Mitch didn't trust any of them.

And he couldn't stand the other kids. His stomach churned at just the thought of going to school every day. The creepy building. The musty rooms. Mitch had to do something to calm himself down. So he'd sneak a few drinks from his father's liquor cabinet in the morning. Scotch, bourbon, Grey Goose, and a variety of wines. He always made sure he never drank too much from any one bottle. And after a while he had actually become a bit of a connoisseur.

Then he met Sonja Belotti in his sophomore year. Her parents were rich and divorced and tossed her between them like a hot potato. Neither one seemed to want her for very long. She was a bleach blonde with crystal blue eyes who wore tight jeans and black T-shirts. Mitch fell for her hard the moment he first saw her.

And Sonja was every bit his match at getting in trouble. She was the one who had taken his virginity and his heart. Though really, Mitch had given both to her freely and eagerly. And she was the one who had first introduced him to pot.

"You think this is funny?" His father's voice broke into Mitch's thoughts.

Mitch found he'd been smiling. It quickly turned into a scowl. "No. I think you're pathetic."

Mitch's father strode toward him, holding the paper in front of him, shaking it. "You think I'm paying for you to goof off and get high? I've got news for you, kid. You are going to straighten up or so help me, I'll—"

"Shut up!" Mitch punched his palms into the man's chest, throwing him back across the garage. "You think I'm afraid of you anymore? I'm not afraid of you!"

Mitch's teeth were clenched so tightly his jaws ached. Rage boiled up inside him as he lunged after his father. But he stopped suddenly, staring into the shadows of the empty garage. His chest heaved.

They were doing it to him again. Messing with his mind. Throwing these hallucinations at him and probably watching how he would react. Maybe they were off somewhere watching him on a monitor, laughing their heads off.

Mitch shook his head. His anger and frustration were

building, but now he had nowhere to direct it. He swore at the shadows of the garage.

His tirade was cut short by a thunderous noise outside. The monstrous roaring he'd heard before. Part beast, part machine, and unlike anything Mitch had ever known. He spun around to see an enormous black shadow sweep past the bay door windows, around the side of the building, out of sight.

Mitch scrambled to the window to get a glimpse outside. He had to get out of here. If that thing had found him, he'd be a sitting duck in the garage.

The building shuddered as something pounded the roof. Mitch could hear the joists and rafters cracking. Dust and dirt poured down as a second blow shook the building. He slid open the bay door and ran back to his bike.

Another explosive bellow blasted from outside.

Mitch thumbed the starter and kicked the bike into gear as a huge black limb crashed down through the roof in a shower of metallic and wooden debris. He jerked the throttle and squealed out of the garage, onto the road. Mitch glanced in the mirror to see the black creature huddled over the gas station, one of its arms jammed through the roof.

He turned forward in time to see a flash of light coming right at him. He ducked instinctively as something like a large flare streaked over his head, leaving a trail of smoke tracing behind it. Mitch swerved the bike, skidding to a halt. He glanced over his shoulder as the flash impacted with the creature. A moment later came a burst of light and a thunderous explosion as the creature disintegrated—along with the gas station—in a billowing plume of fire. Chunks of concrete and glowing metal shot up and outward.

The shock wave knocked Mitch off his bike and sent him rolling onto the asphalt. He covered his head as flaming debris rained down across the entire town. His ears rang with a dull hum. He fought for breath, feeling like he'd been socked in the ribs with a bowling ball.

Groggy and disoriented, Mitch struggled to his knees. But he felt the ground shifting beneath him. The ringing in his ears began to fade and he managed to suck in an agonizing lungful of air.

In his haze, Mitch glimpsed someone walking toward him through the smoke, from the direction the flare had come.

29

CONNER PULLED UP to the hospital in Winthrop Harbor. It was just after seven o'clock and he figured he should be able to get into the ICU to see Mitch without much difficulty. That is, if everything went smoothly.

During the last two months, Conner had managed to sneak into Mitch's room on two previous occasions, but only for brief visits. He had to plan his arrival within a ten-minute window during the change in nursing shifts. Security tended to wane a bit during those times, and Conner found that if he could make himself look like he belonged in the hospital—like someone in the health care profession—he could go just about anywhere he wanted without raising suspicion.

He wasn't exactly new at this stunt either. He had purchased a white lab coat and stethoscope when he'd first graduated law school. A clipboard with several sheets of miscellaneous legal forms completed the masquerade. It had served as a pretty reliable method for drumming up business in those early years. Making contact with injured potential clients was always a challenge. A task that called for creativity and innovation.

Conner stopped in the men's room to change, then made his way to ICU. He felt a twinge of guilt but quickly buried it in the rationale of his mission to help Mitch. He hoped the end justified his means.

Conner loitered around the entrance to ICU until someone came out of the doors; then he walked through with a nonchalant but hurried gait, reading feverishly from his clipboard.

He located Mitch's room and passed by twice when he glimpsed someone else in the room. A nurse stood at Mitch's bedside, checking the IV. After she left, Conner slipped inside.

Mitch lay there motionless, his arms and chest connected to a network of tubes and electrodes. His head was wrapped in gauze and his face was scarred. A breathing tube from the bedside ventilator had been inserted into his throat and taped at his mouth.

A slight chill washed over Conner and he caught a flash of movement from the corner of his eye. He thought at first the nurse had returned, but except for him—and Mitch—the room was empty.

Conner turned back to Mitch and watched him for a moment, listening to the quiet humming and beeping of the various monitors and pumps. He bent down to Mitch's ear.

"Mitch?" he whispered, watching for the slightest twitch or sign of acknowledgment. He glanced over Mitch's chart, trying to make sense of the information, searching for any report of treatment or any indication that he'd been scheduled to be disconnected. He couldn't find anything relevant.

He bent down and whispered again, "I'm not going to let you die."

"That's what I tell him too."

Conner straightened and turned to see a young woman in the doorway. She was in her early twenties, Conner guessed, and thin, with straight brown hair and large brown eyes.

She offered him a meager smile as she entered. "I talk to him too. They said it can't hurt, right?"

Conner swallowed, not sure what to say. "Umm," he stammered, "it's been known to help."

She leaned over Mitch and kissed him softly. "Anything new? Any improvement?"

Conner remembered his doctor's garb and tried to recover. He cleared his throat and did his best to sound aloof and professional. "Uh . . . yes. Nothing noticeable, but I'm still optimistic." He started to sidle toward the door.

The young woman turned and held out a hand. "I don't think I've met you yet, Doctor . . . ?"

Conned smiled and shook her hand, trying to hide his discomfort. "I'm . . . Dr. Hart . . . man."

"Dr. Hartman? Linda. Linda Wilson."

"Ah, yes." Before Conner could stop himself, he blurted out, "His fiancée."

She blinked and frowned. "No . . . we weren't engaged. We were dating for a while. But . . . how did you know?"

Conner felt as if a hundred icy needles had suddenly

pricked his neck. "Oh, I . . . I'm sorry. I must've . . . I just assumed . . ."

Linda waved it off with a smile. "That's okay. I don't think he was quite ready to make that commitment yet." Then her smile faded. "I just hope he can remember me when he gets better."

Conner bit hard on his cheek, cursing himself. Mitch had mentioned that he'd been on his way to propose the night of the accident but never actually made it. He had to get out of here quick, before he made any further gaffes. "Well, we're not giving up hope yet."

Linda's eyes lit up. "Really? I . . ." She glanced out into the hallway and lowered her voice. "I get the feeling that no one else around here seems to think he'll get any better. Are you that specialist they were going to bring in?"

"Specialist? No. I . . . I had heard about Mi—uh . . . this case and wanted to stop by to familiarize myself with the, uh, with the charts. No. I don't, I don't really know anything about this case."

Linda narrowed her eyes. "But I heard you talking to him, telling him you weren't going to let him die. I assumed you were going to be treating him."

Conner found himself nodding and sweating. "Yes, well I just wanted to, y'know, offer a word of . . . encourag—"

"You're not really a doctor, are you?" Linda's eyes grew cold.

Conner offered up a laugh. "Umm, yeah, but I was . . ."

"What do you want with him?"

Conner continued backing toward the door. "Nothing. No, I was just making my rounds and wanted to . . . y'know— this is an interesting case. So I stopped by for a minute."

Linda's frown turned to a scowl. "I'm calling the nurse." She pushed past Conner, out into the hallway.

Conner caught her arm. "Look," he said in a low voice.
"I'm a friend. Okay? No, I'm not a doctor. I . . . I just wanted to
see him. I don't want anything."

"Who are you?"

"I told you. Just a friend."

Linda's eyes were still icy. "I thought I had met all of
Mitch's friends. How come I've never met you before?"

Conner shrugged. "I only recently got to know him. I'm
a lawyer, and I was trying to make sure—"

"Is he in trouble?"

"No. No, I just want to be sure he's getting the care he
needs."

"A lawyer? What did Mitch need a lawyer for?"

Conner rubbed his eyes. "He's not in trouble. I'm a friend
of the family. Sort of. And . . . it's a long story."

"You don't think he's getting the treatment he needs?
Are you working on some kind of lawsuit?"

"No. I just feel like . . . I get the feeling that Mitch's father
may be preparing to disconnect. He may be giving up."

Linda's eyes widened. "How do you know that? Who told
you that?"

"I've been trying to contact Walter Kent—"

"He's very sick."

"Yes, I know. I've been trying to warn him . . . to tell him
not to give up hope. I can't explain it, but I really believe Mitch
will recover."

"But who told you they were going to disconnect him?"

Conner rubbed his eyes again. This was getting out of
hand. He should've left when he'd had the chance. He never
should have started talking to this woman. How much more
could he reveal to her? He couldn't tell her everything. She'd
think he was crazy for sure.

"I spoke to Mr. Kent's assistant today. And she mentioned something about . . . final arrangements."

Linda backed away, shaking her head. "Final arrangements? What does that mean?"

Conner sighed. "I don't know. That's why I snuck in—to see if I could find any more information."

Then a thought struck him. "Wait a minute. How come you're here? How did you get permission to visit?" The policy was immediate family only inside the ICU. And Kent had made sure the hospital clamped down hard on that rule.

Linda hesitated before answering, looked down. "I . . . I used to volunteer here. I know some of the nurses and they let me visit in the evenings. They knew we were dating, so they let me come see him when no one's around. I just come and talk to him in the evenings. And pray."

Conner drew a long breath and glanced at Mitch. "Maybe that's the best either of us can do right now."

30

SMOKE SWIRLED AROUND the approaching figure. Mitch's vision was still blurry, but after a moment the figure came into focus.

Nathan strode through the smoke. He was wearing a long black overcoat with what looked like a rocket launcher resting on one of his shoulders. He grinned. "Hey, pretty good shot, huh?"

Mitch staggered to his feet. "Except that you nearly killed me along with it. Are you nuts?"

Nathan chuckled. "You still don't get how this all works, do you? I can't kill you. I couldn't kill you if I tried. . . . Not here at least."

"Yeah, yeah. I'm dead already. I know that."

Nathan dusted him off. "You didn't listen to anything I told you. You're not dead. You're in a coma. This—" he patted Mitch's shoulders—"is not your body. This is just a pseudo-corporeal construct generated by your spirit. It's pure energy. You don't have any bones to break, no blood to lose. No heart to stop. Get it?"

Mitch groaned and rubbed his neck. "Odd that I should feel such vivid pain from a simulation."

"Ah, but that's because pain is really just energy." Nathan helped Mitch hobble back to his motorcycle. "In your physical body, pain was merely a set of electrical signals transmitted through your nerves and interpreted by your brain. And now your spirit remembers what your brain used to tell it. Like Pavlov's dogs, you're just responding to perceived stimuli."

Mitch tried to lift the Road King off its side, but it wouldn't budge. He glanced up at Nathan. "Little help please?"

"You're not listening." Nathan motioned for Mitch to step aside. Then he grabbed the handlebar with one hand and tilted the bike upright.

Mitch blinked and stepped back. "Whoa. Dude. How . . . how did you . . . ?"

Nathan sighed. "Because it doesn't actually weigh anything. Or more accurately, it doesn't have to weigh anything. You keep thinking you're in the physical world. This ain't it."

Mitch stared at Nathan, then back at his bike. He grabbed hold of the handlebars and tried to shake the motorcycle. He could feel its weight. He could feel its substance. "I don't get it."

Nathan patted Mitch on the shoulder. "Don't worry. We'll work on it. But we should get going." He glanced at his watch and gestured to the smoldering gas station. "Just like I can't kill you, I can't kill your friend over there either."

Mitch stared at the rubble. He thought he saw something moving in the debris. Something that looked like a charred piece of wood shuddered. It rolled and twisted itself through the clutter toward another similar-looking black stick. The two pieces slowly touched and then conjoined into a single piece.

"What is that thing?"

Nathan rubbed his jaw. "Not sure exactly, but I believe it's called a Keeper. Think of it as kind of a guard dog. It's one of the ways this place tries to prevent you from leaving."

"Why haven't I seen it before?"

"Because you never tried to leave before. As long as you stayed on the farm, numb and tranquil, everything was okay. But now that you tried to leave . . . well, let's just say it won't let you go without a fight."

"So what did you do to it?"

"All I did was temporarily disrupt its unanimity. But we should get going before it coalesces again. C'mon, let's put some miles between us."

Nathan turned and headed to a waiting car. Mitch stopped in his tracks when he saw the spotless red Ferrari F430 through the clearing smoke.

"Whoa. Where'd you get that?"

"Same place you got your bike . . . kind of." He flashed a smile. "Only mine was intentional."

Mitch frowned. "What's that supposed to mean?"

His gaze traveled along the F430's sleek profile. A bright red Spider convertible with a tan leather interior. Beneath the surface lay a 4.3-liter flat crank V-8. It could easily do zero to sixty in under four seconds.

Nathan started it up, gunned the accelerator. "You coming

or not?" He slid the car in gear and tore off in a fishtailing spray of gravel and smoke.

Mitch whistled to himself as he watched the Ferrari rocket down the road. Then he shook his head and started up his Road King. A moment later, he took off as well, following the Ferrari west along the highway.

Behind them, amid the smoldering debris, several black shapes were slithering toward one another.

A SQUAD CAR TURNED LEFT onto Jefferson and rolled past the gravel parking lot toward Hubbard. Its headlights shone momentarily into the windshield of the Ford Tempo, parked near the railroad overpass. Devon slumped down and held his breath as the car flooded with light. The squad passed without incident. Without even slowing down.

Devon sat up again. He was camouflaged well enough here, off the street, huddled amid a half-dozen other cars. He reclined the seat and cracked open the window. His mother would have reported the car by now. But really, it was just a beat-up old Tempo and wouldn't be high priority for the cops.

Devon knew he should probably close his eyes and get some rest. But his mind was still buzzing. He needed a plan. What was he going to do for cash? The car would get him only so far. He'd need to dump it eventually. Plus, he'd need to get some more food. The cold remains of a few french fries littered the seat beside him with the crumpled wrapper of the cheeseburgers he'd ordered at a McDonald's drive-through. It was all he'd had since breakfast. Now he sipped down the last drops of his Coke.

On the other side of the tracks was a six-dollar parking lot with one of those port-a-johns for the attendant. At least he wouldn't have to go into a gas station or restaurant to use the bathroom. Less chance of being seen.

He leaned his head back and closed his eyes.

"That's right," a voice said from the backseat. "Try to get some rest."

Devon glared in the mirror at the pale-skinned figure behind him. "Get outta my face."

"I'm not going anywhere. Besides, you've got a big day tomorrow."

"Doing what?"

"Well, first you need to visit your boss. You need a gun."

"He ain't gonna give me no gun. And I ain't gonna kill no one."

Pale Man sighed. "Anybody ever teach you about using double negatives?"

"Double what?"

"Forget it. It's kind of endearing."

"Man . . . just leave me alone."

"Alone?" Pale Man snorted. "If it weren't for me, you'd still be sitting in your cell."

"All you've done is get me in more trouble than I was already in."

"Son, you have no idea how much trouble you're in."

"And I ain't your son, either."

"Quit your bellyaching, chief, or I'll walk you off a bridge. You should be thankful you're even alive."

"Why are you doing this to me?"

"Because I can." Pale Man leaned forward. "You came into our world and got back out alive. You're one lucky kid. You should've ended up like your buddy Terrell."

"Shut up!"

"Know what he's doing right now?" Pale Man started to giggle. "Screaming his fool head off. He'll be doing that for, like . . . forever."

Devon clenched his jaw. His eyes stung.

"Oh . . ." Pale Man's voice softened. "Oh, I'm sorry. Am I upsetting you? I'll try to be more sensitive from now on. Really. We'll be friends. We're going to be great friends, you and me. Before you know it, you'll forget all about Tyreek . . . er, Tyrone. You know . . . what's-his-name."

"I don't have to listen to you."

"Of course you don't, kid." Pale Man leaned back again, laughing. "You came back to life, all right. You just didn't come back alone."

VALLEY OF THE SHADOW

32

THE AFTERNOON DREW OUT toward
evening as Mitch followed the Ferrari
west. Or at least what he assumed was
west. Without reference to the sun, it was
impossible to be sure which direction he
was headed.

The highway cut a straight path
through miles of farmland, past the
occasional cluster of drab houses and
through several abandoned towns.
Before long, everything along the
road began to look alike to Mitch, like
they were traveling the same section
of highway over and over. It was as if
Indiana were stretching on for eternity.
They traveled for more than three hours
until at last Nathan pulled to a stop in a
secluded wayside.

"Mind telling me exactly where we're headed?" Mitch said as he pulled up alongside the Ferrari.

"West," Nathan said, pointing ahead.

"I know west. I mean west where? Where specifically?"

Nathan got out of the car and stretched. Then he stared into the distance for a moment and breathed a sigh. "To the edge of the world. The only place you can get back to your body from here."

"The edge of the world, huh?" Mitch snorted. "And I thought Howard was a little crazy."

Nathan flashed a smile. "I know you're still having some trouble getting your head around this whole thing. That's why I thought we'd take a slight detour."

"Nice. Where to?"

"Someplace that should provide you a little perspective."

"Dude, why can't you just give me a straight answer? Like 'Hey, we're going to Kansas' or something. 'Cuz all this oooh-I'm-so-mysterious-and-insightful stuff is starting to get a little old."

"Sorry, Mitch." Nathan looked as if he was repressing a laugh. "It's just that some things you really do have to see for yourself in order to understand. Besides, this place I want to show you doesn't have a name."

"Whatever."

Nathan glanced at the sky. "It's going to be dark in a little while. We should get going."

"You do know those creatures all come out at night, don't you?"

"Yep. But they can't really do anything to you."

"Oh, really?" Mitch's eyebrows went up. "Because you obviously haven't encountered the same ones I have."

"I mean they can't drag you away like the others," Nathan

said as he climbed back into the Ferrari. "See, if it's not your time to go yet, they can't do anything to you. Not until you reach the final stage."

"Final stage?"

"That point where you're beyond any hope of revival. I mean, don't get me wrong, they can put on a pretty scary act, but they can't really touch you. Not yet." Nathan fired up the car, gunned the engine, and grinned. "Until then, it's all just a show."

He stomped on the accelerator and tore out of the wayside. Mitch watched him go and rolled his eyes.

"Oooh, I'm so mysterious," he muttered and swung a leg over his bike.

Mitch pulled onto the highway and accelerated to eighty-five but still wasn't closing the gap on Nathan. He pushed his speed to ninety and slowly found himself gaining. After several minutes, he was close enough to see Nathan lift his hand and point to the left.

Mitch glanced in that direction, then slowed the bike and peered over his glasses. The horizon was hazy, but he could see a long, jagged mountain range to the south. Dark purple against the gray sky. Most of the peaks looked so tall that they disappeared into the canopy of clouds.

Mitch frowned. Mountains?

In Indiana?

He knew they had come a long way, but they hadn't traveled that far. And while he was no geography whiz, he did recall that Indiana had no mountains.

Up ahead, the Ferrari's brake lights flashed. The car skidded through a sharp left turn, kicking up a cloud of dust, and proceeded south along a side road. Mitch pulled to a stop at the intersection and stared down the road. The red Ferrari was now just a cloud of dust headed into the mountains. The terrain that spread out before Mitch was flat and low, peppered by miles and miles of stubby sagebrush.

Mitch's frown deepened. One thing was clear.

They weren't in Indiana anymore.

33

CONNER FOUND HIMSELF once more fighting his way through the black forest of his nightmares. Trees loomed like sentries, tall and blackened, their barren branches twisted and gnarled. Ahead of him, the cabin sat amid the shadows, its orange light shining dimly in the woods.

Conner fought his way through the undergrowth and stood at the entrance. Again.

Help me!

He could feel the voice calling out to him, more than he actually heard it. It was like some invisible force drawing him toward the cabin. Always back to the cabin. His heart pounded and his palms felt cold and moist.

He slipped inside and glanced around. "Mitch?"

Nothing moved. All he could hear was his own heart pounding inside his chest. The wind moaned through the trees outside, rattling the windowpanes and the door. But Conner could feel a presence outside. As if someone was watching him.

The cabin's porch creaked and a dark shape moved past the front window. A second one followed it. Then a third.

"What's going on? What do you want?" His voice sounded weak and shaky.

He could see them now. Dark shapes huddled outside the window. There must've been dozens of them out there. Surrounding the cabin. They just stood there, as if watching him silently.

Conner crouched in the corner. "What do you want?"

Then the voice came again.

He's coming!

Outside, Conner could hear the snapping of sticks underfoot. A wave of terror descended on him and he pressed further against the wall, away from the door.

The footsteps drew closer. The floorboards of the porch creaked. A shadow moved outside the bottom of the door. The old brass knob turned and the door swung open.

Conner caught his breath. A tall figure loomed in the doorway, a motionless silhouette.

Conner could manage only a hoarse whisper. "Mitch?"

But the figure didn't move. After a moment, the stranger stepped inside and the glow from the stove fell on his face.

Conner stammered. "H-Howard?"

Howard Bristol stared down at Conner with white, lifeless eyes. His gray hair was disheveled. He looked thinner than Conner remembered. His cheeks were sunken and his mouth

drooped in loose folds at the corners. His jeans and red flan-
nel shirt hung loose over his gaunt frame.

A stench filled the tiny room. The odor of rot overwhelmed
Conner. "What do you want?"

Howard's thin lips parted in a demented smirk and a voice
whispered, "There's a hole in the sky."

At that, the other figures outside began to crowd into the
room behind the tall farmer. Howard just stood there grinning
as they scurried around him. These weren't the hideous gray
creatures that Conner remembered. They were human. Men
and women. More than a dozen of them, moving with lurch-
ing, jerky movements. Their eyes too were white and soulless.
They were upon him in a moment, clutching his arms and legs.
Hands closed around his throat.

Conner tried to scream. . . .

He sat up in bed, sucking air into his lungs. Heart
pounding.

Gray, early morning daylight shone in around the edges
of the window blinds.

Marta rolled over. "You okay?"

"Yeah."

Conner tried to slow his breathing. Another nightmare.
Though this one was different. This was something he hadn't
seen before. Howard had never invaded his dreams before.
What had he meant about a hole in the sky? And what about
all of the other people in the cabin? Conner wondered if these
things had any significance or if it was just his subconscious
playing tricks on him. Or if there was something he was supposed to figure out from it.

Conner felt completely alone. Like he was in a foreign
country, trying to understand a new language. A country
where everyone seemed to be talking earnestly—their faces

showing urgency but their language remaining incomprehensible to him.

Did this mean something? What was he supposed to do?

He lay back and wiped the sweat from his forehead. He closed his eyes and tried to pray. It was an entirely new experience for him, and after two months, he still didn't feel comfortable with it. Marta often encouraged him to pray with her. And he had to admit, she was much better at it. More comfortable with talking to an invisible God. It seemed like she was carrying on an actual conversation. Like talking to a friend. But Conner still found it difficult to pray out loud. Especially in front of her.

He could speak in front of juries and judges, even improvising as the occasion warranted. But he couldn't for the life of him get the hang of prayer.

He believed. At least he knew he wanted to believe. But in so many ways, he felt ill-equipped to handle talking to the Creator of the universe. A God who could see right through him. Who knew his thoughts.

Maybe that was the problem. Conner's career had trained him to be so polished. So rehearsed. Even his improvisation was still for the sake of performance. All just to elicit an emotional response from his audience and direct them to make the decision he wanted. Not that it was all fake, but it was often an act. Trials, after all, were about who could put on the best show.

But with God it was different. Conner knew God didn't want any of that. No pomp or pretense. Just simple, sincere communication. Just come and talk to Him. Humble and trusting like a child.

Conner had forgotten what that was like.

Marta had fallen back to sleep and Conner could hear her

rhythmic breathing. He sighed and tried again to speak with
God in the quiet of his thoughts.

*Look, I apologize if I sound a little unpolished. I know You
know what I'm thinking. I just feel like I'm going crazy. I know
You saved me for a reason, but I don't get why You're making
it so hard to figure out what it is. I feel like I'm at the end of my
rope here. I want to be useful. I want to be obedient. Just give
me a sign. Give me something. Some kind of direction.*

Conner closed his eyes again. He didn't know what more
to ask. Even his talk with Pastor Lewis hadn't given him any
concrete direction.

Then it struck him. What had Lewis said? That God's plan
might not be about Mitch, but maybe it had something to do
with Howard?

Conner sat up. Each of his nightmares had been about
the cabin. On Howard's farm. And now he'd dreamed about
Howard himself. A sickening realization was starting to gel
inside Conner. It was a thought—an idea so completely ludi-
crous and frightening that up until now he'd managed to keep
it well at bay. Locked away deep inside the realm of impos-
sibility. But somehow Lewis had unlocked the door and that
idea had crept out. And now it was sitting there. Just sitting
there, waiting for him to notice it.

He had to go to Indiana.

He had to go back to the farm.

VALLEY OF THE SHADOW

IT WAS NEARLY DARK by the time
Howard arrived back at the farm. He'd
spent the better part of the day driving
aimlessly, unsure of his next move.
But as the afternoon wore on, his frustration had only grown. He stormed
into the house and slammed the door.
He paced across the kitchen, muttering curses. After everything he'd done
for that kid, all those years of watching over him, this was the thanks he
got. No appreciation, no acknowledgment, not even the courtesy of an
explanation.

He slammed his fists into the cupboards, flung open the pantry door, and
hurled cans across the room, sending

them crashing through the plaster and the windows. He whipped boxes of oatmeal and granola off the shelves, showering the linoleum with their contents. He threw plates onto the floor, shattering them into pieces.

His tirade lasted for several minutes until every drawer and every cupboard lay open, empty, or broken. He stood in the middle of the mess, red faced, his chest heaving.

His gaze beat a trail across the room until it came to rest at last on the cribbage board on the table in front of him. The wall held the tally of five years of games. He had yet to win a single one.

Howard picked up the board and hurled it at the wall, where it embedded in the plaster. Then he sank into the chair and put his face in his hands. He was alone again. He had been alone before, though now he felt it more keenly. After the last five years, the farm seemed all the more empty.

A breeze wafted through the broken window, fluttering the curtain slightly. A soft voice followed on its heels. Nearly a whisper.

"Beloved."

Howard looked up and shook his head. "I tried. I . . . I really did. I thought the Keeper had scared him outta leaving. But he just up and left anyway."

"We cannot let him go."

"What do you want me to do? I couldn't force him to stay. I couldn't chain him up here. He went and got one of them motorcycles running and just took off."

"He's not alone."

"What?" Howard caught his breath. "What do you mean?"

"The Enemy is moving again. Helping him. We feel it."

"The Enemy?" Howard stood. "He . . . He's back?"

"He has sent a surrogate."

"So . . . you think Mitch knows the truth now? Do you think they showed him?"

"Perhaps, but it will not matter. They cannot help him in time. We must see that he does not go back. We must follow him."

Howard frowned. "We? What do you . . . ?"

"Come to us, Beloved."

"But . . . but . . ." Howard's voice broke as he stammered. "You don't need me to go after him."

"With you he may yet be persuaded."

"But the Keeper won't let him leave. It'll follow him to the edge of the world."

"If it fails, we cannot allow him to escape. Not with the Enemy helping him."

"Are . . . are you sure? I mean, as long as the Keeper—"

"The Keeper could fail!" The voice flared into a biting tone. The cupboards and walls rattled. "We cannot allow him to go back! We cannot allow the Enemy to succeed."

"Forgive me." Howard sat down again. His anger drained from him. "I guess . . . I suppose you know best."

"I do, Beloved. I only ever do what is best for us."

Howard stared at the rubble in the kitchen. The shattered plates and glasses. His chest ached as a sudden wave of emotion hit him. He missed his wife and son. It seemed more than a decade since they had last been together.

He would sometimes dream of Clarice. She would be standing on the porch, calling him in for supper. And Owen would come out from the barn, smiling. Then they would all go inside for a meal. Howard longed more than anything to join them again. To be together once more, like they promised.

"How much longer must I endure this place?"

The voice softened. "Soon, Beloved. Very soon now."

VALLEY OF THE SHADOW

**35**

MITCH FOLLOWED NATHAN through
the flat desert terrain toward the base
of the mountains. Within fifteen minutes the dirt road curved sharply and
headed up into the foothills. They followed it as far as they were able, until
the road grew too narrow and steep to
travel. Nathan stopped at a point where
the road curved and got out.

Mitch guessed they must have
been a thousand feet over the desert
floor. He could see the narrow ribbon
of road winding back down the slopes.
Below, the desert spread out into the
distance like a carpet. It was nearly sun-
set and the gray gloom was deepening.

Ahead of them, the road narrowed

further and turned back on itself as the grade increased dramatically. Mitch knew he wouldn't be able to get the Road King up that steep a slope. And the Ferrari certainly wouldn't be able to make it either.

"We're going to have to hoof it from here, buddy," Nathan said.

Mitch was less than enthused by the prospect. He peered up the path as it wound its way out of sight. "How much farther?"

"Maybe another half a mile or so, but it's mostly straight up."

"Great."

Mitch untied his duffel bag from the bike and slung it over his shoulder. He noticed Nathan wasn't carrying anything with him. No supplies, no extra clothes. Nothing. They were hiking into the wilderness, and all this guy had with him was the clothes he wore.

"Dude," Mitch grunted, "doesn't look like you came prepared for mountain climbing."

"Looks are deceiving here, Mitch."

"Oh, right. I forgot. Are we at least going to come back this way?"

"That's the plan."

"You got a flashlight or anything?"

"Nah. Won't need one."

They followed the path up a boulder-strewn slope. Mitch found himself growing more and more uncertain of his predicament. To be sure, Nathan had rescued him from the creature—what had he called it? A Keeper? But still, this situation was becoming altogether too strange. It was getting dark and they had no flashlights, little food, and no shelter. Yet for all this lack of resources, Nathan seemed completely unfazed by the danger they were obviously in.

Mitch huffed as the incline increased sharply. He scrambled around boulders and pulled himself up jagged outcroppings. Then to make matters worse, he found himself suddenly surrounded by a dense fog. They had entered the cloud cover.

Mitch could barely make out Nathan's shape in front of him. He was no more than a few yards back, but at times Mitch could not even see the guy.

"How much longer?" Mitch said between breaths.

"Just a little farther." Nathan's voice came back out of the fog.

"Dude, the sun's going down."

"Yep."

"We don't have any flashlights."

"I know."

"But you know where you're going?"

"Yep."

"So . . . you can find your way in the dark?"

"Won't have to."

Mitch struggled up the slope. The air was growing thinner, but he could tell that the fog seemed to be lifting a bit. "Why not?"

Mitch took seven more steps and gasped. The fog was completely gone. The slope had leveled off, and Mitch found himself standing on a wide, level section of rock. Nathan stood at the edge, facing him. Smiling. He held out his arms.

"Because we're here."

Mitch looked around; his jaw hung open and he could only manage a whisper.

"Whoa."

VALLEY OF THE SHADOW

36

"WHAT ARE YOU DOING, DAD?"
Rachel stood in the entrance to
Conner's study, rubbing her eyes.
It was just after six o'clock.

Conner looked up from his computer. "Sorry, did I wake you up?"

Rachel yawned. "I saw the light on.
You working on a Saturday?"

"Umm, just doing a little . . .
research."

"What for?" She came around his
desk and rested her arm on his shoulder.

Conner shrugged. He didn't want to
tell her everything, but he didn't want
to appear like he was hiding anything
either. "Getting driving directions. I
have to run down to Indiana today."

"Indiana? What's in Indiana?"

"Uh, need to take a deposition." Conner winced inwardly. He couldn't believe he was lying to his daughter. It used to be so easy. Now it bothered him. But he didn't want to get her involved in his goose chase. Really, it was for her own good.

"Are you going to be back home tonight?"

Conner looked up again and paused before answering. He honestly didn't know how long it would take. He didn't even know exactly what he was going to do when he got there. He was figuring this thing out one tiny step at a time. Finally he gave her a half nod. "Yeah, I'll probably be home by supper. You know, unless something unexpected comes up."

Rachel kissed him on the cheek. "Well, good luck on your deposition."

She left and Conner clicked back off his Web browser. He had downloaded the latest version of Google Earth, a program containing a satellite map of the entire globe. He used it occasionally for fun, but now there was something he wanted to see. Something he needed to see.

For two months Conner had completely ignored all of the information about Howard Bristol that Nancy had found. But after his latest dream, he decided to dig out the yellow legal pad from his drawer. He entered the Bristols' latest home address into the map coordinates and hit Enter.

The image of the earth on his screen rotated and zoomed in. Like he was flying in a spaceship, entering from orbit, descending over the eastern seaboard of the United States, moving west. It crossed over Pennsylvania, Ohio, and then zoomed in rapidly on Indiana. In a matter of seconds, the viewer came to rest, hovering over an area of land at what looked like an altitude of 1,500 feet.

He could see a patchwork of farm fields and towns, spread

out like a view from an airplane. Conner clicked the zoom control and the image zoomed in to three hundred feet. The resolution increased and the image came into better focus.

He could see the top of an old farmhouse with a long driveway running out to what looked like a county highway. Behind the house were three outbuildings and a silo. Beyond the barn was a wide stretch of land that ended at a large patch of trees.

It was exactly like he remembered.

He'd seen this before.

He had been there before.

Conner scrolled the viewer slowly over the wooded area behind the farm. The satellite images were probably a few years old and looked as if they had been taken during the early spring or late fall. The trees were still bare but there was no snow on the ground. Conner scrolled a little farther and stopped. His mouth went dry.

He could see a blotchy image that looked like a small building, nestled among the trees.

VALLEY OF THE SHADOW

MITCH STARED AT THE SKY. His mouth hung open.

The vast black canopy of space spread out above him, flooded with myriad pinpricks of light. Each one different in size and color. No two looked the same. Mingled among them swirled thousands of galaxies of all shapes and sizes. And directly overhead, like a backdrop stretching from one horizon to the other, lay a brilliant purple nebula. Its massive billows and plumes were so clear and vivid, they looked close enough to touch.

Nathan stood at the edge of a cliff, facing Mitch. He spread out his hands. Behind him, the cloud cover rolled out like a carpet. While from below, it had appeared as a drab, lifeless gray hue, from here above, it reflected the purple light of the nebula. Jagged mountain peaks jutted up through the mist like black islands of rock amid a vast purple ocean.

"Whoa," Mitch whispered again. His sarcasm was gone and he found himself—maybe for the first time in his life—at a loss for words.

Nathan just smiled and pointed to the sky behind Mitch. Mitch turned and froze. The cloud carpet spread out in a long, wide swath toward the eastern horizon. And above the edge of that horizon loomed a vast swirl of light so enormous it took up the entire eastern sky—if in fact it was east. The light was like a massive spiral galaxy tipped on its edge, spinning slowly in space. Its arms swirled up and dissolved into the darkness. Its lower half disappeared below the horizon line and its center glowed with a dazzling spectrum of colors. Colors Mitch could not even recognize. He had never seen them before.

Mitch found his knees growing weak as he gazed into the massive vortex. A sudden wave of vertigo washed over him and he knelt down to steady himself. His breath puffed out steamy tendrils in the cold, crisp air. "I'm . . . I'm genuinely impressed."

Nathan chuckled. "Thought you might be. See what I mean about perspective?"

Mitch nodded, unable to take his eyes off the eastern sky. "Um . . . yeah."

After several minutes, he turned around. "Okay, so . . . we're not on Earth anymore?"

"Man, we're so far from Earth you can't even see the farthest spot from which you *could* see Earth."

"What?"

"We're at the edge of the universe." Nathan nodded toward the glowing vortex. "On the doorstep of eternity."

"How . . . how did we get here?"

Nathan spread his palms and shrugged. "Time and space don't present the same barriers for the spirit as they do for the body."

Mitch looked down at his hands. But he had a body. He rubbed his arms. He felt solid to his own touch.

"I know what you're thinking," Nathan said. "You can feel yourself. You still think that's your body you're touching."

"But it is. I'm solid to the touch."

"Hey, you've spent your entire life inside your flesh. It takes a while for your spirit to grasp the fact that it can exist apart from that as well. Your mind is just creating the sensation of a body because that's all it's ever known. Like a security blanket."

Mitch stood again. The cold and the altitude were making him feel light-headed. He tried to concentrate. He looked out over the clouds. The line of mountains they were on seemed to run laterally east to west. The clouds spread out to the north and far off, he could see another distant row of peaks running parallel to them. Two mountain ranges ran east to west with this sea of clouds between them.

And below the clouds, down where everything was gray and colorless . . . It wasn't Indiana. It wasn't even Earth.

Mitch spread his arms. "So where exactly are we?"

Nathan moved to stand next to Mitch. "They call it Interworld. It's like a passageway between life and death. Between the material world and the spiritual. Some people see it as that long dark tunnel with a light at the end. For others it's a place that looks just like Earth, or at least their little section of it, anyway. Some people spend days here, terrified and alone.

Others pass right over and hardly even notice it. But sooner or later, everyone travels through it to the other side."

Mitch shook his head. This morning he thought he'd woken up on a farm in Indiana. Now he discovered he wasn't anywhere near Indiana. Not even in the same galaxy. He was in . . .

"So then is this . . . y'know . . . some kind of purgatory? I heard about that in one of my classes at school."

"You're not here to pay for any sins. It's way too late for that."

"Then what? I don't get it."

"It's not life and it's not quite death. It's the place everyone travels through on their way to eternity."

Mitch was growing weary. This had to have been the strangest and longest day he'd ever experienced. He rubbed his eyes and looked again at the stunning view of space.

And at that moment he saw something moving along the horizon off to the west. Coming right toward them.

THE WAREHOUSE WAS BUILT sometime in the 1920s, they said. And it looked every bit its age. It was owned by a holding corporation that existed only on paper. If anyone tried to track down any of its officers or board members, they'd find themselves pursuing paper phantoms. Names and social security numbers from people long dead. Addresses and phone numbers that only led to more dead ends.

Devon pulled into the empty parking lot and drove around to the back. Pale Man sat in the backseat humming to himself. Devon thought it sounded like AC/DC's "Highway to Hell" but he couldn't be sure. He hated heavy metal anyway.

"Man, this is stupid coming back here. This dude ain't gonna just give me a gun."

"O ye of little faith," Pale Man sighed. "Have I led you wrong yet?"

"I'm just sayin' he ain't gonna give me no gun."

"Well, he ain't gonna have no choice. Let's go, chief."

Devon got out and knocked on the rear entrance. A brown steel door next to a row of big garage doors along a loading dock.

A minute later the door opened and a tall, burly white guy with a crew cut glared at Devon. He didn't say anything.

"I just need to talk to Mr. Karenga for a minute," Devon said.

The man turned away and relayed the information through a radio device in his hand. A moment later he received a reply in his earpiece and let Devon inside.

He led Devon across a wide loading dock, into the main warehouse. The place was packed with yellow industrial shelving units loaded with plain brown corrugated boxes of various sizes. They moved down several aisles until they came to a narrow set of stairs leading up to a mezzanine office area.

They climbed the stairway. Pale Man followed, whistling to himself. "Wow, this guy must be pretty important."

Devon didn't say anything. He knew better than to act cocky here.

The guard led Devon to a small, sparsely furnished office and told him to sit. Pale Man leaned against the wall. "S'matter, little chief? You seem somewhat subdued. You're not nervous or anything, are you?"

"Man, you don't mess with this guy. That's all I'm saying."

Pale Man chuckled. "I think that'll change. Greater is he that is with you than he that runs this little show."

Devon wrinkled his forehead. "What?"

At that point the door opened and a wiry black man entered, wearing tan slacks and a dark brown sweater. With thinning hair and small, wire-rimmed glasses, Oswald Karenga may not have been physically imposing, but Devon knew what the man was capable of. He'd only met him once before. More accurately, he'd only been in the same room with him once before. He'd never actually had direct dealings with him.

The guy was from South Africa or someplace. Devon had heard bits and snatches of his history and reputation. He had numerous international connections, involved mainly in imports. Diamonds mostly, but a whole host of other products as well.

He was the guy who supplied the suppliers' suppliers. Several levels removed from anything Devon had ever been involved in. The fact that he was even willing to see Devon unannounced was either very good news . . . or very, very bad.

"Mista Mahshall, yes?" Karenga's accent was thick.

"Uh, yeah. I . . . look, I wouldn't even be bothering you except I'm a little desp—"

"That was a nice escape yesterday," Karenga said. "My people were quite impressed."

"You . . . you heard about that already?"

"Oh yes." Karenga chuckled. "I keep a very close eye on my employees. At all times. Now then—" he sat down behind his desk—"you have something for me?"

Devon felt his stomach churn. Something for him? His mind was blank. What was the guy talking about? Devon looked up at Pale Man, who only shrugged.

"Sounds like you've gotten yourself in a bit of trouble, chief."

Karenga leaned forward. "Don't give me that look, like you don't know what I'm talking about. Where is it?"

"Yo, man . . . look, I'm serious here. I—I don't know what you're talking about."

Karenga leaned back, opened a drawer, and produced several photographs. He slid them across the desk. Devon glanced at them. His eyes widened.

It was J.G. and Apollo—Devon's immediate bosses—lying faceup on asphalt in pools of blood. Their eyes open but empty.

Devon swore. "Hey, man, I'm telling you, I don't know what's going on."

"Apparently, neither did they," Karenga said. "Now you were the only other party involved in the transaction, and I want to know where the item is."

"Transaction?"

Pale Man chuckled and started mimicking Karenga's accent. "Apparently you 'ave someting thees man wants. It ees d'only reason you ah steel alive. And you 'ave dat infahmation locked up inside yo'ah leettle head."

Devon's mind was reeling. He said to Karenga, "I—I can find it. I can get it for you. But I need a gun first. I'll get it for you. I mean . . . that's why I broke out. So I can get you the . . . the item."

Karenga's expression darkened. "You're not trying to bargain with me, are you? Is that what you are doing?"

Pale Man bent down. "See, the night you got shot, you were involved in a certain transaction. You and your little friends there were in charge of a sizable donation from Mr. Karenga, which you were supposed to exchange for a small item of considerable value. But something went bad that night. And now he's out his money and no one seems to know where the item is. Well, except for you. Supposedly."

Devon shook his head at Karenga. "No, sir. Straight up, I'll get it. I just need a gun."

Karenga laughed. "If you think you will be getting anything from me before I see the item, you are sadly mistaken."

Pale Man sighed. "Come on, chief. Show some backbone. He won't respect you otherwise."

Devon felt a surge of anger inside him. His hands trembled and suddenly everything looked red. He felt himself leaping forward onto the desk and clutching a surprised Oswald Karenga by the throat. But now Devon wasn't thinking. He was acting purely on impulse. He stood up on the desk, lifting Karenga out of his seat.

Karenga's eyes bulged; he struggled for breath.

Devon pulled the man close. His voice deepened an octave. "You won't get anything unless you give me a gun."

He tightened his grip, cutting off all air to Karenga's lungs.

Then he heard a whisper in his ear. "Careful, chief. We need this guy a little while longer."

Devon hesitated a moment, then dropped Karenga into his seat, unconscious. Devon got down and searched the desk. He found a gun inside one of the lower drawers. He popped out the clip to verify it was loaded, then snapped it back and quietly left the office.

Karenga had two personal bodyguards posted at the bottom of the stairs.

"I'll take care of them," Pale Man said and disappeared down the grated steps.

Devon watched quietly. After a few moments, the guards seemed to become agitated about something and moved off into the warehouse. Devon slipped quickly down the stairs and back outside.

He started up the car, and the next thing he knew, Pale Man was sitting behind him. "Don't say I never did anything for you, chief."

Devon put the car in gear and tore out of the parking lot.

39

A TINY SPARK OF LIGHT had popped
up over the western horizon and
cruised in a graceful and swirling
path toward them. Mitch had no idea
of its size, composition, or identity,
but it continued to grow larger as it
approached.

"What is that?"

Nathan smiled. "That's what I
brought you here to see."

After a minute it passed by no more
than fifty feet overhead. Mitch stared,
openmouthed. It was long and slender, maybe five or six feet long, and it
glowed with an intense yellow light—so
bright that Mitch couldn't make out any
other details. It left a long, shimmering

trail in its wake as it continued on a course toward the rainbow vortex in the east. It shrank into the distance until at last it was a pinpoint of light again. Then it started to accelerate, as if the vortex itself was attracting it somehow. Drawing it inside.

A moment later, it disappeared completely, lost within the brilliant expanse.

Nathan wore a soft grin. He stared at the vortex and shook his head. "You know what that was?"

Mitch shrugged. "Not really. No."

"A spirit," Nathan said. "A soul on its final journey home."

"A spirit? So then that's . . . heaven?"

"Not exactly." Nathan chuckled. "That's just the front door."

Mitch spotted a second spark in the sky, moving toward them. "There's another one."

The second spirit drifted past at a much higher altitude, spiraling around as if in giddy excitement, toward the vortex. It too was sucked inside and vanished from view.

After several more minutes, a third spirit appeared on the horizon. This one swooped side to side in long, gentle arcs. It dipped low, skimming the clouds like a heron gliding over a lake, trailing its feet in the water. Then it accelerated right past them, ascending high above them.

Nathan climbed onto a rock and waved his arms wildly. The spirit paused in its flight. It turned and descended toward them, curving around on a graceful arc, like an eagle gliding on an air current. Nathan stretched his hand up. The spirit approached and hovered over him.

Mitch could see more detail now. It was human . . . in a way. He could see a face, of sorts, though not a face of flesh and bone. This was a face of pure light. As though light itself had become a solid mass. But it seemed to convey expression and emotion in a way Mitch could recognize, though he wasn't sure exactly how he was able to recognize it. It was unlike anything he had ever seen before. It was more luminous, more intense, and more graceful than any human being he'd ever seen on Earth.

Entranced, Mitch instinctively touched his own face. Its cold and meaty features felt like a dead fish. A sudden pang of embarrassment washed over him and he flushed with shame to be in the presence of something so beautiful.

Was this what resided inside every human being? the spirit that every human body contained? As if all their flesh and bone were simply part of a dismal cocoon that masked something far more wondrous.

The spirit extended a glowing appendage that looked vaguely like an arm. The light seemed to form itself into a slender hand that reached down to touch Nathan's out-stretched fingertips. And for a moment, Nathan's entire body was bathed in a warm, orange glow. He closed his eyes. His clothes rustled as if a strong breeze were rushing past him. Then the spirit looked over at Mitch and . . .

And smiled.

Mitch blinked. He felt something growing inside his chest, pressing against his ribs with an almost physical force. It flowed up into his neck and his face.

Before he knew what was happening, Mitch's eyes were pouring tears. He couldn't stop himself yet he couldn't look away. It was like someone had turned on a spigot and his emotions were gushing out uncontrollably. His legs buckled and he sank to his knees.

The spirit glided closer and hovered over him. Luminous fingers brushed against his cheek. Mitch felt something like a jolt of electricity rush through his body. The hair on his arms stood up. His skin flushed with warmth. For that brief second, every neuron in his body fired as though his entire nervous system was electrified. But there was no pain, no discomfort of any kind. Just a tingling rush of warmth and an overwhelming sense of joy. Complete and perfect.

The spirit zoomed up again, accelerating toward the door of heaven. Mitch watched, his cheeks glistening, until it reached the vortex and disappeared.

Mitch found himself physically shaken. His emotions were completely jumbled now, battering around in his head like the Ping-Pong balls inside one of those lottery machines. He felt an alternating mixture of joy and awe that quickly settled into a profound sense of emptiness. A feeling that he had lost something incredibly precious that he would never see again.

He wiped his eyes. He suddenly felt embarrassed that he'd been blubbering like a child. He struggled to regain his composure and felt Nathan's hand on his shoulder.

"It's a beautiful thing, Mitch. To finally be free from our mortal failings. Every petty and selfish thought. Every shred of hate."

Mitch stood, wrestling his thoughts and emotions into line. It was like trying to herd a flock of spooked sheep back into a pen. He rolled his neck and took a deep breath. "Is that what we happens when we die?"

Nathan didn't respond at first. Then he said softly, "For some."

"What do you mean?"

"That's not our natural condition, Mitch. Most people never get to that state." He nodded back down the mountain. "Most humans never rise above their own selfish nature. They won't even acknowledge their true condition. They live their entire lives in a delusion, thinking everything's okay. Thinking they're okay."

Mitch looked back down the path they had climbed. It disappeared into the mist. Below it lay a gray, lifeless country of souls wandering about. The walking dead. Not really knowing what was happening to them. Unaware of the danger they were in. Doomed to wander a time until there was no hope of returning. No chance of ever going back.

Until the creatures came from the shadows and dragged them away. Dragged them off to the forest. To . . .

To where?

"What happens to them?" Mitch said. "Down there. What happens to those people? Where do they end up?"

Nathan's eyes lowered. He turned away. "You don't want to know."

"Yes, I do!" Mitch flared with anger and spun Nathan around. "Where do they end up?"

Mitch could see pain in Nathan's eyes. They shifted back and forth, as if he was trying to think of an answer. "There's a place . . ."

"Where?"

Nathan's gaze lifted. "There at the edge. A chasm. I can't describe it more than that. But I can feel it. I can sense it from here. Fear and anger. Lost in unending darkness."

Mitch blinked and stood back. "What are you talking about? Hell?"

Nathan just stared at him. Then nodded.

"Hell," Mitch repeated, shaking his head. "You're telling me this place—down there—it leads to hell."

"For most."

"So all of those people down there that've been dragged off by those . . . things. They're all in hell now?"

"I told you, you didn't want to know."

Mitch's breathing grew labored in the thin air. Sin and

hell. He felt like he was back in church again. Trapped in his father's religion. He sat down and tried to calm himself. "I don't feel so well."

At that moment another glowing spirit whizzed past overhead. They watched it disappear into the vortex.

Nathan shook his head. "We better get back down. We got a long way to go."

40

IT WAS SHORTLY AFTER TEN O'CLOCK Saturday morning when Conner pulled into the LaPorte County Nursing Home five miles outside of Westville, Indiana. It was a low, brown brick building designed with three wings around a central common and office area. It sat on ten rural acres surrounded by towering oak trees, now nearly void of leaves.

The parking lot was only sparsely populated, and Conner figured he had arrived before the peak visitation time. Though this far out in the country, he doubted there was ever a real peak visitation period. Besides, it was a nursing home. Conner guessed that most people—who weren't residents, anyway—tried to spend as little time in here as possible.

The place reminded Conner of the nursing home in which his own father had spent several weeks recuperating from heart surgery five years earlier. Conner recalled his seventy-eight-year-old father steadfastly refusing to eat in the cafeteria with "all those old people." He eventually got well enough to return home. But six months and two strokes later, he was dead.

Conner's fingers felt cold and moist as he sat in the car, staring at the nursing home entrance. He hadn't been completely honest with Marta and Rachel about where he was going. They'd already made plans for most of the day anyway. Still, Conner had kept his cell phone off during the drive down. And he decided to leave it off awhile longer. He was still a little embarrassed, and for some reason he felt compelled to come here alone. Part of him felt it was better not to put Marta and Rachel in danger. Although another part of him thought that was a crazy excuse. After all, what real danger could an old man in a coma be to him or his family?

With that, Conner said another prayer, gathered up his nerve, and got out of the car.

"Umm . . . you want to see Howard Bristol?" the nurse's aide behind the sliding window repeated once Conner gave her the reason for his visit. She was young, maybe just out of high school, with long blonde hair pulled into a tight ponytail. Her plastic name badge read *Julie*.

"He was transferred from the Merrillville Hospice a few weeks ago," Julie went on. Her face was serious. "I'm afraid he's . . . he's not really able to . . ."

Conner nodded. "Yes, I know. He had a stroke and he's been in a coma the last several months."

"And you're a relative?"

Conner took a breath, resisting the urge to lie. "No. Actually, I'm just an acquaintance. I was driving through and wanted to . . . y'know—" he lowered his voice—"pay my respects."

Julie nodded, looking around. There was no one else in the office. "So . . . do you just want to stop in his room and see him?"

"Yeah, just for a minute," Conner said. "Actually . . . has Mrs. Bristol been by to see him yet?"

"Oh, she comes by pretty much every day. Usually spends a couple hours in the afternoons. That's why they moved him here. To be closer to their home. So she wouldn't have to drive so far."

"I see. Is he undergoing any therapy?"

Julie hesitated. Conner could tell she was trying to be judicious in her answer. "They, umm . . . they do some limb movement. Mostly to prevent bedsores. But not much more. He's catheterized and has a feeding tube. Mrs. Bristol hasn't authorized its removal just yet."

"Mmm . . . ," Conner said. "Has she been advised by their doctor to keep it in?"

Julie winced and glanced around again. "I believe he's been trying to get her to let him go. Apparently there's too much damage and there's nothing they can really do for him. But she won't authorize anything. She still thinks he's going to get better. But he's just been . . . lingering."

"Ah . . . ," Conner said knowingly. He could tell he had gained Julie's trust and now wanted to see how much information she would offer up. "Yeah, that is sad. I think when you've been with someone so long, for so many years, it's just very hard to let them go."

Julie went on. "But it's gotta be putting her in the poorhouse. I don't think his Medicare is covering everything. I don't know how she affords it all now."

Conner tightened his lips and nodded. It was a good question. Ultimately it was just a matter of time. Either Howard's body would give out or his wife's finances would. It was sad, however, to see an elderly woman bringing herself to financial ruin because of circumstances like these.

"Does he have any other family? Does he get many visitors?"

"Just his wife. And sometimes their son comes with her." Julie leaned close. "I saw him once or twice—kind of a creepy-looking guy."

"What do you mean?"

"I don't know . . . just creepy. He's real tall. A big guy. And he's got real long hair, and he just sort of stares at you. Like he's not all there or something. I never heard him talk at all." She shrugged—or maybe it was a shudder. "He just creeps me out."

"I see." Conner rubbed his jaw. "Does he live with his mom on the farm?"

"I don't really know. I think so. She usually drives herself, but sometimes she comes with him."

Conner took a deep breath. "Well, I don't want to bother you. I just wanted to see him briefly, and then I'll get out of your hair."

Julie smiled and gave him directions to the room. Conner thanked her and made his way down the corridor.

Room 427 was darkened. The shades were drawn so only thin stripes of sunlight streamed through the blinds. Conner could see a long, thin mass beneath a linen sheet. He took another step into the room where Howard Bristol lay obscured in shadows.

Conner's heart was pounding now. Thumping hard against his ribs. He took a few deep breaths, tried to calm his thoughts, and moved in for a better view.

He could barely recognize the old man lying in the bed. Wisps of white hair lay in unruly tufts across his pale, spotted scalp. The color around his eye sockets was a sickly mix of purple and yellow. A feeding tube ran into one nostril, and his toothless mouth hung open, sucking in air with shallow breaths. The skin of his face hung in loose folds at the corners of his mouth and around his jowls, like a deflated balloon covered with several days' growth of gray stubble.

Conner caught the whiff of death in the room. A slightly septic odor, thinly veiled by a forest pine air freshener hanging from an overhead light. A few potted plants were set near the window. Probably left there by Mrs. Bristol or some other friend.

Conner shook his head. He'd half expected the room to be shrouded by an enormous shadow of pure evil. But instead, all he saw was an emaciated old man.

A soft rustling sound behind him caused Conner to spin around. A hunched, impish figure stood in the doorway. An elderly woman with a tight mouth and a long, hawkish nose. Her silvery hair was pulled back in a bun with a few haphazard strands hanging in her face. Her eyes were large and brown, gazing at Conner from behind wire-rimmed spectacles. They seemed to flare with emotion for a moment. A flash of anger.

She took a step forward and wagged a thin forefinger at Conner.

"I know who you are."

VALLEY OF THE SHADOW

MITCH AND NATHAN made their way back down the path through the fog. Nathan moved deftly along the jagged slope to the road, even though Mitch struggled at times to keep up.

Something was confusing him. By his reckoning, it should be the middle of the night, yet the fog around him was still lit up brightly. Eventually they emerged from the clouds onto the road, where the Ferrari was parked with his motorcycle beside it.

Mitch stopped to catch his breath. "What time is it? It can't be morning already. There's no way we were up there all night."

Nathan glanced over his shoulder. "Day and night don't exactly work the same here, Mitch."

"So what now? Don't we get a chance to sleep?"

"I don't think you'll need it for a while."

"What?" Mitch realized that he wasn't actually tired. In fact, at the moment, he felt wide-awake. As if he were on a caffeine rush or something. Maybe it was just the adrenaline from the experience he'd had at the top of the mountain. But he figured that would wear off soon enough.

Nathan wiggled his fingers. "We just got an infusion of life. That'll keep us going for a while longer."

Mitch thought about the spirit that had touched them. Maybe some sort of spiritual energy had been transferred. Could that be what was coursing through him right now?

He shrugged. And why not. He remembered hearing once that in heaven there was no day or night. No need to sleep. Probably no need to eat. Those were physical requirements, after all. Needs of the flesh. Their bodies needed fuel and sleep, but not their spirits. Now devoid of the body, did they need any sleep at all?

For five years, he'd been sleeping at night, though never feeling very well rested. He'd been eating and drinking but never felt satisfied. But if he was just a spirit—a ghost—then what explained the fact that he had gotten tired and hungry? And why was he almost always thirsty?

Maybe that was a side effect of being down below the clouds. Down in the valley. Or maybe it had something to do with what Nathan had said. That those spirits up above were different. They had been changed. Nathan had said that God had made them new. And now they were free from all of the negative influences that once plagued them. Free from all hate and envy and . . .

And sin.

But all the souls here below were still trapped. Maybe their bodies hadn't passed away completely, but their spirits were essentially dead. And now they were suffering from the same weaknesses they'd had in life. Or worse.

Mitch swung a leg over his bike. "So what's the plan? Where do we go from here?"

"West." Nathan pointed off toward the distance. "You remember where we saw those spirits coming from?"

"Sort of, yeah."

"That's where we need to be. Every time a spirit passes through this place into heaven, a doorway opens up."

"A doorway?"

"Yeah, like a portal. From the physical world. That's how we get you back into your body. When a portal opens up to let some spirit through, you jump into it."

Mitch laughed. "Dude. That's your plan? You dragged me off the farm for that?"

"So it sounds a little crazy," Nathan said. "It's your only chance. Besides, I don't think you really want to go back, do you?"

Mitch considered that option, but the thought of returning to Howard's farm was definitely out of the question.

They drove down from the foothills onto the highway. Mitch followed Nathan's Ferrari through the endless, flat desert peppered with sagebrush as far as the eye could see. Along with an occasional gnarled cactus.

They drove for what felt like hours until they arrived at an abandoned gas station in the middle of nowhere. Mitch filled up, not surprised to find that the antique-looking pumps still worked. It was just one of those things he'd come to accept.

Besides, his mind had been working on the idea of this

doorway at the edge of the world. What was it like? How did it work? And what exactly would happen to him once he jumped through?

Nathan could only offer a shrug when Mitch asked him. "Not sure what's going to happen to you. I assume you'll wind up back inside your body, but there's still no guarantee you'll come out of your coma. This is all pretty new to me, too."

"New?" Mitch frowned. "But I thought you were like, y'know . . . an angel or something."

"Angel?" Nathan laughed. "I'm no angel. That's for sure."

"Well . . ." Mitch felt a slight prickle of embarrassment. He had just assumed the guy was some kind of angel. Or something like that. A leprechaun or a magic elf. He seemed to have so much knowledge of everything. "All right, then, exactly what are you?"

"Just a guy, like you. I was in an accident, like you were. And they have my body on life support. So in a way, I'm stuck here too. Just like you."

"How long have you been here?"

"Don't know for sure. I lost track. Seems like it's been a while."

Mitch's frown deepened and he folded his arms. "So how is it you know so much about this place, then? What's up with that?"

"Like I said, I was in an accident. Lost control of my vehicle one night and went off the road. I hit a tree and went through the windshield. The next thing I know, I could feel myself floating, away from the crash site and out into space. Then I started to accelerate faster and faster. And when I looked up again, I saw that vortex opening right there in front of me." Nathan stared at the clouds for a moment and sighed. "But then something else happened to me and I started to slow down. I felt myself growing heavier and heavier. I knew they were doing something to me. I could feel them. Working on my body. Trying to revive me. But instead of going all the way back, I suddenly felt myself sinking. And I couldn't do anything about it. I was falling. I fell through those clouds and sort of crashed in the mountains."

"Crashed, huh?" Mitch narrowed his eyes. "I didn't think that could happen. I thought this place was only for us sinners."

"I don't know what to tell you. I don't think it's ever happened before. Or at least not very often. But right after I landed in the mountains, I heard God speaking to me. He said He had a job for me to do here and that's why He didn't let me go back."

"A job?" Mitch recalled what Nathan had told him in the bookstore when they had first met. That God had sent him.

"Yeah. To help you get back."

"You're telling me God sent you here just to help me get back into my body?"

"That's what I told you before."

"I didn't believe you before," Mitch said. "What does God want with me?"

"I figure He wants to give you a second chance."

"To do what?"

"Mitch—" Nathan smiled—"a second chance at life. A chance to break away from the consequences of your past and change the direction your life is headed. To follow a new course."

Mitch's lips tightened. Exactly how much had God revealed to this guy about him? Mitch had managed to keep most of those dark memories boxed up. Locked away, out of mind. But they would sometimes try to haunt him. At night, they would burst into his dreams like uninvited guests. And he would see his mother again—emaciated, pallid, and suffering. He would feel her again, struggling under the pillow. Struggling against him.

But then he would wake up in a cold sweat and lock those memories away. Back inside. Deep inside.

"What do you know about my life? What makes you such an expert?"

Nathan removed the blue stick of chalk from his coat pocket.

Mitch rolled his eyes. "Oh, that's right. The magic chalk."

Nathan smiled. "Yep. The magic chalk." Then he looked at his watch. "I think we can spare a few minutes. Why don't you let me show you something?"

They went inside the abandoned gas station. Mitch could smell the musty odor of old wood inside the cramped shop. It reminded him of his grandfather's attic. After countless years of exposure, sand had encrusted the windows, blown in through the broken glass, and dusted the buckled and uneven floorboards. On the walls hung a few rusted tools, a couple of fan belts, some cans of oil, and an assortment of other antique automotive supplies. The place reminded Mitch of something from the Depression era. Out in the dust bowl of Oklahoma.

Nathan found a clear spot along one of the walls and drew another circle. After a few moments, the chalk line began to smoke as it had before inside the bookstore, the first time Mitch had seen this trick. Nathan punched away the plaster to reveal another shimmering, quivering, luminous window.

Mitch slipped his sunglasses on and looked inside. A moment later, his eyes widened and he shook his head.

"That's . . . that's not what I think it is. . . . Is it?"

CONNER STARED AT THE OLD WOMAN,
his mouth open. How would she know
who he was? What kind of creepy
woman was this? some kind of psychic
or a witch? Had she managed to get in
contact with her husband while he was
in a coma?

She walked into the room still
wagging her finger. "I know exactly
who you are."

"Y-you do?"

"You're that psychiatrist my doctor
was talking about. Gonna try to talk me
into removing that feeding tube."

Conner relaxed. Maybe she was a
little nuts, but she didn't appear to be
clairvoyant. "Uhh . . . ma'am—"

"Well let me tell you something, mister doctor, I am not gonna do it. You hear me? So you can just get right out of this room. I only want positive thoughts in here. Positive energy. Because my Howard is getting better. Stronger every day. And you'll see. One day soon, he's gonna wake up again. Right as rain!"

Conner smiled and held up his hands. "Mrs. Bristol, I'm not . . . I'm not a doctor. I don't want to convince you to do anything. I just . . ." Conner paused. What kind of excuse would he use now? He could try telling her the truth: that her husband was really trapped in a ghostly Interworld, perched on the brink of hell and working in concert with the powers of darkness. Right. "I just . . . stopped by for a visit. I wanted to stop in and say hello."

Mrs. Bristol stopped jabbering and narrowed her eyes. Her finger froze midwag as she stared at him. "Do I know you?"

"Uhh . . . no, no but I knew your—know your husband, Howard. Know of him, I mean."

Mrs. Bristol's forehead wrinkled further as her brows came together. "Know of him? What do you mean?"

Conner's mind raced. He was slipping back into his former mold. "I—I mean, my father knew him. Knew him from way back. Went to school together . . . uhh, I think. And I wanted to come down and see him. Just maybe say hello is all."

Mrs. Bristol's eyes seemed to light up. "Oh . . . are you Stewart's boy? Felix? From Minneapolis?"

Conner froze, cursing himself silently. How had he gotten himself in this situation again? And how should he answer this one?

"Yyyyes." His head came down in a hesitant nod. "Yes . . . I am."

And he immediately knew he'd made a mistake. Again.

Mrs. Bristol patted his arm. "Ohhh . . . it's so nice to see you. Why, the last time I saw you, you were just a child. That must be more than thirty years ago now. How is your father doing?"

Conner nodded again. His eyes like a deer's in the glare of oncoming headlights. "Oh . . . fine. He's doing fine."

She shook her head and clicked her tongue. "But I'm sure he misses your mother these days."

"Yes . . . well, it . . . it was a big loss for him. But at least he still has us—me. And we're helping him through . . . this difficult . . . adjust . . . ment . . ." Conner knew instantly something had gone wrong.

Mrs. Bristol's face was white. Her eyes grew wide and moist. "Oh, dear!" She gasped, her hand over her mouth. "She passed away? Oh, my dear, when did that happen? It wasn't during her trip, was it? Please tell me she didn't pass away in Norway."

Conner could only offer up a blank stare. Moments creaked by. "Oh . . . you meant my mother. I . . . I thought you said . . . y'know . . . *his* mother."

Mrs. Bristol stared back at him. Her brow was furrowed again. Then her eyes rolled up. "Felix! You just don't change, do you?" She slapped his arm and laughed. "Oh, you nearly gave me a heart attack. You wicked boy! You haven't changed at all."

Conner swallowed and did his best to laugh as well. "Uh . . . well, I'm sorry, Mrs. Bristol. . . . I didn't mean to . . . I . . . I didn't mean to be disrespectful . . . here."

"Nonsense," she said, dabbing her eyes with a tissue she had produced from somewhere. "Here is where it does the most good, dear. Laughter is strong medicine, you know."

Conner breathed a sigh. He'd dodged one bullet. "Yes. Yes it is."

Mrs. Bristol took his arm and drew him up to the bedside. She patted down Howard's hair and left her hand to linger on his forehead. "Howard, dear. Guess who's here? It's Felix Grady. You remember? Stewart's boy." She glanced at Conner. "Say hello, Felix."

Conner hesitated until Mrs. Bristol shook his arm. "Go on."

Conner bent stiffly and mumbled, "Uhh . . . hello, H-How . . . Mr. Bristol."

Mrs. Bristol went on talking. "He played the cruelest prank on me. Just cruel. Tried to tell me Anna had passed away on her trip. You remember she was going back to visit her mother's hometown in Norway."

Mrs. Bristol went on talking like that for several minutes. Her hand clutched Conner's arm so tightly he could not manage to back away. Every so often, she'd have him say something to Howard as well.

After what felt like a half hour, Conner managed to extricate himself from her grip with the excuse of having to use the bathroom. Which wasn't untrue at all.

As he washed his hands in the sink, he stared at himself in the mirror and sighed. What was he doing? Why was he here? He'd come all this way because of a dream and he had no idea what he was supposed to do.

Conner knew he couldn't stay in the bathroom forever. He racked his brain for an excuse to leave. Mrs. Bristol would no doubt invite him for dinner. After so many years, she'd never let "Felix" leave without a good home-cooked meal. But he couldn't do that. That would be far too risky. Maybe he could say he was on a business trip and he could stay only a few minutes. He had to drive to . . .

Ohio . . . and he had to get there by suppertime. That
was it.

Although, an invitation for lunch could be the perfect
opportunity to see the farm. But once there, how would he
manage to sneak off and look around?

He shuddered as he recalled his nightmare and Howard's
zombielike presence. He closed his eyes. Maybe God would
present the next step when it was time to take it.

Conner came out of the bathroom to find Mrs. Bristol
waiting for him, clutching her purse. She looked as if she was
ready to leave.

"Now, Felix," she said, "you do have time to stay for a
visit, don't you."

Conner shook his head. "Oh . . . I'm real sorry. But I've got
this . . . I'm going for a job interview in Columbus, and I need
to get down there today. So I really have to get going."

"Job interview? On a weekend?"

"Well, no. I'm . . . I wanted to drive around and get to
know the community a little bit tomorrow. The interview itself
is on Monday morning. Bright and earl—"

"Oh, good! Then you have some time," she said.

Conner rubbed his eyes. He was getting nowhere with this
woman. "Mrs. Bristol, I'd love to visit—I really would—but I
don't have—"

"Just stay for some lunch, then."

Conner was feeling faint. Something inside him was
pounding. *Get out of here. Just make an excuse and leave!
You're good at excuses. Make one and leave.*

She pulled him by the arm, out into the corridor, still talking away. Something about Columbus and how it was only a
few hours from there—much closer than Minneapolis. And
now he wouldn't have any excuses for not coming to visit. That

is, if he got the job, of course. And by the way, what kind of job was it?

Conner groaned inwardly. This wasn't a good idea. He knew it. But there was also a part of him—like a gentle voice—that prodded him onward. Telling him to stay the course and see the farm for himself. As if all his nightmares for the last two months had led him here and he knew he couldn't go home without at least seeing the place.

Mrs. Bristol led him out to the parking lot and Conner hoped she wouldn't notice the Illinois license plates on his car. Which she did. Illinois? Yes, Conner said he'd flown into Chicago from Minneapolis and then rented a car, just so he could stop in to see poor Howard on the way to Columbus. Fair enough.

Mrs. Bristol clambered into her gray Chevy pickup and pulled the door closed, waving for Conner to follow her in his car. He would stop by the house for lunch and a short visit and then be on his way.

Conner got into his Mercedes, started it up, and against every natural instinct inside him, followed her.

43

THE GLOWING PORTAL OF LIGHT grew
still and the images came into focus.
Mitch could see a child sitting at a
dining room table. In a cavernous,
ornate dining room that Mitch recognized right away.

It was his father's house. The
boy was a younger version of Mitch.
He was sitting at the table, hunched
forward, head down, hands folded
on his lap. Suddenly a voice boomed,
causing ripples in the surface of the
window.

"This is what you do with your
time?" Mitch's father moved into view.
Tall and broad shouldered, he loomed
over the boy, nearly casting a shadow

over the entire room. He slid a sheet of paper across the table toward his son.

Young Mitch glanced at the paper, then up at his father and back down again. Mitch craned his neck for a better view. The vantage point of the image shifted to the table, where Mitch could make out something scrawled on the paper. A picture. A cartoon.

Walter Kent's voice sounded again. "Do you care to explain that?"

The boy said nothing.

"Mrs. Tompkins said she caught you drawing this during class."

Now Mitch recalled the incident. The cartoon was of his Sunday school teacher. Round and stern and always smelling too much like flowers, Mrs. Tompkins ruled the class with an iron fist. She'd always seemed to expect more from Mitch because his father was someone important, and so she would single him out to read verses, call on him first for answers, and critique him more harshly for being wrong. So Mitch found himself quietly building up resentment. Little by little. It started at first as harmless cartoons but then grew into silent impressions to the class while her back was turned. Her bulging eyes and tiny, puckered mouth. He had her down pat.

Mitch smiled even now as he recalled her growing paranoia brought on by the children's stifled giggles every time she turned her back on them. He'd taken great delight in driving her crazy.

But all good things must come to an end.

One day she caught a glimpse of his artwork. A hippopotamus onto which Mitch had added lipstick and a mop of hair in the same style Mrs. Tompkins wore. It brought out a chorus of snorts and giggles as he showed it around before class one Sunday. He was still proudly showing it off when Mrs. Tompkins entered the room behind him. She snatched the sheet from his hands, looked it over with nothing more than a slight pucker of her mouth. Then she folded it neatly and slipped it into her Bible.

Mitch recalled vividly the feeling of being caught. Nabbed. Red-handed. His cheeks flushed hot with blood as he took his seat. The class was silent. And that lesson was the longest one he'd ever experienced in his life. Mrs. Tompkins improvised that day, teaching on Numbers 32:23: "Be sure your sin will find you out."

Through the window, Mitch could see his father glaring at his son. The boy didn't look up again.

"Well?"

The boy shrugged but said nothing.

"Don't you have anything to say for yourself?"

The boy shrugged again and mumbled something.

"What?"

"I didn't draw it during class," young Mitch said. "I drew it before."

His father blinked, as if in disbelief. "It doesn't matter when you drew it. The fact is you drew it!"

Walter Kent grabbed his son by the hand and led him out of the room. Mitch didn't need to see any more. He knew where they were going. He remembered vividly the beating he'd gotten.

He turned to Nathan. "So . . . what? You've watched my entire life through these windows? Now you think you're here to help me? You think you understand everything about me?"

Nathan looked away for a moment. "I know what happened to your mother. The cancer."

"That's none of your business."

"And I . . ." Nathan hesitated. "I know what happened with you. What you did to her."

Mitch suddenly felt his rage releasing. "I helped her." He leaned into Nathan's face. "I put her out of her misery!"

Nathan didn't back down, but his voice was soft. "I know you think you meant well. But, Mitch . . . sometimes you can do the wrong thing with the right motive."

Mitch's jaw tightened. Who was this guy to judge him? What right did he have? It was typical, though, of zealots. Religious fanatics. Everyone else was wicked. But not them. They were saved. They were God's special children in their little club on their way to heaven while the rest of the world was destined for hell.

"I suppose God appointed you to be my judge now."

"I'm not your judge, Mitch. He just wants me to help you get out of this place. But I want you to know that I don't think any less of you. We all have things hidden in our pasts. I do as well. The only difference is, my sins were . . . well, they were erased. Every last one of them."

"Well then, that's the difference between you and me," Mitch said. "I don't think what I did was a sin."

Nathan sighed and looked down. "You're right. That's a huge difference."

Mitch went to the doorway and stared out across the desert, struggling to calm his temper. For a moment, he was tempted to get on his bike and drive, no thought for where he would go or what might happen along the way. Just leave this guy and drive away.

But then he remembered the amazing sight he'd seen on the mountaintop. If it had been real—if there really was a heaven like he'd heard about all his life—then maybe all of this did matter. Maybe there was something to it after all.

Maybe . . .

He turned to see Nathan huddled on the floor, staring into the portal. It still glowed softly. But Nathan's shoulders were moving. Mitch looked closer. The man was crying.

"Hey . . . what's wrong?"

Mitch stood behind him. The scene inside the window had changed. It was a hospital scene again. Mitch thought for a moment that it was his own, but then he saw a young woman he didn't recognize standing at the bedside. The figure in the bed was enmeshed in tubes and wires, a thick brace around his neck.

Mitch pointed. "Is that you?"

Nathan wiped his eyes. "Yeah."

Mitch could see three children in the room as well, standing around the bed. His shoulders slumped. "Dude, you never said you had kids."

Nathan nodded and pointed to each one. "That's Nathan Jr. He's ten. Joleen is eight and Michael's six. And that's my wife, Val."

Mitch looked closer. Val was clearly comforting her children. She had her arms around Joleen and Michael, hugging them close as they wept with abandon. But Nathan Jr. stood apart from them at the foot of the bed, just staring at his father. The boy showed no emotion. Other than a tear welling up in his eye. His lips were tight. He looked almost angry.

Nathan shook his head. "I never had a chance to say good-bye. That's the thing about accidents. They just happen so suddenly. They take you away right in the middle of everything. You leave so much unfinished business. Conversations you assume you'll pick up again later."

Mitch rubbed his neck. "Hey, I watched my mom suffer for months. There's never a good way to lose someone you love."

"Yeah. I guess so."

Mitch pointed to Nathan Jr. "I know that look. I had that same look at my mom's funeral."

"He's angry," Nathan said. "He's going to blame God for this. He's too young to really understand but he's old enough to be bitter."

"You worried he's going to end up like me?"

Nathan shrugged his shoulders. "I don't know what's going to happen to him. I really tried to show him what I believed, though. You know? I really wanted for him to know that God was more than just about rules. That He's a real person—a Father who loves him. I never wanted to just teach my kids about Christianity. I worked hard to live it out, too." He sighed. "But, man, I failed. You have no idea how bad I failed sometimes."

"Dude, you gotta let your kids find their own way. I mean, maybe your religion's just not for them."

Nathan glanced up at Mitch. "Man, I know you mean well. But that's just not true. It's not my religion."

Mitch felt his jaw tightening again. "I'm just saying, sometimes you can tighten your grip on your kids so much that they feel like you're shoving your religion down their throat. And they may end up resenting you for it. To the point that they're just turned off. Maybe even for no other reason than to spite you. So that no matter what you do or say, or how hard you try, they just don't want to have anything to do with . . ."

Mitch found himself ranting. His voice trailed off. Why was he even bothering? He was never going to convince this guy. It didn't matter anyway. They weren't his kids.

Nathan seemed to study Mitch for a moment. "I'm sorry your father wasn't a better example for you. I'm sorry for whatever abuse you might have suffered as a kid. But, Mitch, that's no reason for you to reject what God's offering you. You won't be able to use that as an excuse. Because there's no other way. No other name . . ."

"Yeah." Mitch breathed a sigh. "I know all that. I've heard it all before."

"Knowing it isn't good enough. Not if it's just all up here." Nathan tapped his temple. "For me, the only thing I ever wanted for my kids was for them each to believe it in here." He tapped his chest. "Where it counts. And where it's real. And I just feel like I could've done better."

Mitch had to admit, the guy sounded sincere. And he wondered: if at some point his own father had explained it to him in those words, maybe Mitch's outlook—maybe his whole life—might have been different.

Mitch pushed those thoughts away and shrugged. "Hey, you're talking like you're already dead."

Nathan turned back to the fading portal and shook his head. "Val knows I'm too far gone. There's too much damage. She's held out hope for weeks, but she knows the only thing keeping me alive is that machine. And she also knows that's what's keeping me from really being free. She knows now she's just being selfish, keeping me here. So she brought them in to say good-bye."

"Dude . . . you don't know that."

The portal had faded completely and now just showed a hole in the wall. Crumbling plaster and broken lattice.

Nathan stood and wiped his eyes. He brushed off the dust and bits of plaster. Then he turned to Mitch. "We have to get moving. I don't have much time."

VALLEY OF THE SHADOW

44

LATE SATURDAY MORNING, Jim and Annie pulled up in front of Juanita Marshall's apartment. Jim had met with her briefly a couple of weeks earlier to secure permission to visit Devon at the juvenile center. It was a formality at the suggestion of Devon's probation officer. But this morning, he figured it was as good a place as any to start searching for Devon. Maybe Juanita had heard from him. Maybe not. But she was the only other person that Jim could think of that he might be in a position to help. Annie had come along for moral support, and Jim was glad of it.

"I didn't get a chance to talk to her much the last time," Jim explained as they made their way up to Juanita's apartment. "She didn't have much good to say about her son. I don't even think she realized how close he'd been to dying." He shrugged. He felt bad for Devon. "I don't think she even cared."

Jim knocked on the apartment door. And waited. A minute later, they heard a voice inside.

"Who is it?"

"Juanita?" Jim wasn't quite sure how to begin. "I'm Jim Malone. I'm sorry to just come over without calling first. We met once a couple weeks ago when I stopped by to get permission to visit your son in detention. Do you remember me?"

There was no answer for a few seconds. Then the door opened as far as the security chains would allow. Jim could see Devon's mother staring out at him from the shadows.

"You a cop?"

"No. Don't you remember me? I was the guy who found Devon after he'd been shot. I called the ambulance. I did CPR until they came. You signed a form that gave me permission to visit him at the detention center." Jim could see a vague recognition in her eyes, though shrouded with suspicion.

"What do you want?"

Jim tugged Annie closer to him. Maybe the sight of another woman would ease her apprehension a bit. "I don't think you met my wife, Annie."

"What do you want?" Juanita repeated.

Jim took a breath. "I . . . I don't know if you heard, but . . . Devon escaped yesterday and—"

"I ain't seen him."

"So he hasn't tried to get in touch with you?"

"We ain't exactly on speaking terms."

"Juanita . . ." Jim rubbed his jaw. How could he put this?

"Devon's in trouble. I mean, not just with the police. And I thought maybe you might be able to help us find him."

"Why do you care?"

Jim shrugged. He didn't have a good answer. Devon was still little more than a stranger to him.

Finally Annie spoke up. "My husband saved his life. I'd think you'd show a little more concern for your own son—"

"Don't you go judging me," Juanita hissed. "You don't know what I've been through. You don't know nothing about me!"

Jim tried to keep his voice calm. "Please. We want to help you find him. We think there may be something more serious going on. We don't want him to get in any more trouble."

Juanita stared at them for several seconds without a word and then shut the door. Jim glanced at Annie, who only shrugged. They heard several chains sliding and the door opened again. Juanita beckoned them inside.

She led them to her cramped kitchen, and they sat around her table. Jim eyed a small, framed painting on the wall. A dark-skinned Jesus in a red robe with his arms out at his sides. As if beckoning or welcoming the viewer home. Jim remembered seeing it when he had first come to visit with the probation officer and wondering if Juanita was a Christian. She did appear to have a strong belief in spiritual things, though to him it seemed more a superstition than a real faith. Her slight Caribbean accent was hard to place, and Jim tried to recall which island she was originally from—Haiti, he thought she'd said. She said she had come to America when she was ten years old.

But Jim thought it best not to tell her now that her son might be under some sort of evil spiritual influence. He still barely believed it himself.

He shifted in his seat. "Juanita, I went to see Devon yesterday . . ."

He began to tell her about his brief encounter with Devon the day before. Juanita showed no emotion as Jim described how Devon had managed to escape. She stared at the floor, holding a string of beads around her wrist. Jim assumed they held some spiritual significance for her.

After Jim had finished, Annie spoke up. "He was here, wasn't he?"

A spark of anger flashed in Juanita's eyes. Then it faded and she offered a slow nod. "Yesterday."

Annie pointed down the hall. "I noticed the security chains on your door. It looked like someone tried to break in recently. Was that Devon?"

"He . . . he forced his way inside."

Jim stared at Annie a moment, incredulous, then glanced down the hall. He could indeed see a section of the doorjamb looked as if it had been recently torn away. Splintered, as if the bracket there had been ripped from the wood. He'd completely missed it coming in. But Annie, apparently, had not.

He turned back to Juanita. "What happened?"

She shook her head. "He said he wanted my car. He tried to choke me."

"Did you call the police?" Annie said.

"No. He said he'd kill me if I did."

"Did he say anything about where he was going?" Jim said.

"No. He just said he needed the car."

"Do you have any idea where he might have gone?"

Juanita shook her head and her eyes grew moist. "I can't tell you anything. I don't even know him anymore."

"We're trying to help you." Annie's eyes grew fierce. "Don't you care what happens to him?"

"I can't do nothing about it! I can't stop him!" Juanita glared back at her. "You can go back to your nice little house and your family! But you bring your kids to live in this neighborhood for a couple years and see how you feel! See what they're like!"

Jim inserted himself between them. "Listen, we really do want to help you. We want to help Devon."

"You can't help him. He's already dead."

Jim blinked. "What?"

Juanita's voice softened. "When he got shot. They told me he was dead but they brought him back. Only . . . only he didn't come back alone. Something else came with him."

Jim and Annie exchanged glances. "Why would you say that?" Jim said.

"I've seen it before."

"What do you mean?"

Juanita seemed to shudder. "When I was a little girl in Haiti, I remember a man once who got real sick. They said he had stopped breathing and they revived him. He eventually got better, but he was never really the same after that. Everyone in our town could see he was different."

"Different?" Jim leaned forward. "Different how?"

"He could see things no one else did. He started talking to himself—or to the things no one else could see. One night, he was outside our house, barking and growling like a dog. Like an animal. And when my father went out to make him leave, the man just swore at him. But it wasn't . . . it wasn't a human voice talking."

Jim felt a chill. "And you think the same thing happened to Devon?"

"When he said he would kill me—" Juanita closed her eyes—"it was Devon's mouth, but it wasn't his voice."

They were silent for a moment. Finally Jim spoke up. "When he was in the room with me yesterday, I got the distinct feeling it wasn't really Devon."

Jim told her what he'd learned so far about Conner Hayden and his and Devon's shared experience that night.

Juanita started to weep. "I knew something was wrong. I knew it." She wiped her eyes. "I've been praying for him. I was praying all night."

Annie moved next to her and placed an arm around her shoulder. "Would you like us to pray with you?"

Juanita nodded. "I'm just so . . . so scared for him."

They prayed together, sitting around the kitchen table. Annie first, and then Jim stumbled through his own awkward appeal. It was the first time he'd ever prayed in front of anyone other than Annie. He felt inadequate and unsure of himself. Unsure exactly what to ask for. But hoping God would see past his words into his heart.

He prayed for a mother and her son. Two lost souls who, in the entire world, had only each other. And though everyone else seemed to have given up on them, still he and Annie now found a faint glimmer of hope.

Twenty minutes later, they left the apartment. Jim was shaking his head. "You know, we're still no closer to finding Devon."

Annie nodded. "I think we need to find Conner Hayden. At least let him know what we've found out."

MITCH AND NATHAN CONTINUED
down the highway. The Ferrari kicked
up twin swirls of dust along both shoulders of the road and Mitch skirted
between them, close behind.

He checked his speedometer:
105. Nathan was obviously feeling an
increased sense of urgency since his
latest vision through the window. He
wondered what was going through the
guy's head right now—what it must be
like to know he'd be dead any second.
Mitch wondered how much longer
Nathan had.

And he wondered how much time
he himself had left.

Time was a funny thing. There was

obviously no real correlation—at least no constant—between time in the material world and time in this place. After all, according to Nathan, Mitch had been in a coma for only two months.

Mitch bit his lip. Two months!

Not five years. Five long, dismal years. He tried to make sense out of everything he'd seen. He recalled all the people he'd come across. People who each in their own ways were dying and didn't even know it.

He remembered Conner, Helen, and Devon. They'd spent three terrifying days together. Conner had obviously made it back—that is, if Mitch could trust what Nathan had shown him through the magic window. But what about Helen and Devon? What had happened to them? Mitch remembered Helen had said that Devon had just disappeared into thin air. That must have been the key. When someone's body was revived again, their spirits vanished from this place. But those who had been dragged off . . .

Mitch thought again of Jason. He could still see the guy being dragged away into the forest by the gray creatures. But what lay beyond? What had happened to him? Where was he now? Mitch shuddered at those thoughts.

The day crawled on toward afternoon, and the road stretched through the seemingly unending countryside. At last they came to the crest of a ridge and Mitch looked down the broad vista. Ahead of them rose the hazy shapes of skyscrapers on the horizon.

They were coming up on some kind of city.

Mitch frowned. A city? Out in the middle of this desert?

Nathan seemed to increase his speed. Mitch accelerated as well. The city loomed closer, and soon the road widened to a multilane highway. Before long, they were traveling between the towering skyscrapers. Mitch had slowed and found himself gazing up at the enormous structures.

The buildings appeared to be crumbling. Vacant windows were dark and missing glass. Large portions of the structures had crumbled away. The streets, too, were cracked and uneven. Piles of debris lay strewn everywhere.

In the middle of the city, they came across an interchange. The highway rose to cross over another expressway. Suddenly, Nathan came to a stop in the middle of the overpass. Mitch rolled up next to the Ferrari. The entire bridge had broken off and Mitch looked down a sheer drop and a vast field of rubble on the highway below them.

"Looks like a dead end," he said.

Nathan nodded. "We'll have to find another way through."

From their vantage point, Mitch could see for miles. Everywhere he looked, he saw block after block of towers, buildings, and skyscrapers. Everything was shadowy, vacant, and crumbling. "Dude, what is this place?"

"You don't recognize it?"

"Why would I?"

Nathan raised an eyebrow. "Because you've been here before. But it probably looked a little different when you were here last."

Mitch stared at him for a moment and then back out over the desolate cityscape. It seemed to go on forever. "You mean this is—was—Chicago?"

"Chicago, L.A., Singapore . . ." Nathan shrugged. "Name your town. This is it. The Gray City."

"I don't get it."

"A lot of folks don't even know they're dying. They wake up here all disoriented, thinking everyone else has disappeared."

"Dude, that's exactly what happened to me. But, I mean . . . this isn't how it looked."

"Let me guess," Nathan said. "At first everything looked normal. Sun shining, green grass. Everything looked nice."

"Yeah . . ."

"That's because your mind doesn't know what's happening to it. It hasn't yet grasped the truth, so it creates its own reality. And you think everything's normal. At first."

"But then everything starts to change."

Nathan nodded. "Most people here see what they want to see. They're probably not even aware of you. Lots of them just go on with their routines, until . . ."

"Right," Mitch said. "Until the creatures come along."

"But others start to figure out that something's wrong. And they leave. They head out of the city. Looking for answers."

Mitch frowned. "So how many people are in there? I mean, right now?"

"I don't know. Thousands probably."

"Thousands?"

"Do you have any idea how many people die every day? around the world? every second?" Nathan shook his head. "Sickness, old age, wars, famines, murders . . . everyone's unique. Everyone's experience here is different depending on who they were. How they died. What they believed. What kind of lives they lived."

"Yeah, but they all end up the same."

"Except for the ones that are brought back to life somehow."

"Why can't we see any of them?"

"Oh, they're down there. But most of them are still lost in their own kind of delusion and they see this place the way they want to. Or the way they remember it. Right down to the last detail. Some of them never come out of it before the Reapers come for them."

"Reapers? That's what they're called? The . . . the aliens?"

Nathan offered a shrug and a grim chuckle. "It's what I call them. As good a name as any, I guess." Then his lips tightened. "But we need to get going. We're going to have to find another way through, and it'll be getting dark before long."

VALLEY OF THE SHADOW

46

THE WOODS, THE WOODS. We'll meet in the woods. The woods after dark.

Howard trudged across the open field toward the black forest behind his farm. His flashlight cast a pale cone of light into the swirling mist, slicing left and right and down at the ground.

Howard muttered to himself and his breath coiled out in steamy tendrils. "Meet in the woods. Meet in the woods."

He paused at the edge of the forest. Gnarled branches reached out to him like bony black fingers frozen in place. His heart pounded and he wiped his forehead with his bandanna, then plunged into the woods, pushing his way through the underbrush. There was no path, but he knew the way. He had been here before. It was the place they always came to meet him. To commune. To share their thoughts. Devise their plans. It was a sacred place for Howard. A sort of tabernacle. A sanctuary.

Eventually he came to the small clearing where the dilapidated cabin huddled amid the trees. It was dark and shrouded in shadow.

He stood in the doorway. The cabin was empty. Howard knew they weren't here yet. But they would be coming. They would be here soon. His stomach curled with anticipation. It always sent a chill through him, waiting for them to arrive. A wave of terror and awe. To be so close to such power and yet to be of use to it. It frightened and thrilled him.

Howard closed the door behind him and sat in the rocking chair next to the old iron stove. He sat in silence. Closed his eyes and breathed deeply as he rocked. He had to calm himself. Empty his mind of fear. There was still part of him that wanted to run. To hide. Part of him was desperate to leave this place. And he had to master it. Control his fear. Subjugate it for the higher purpose that drove him to this place.

He breathed slowly. And rocked.

Outside a breeze picked up and moaned through the trees. He could hear them coming. Whispers on the wind. Moaning through the branches. Coming in the mist. Howard resisted the urge to flee. It would have been no use anyway. He had to stay strong. Or he would never see his family again.

The whispers grew louder, and soon Howard forced his eyes open. He let out an involuntary gasp. They surrounded the cabin. He could see them outside. Gray faces. White eyes. Black jaws, gaping open. They crowded around the window. Dozens of them. Hundreds. Just standing there, watching.

Next, Howard heard a deep rumble. Like a distant truck coming closer. His eyes widened. Sweat beaded on his forehead and he wiped it again with his handkerchief. He struggled to control his breathing as the sound grew louder.

The porch creaked. The door handle clicked and turned. The door swung open.

Howard suppressed another gasp. It was always a fearful thing. He would never get used to it.

A cold breeze wafted through the open door, carrying the pungent scent of rotting flesh. A thick black mist flowed into the room, curling and snaking across the floorboards.

"Beloved."

Howard's mouth went dry and he struggled to hide his fear. He bowed his head in a gesture of respect. His hands trembled. The mist curled around Howard's feet and he recoiled instinctively.

"Still repulsed by us, are you?" the voice said.

"N-no." Howard shook his head quickly. "No. Just a little . . . nervous."

"You have been of much use."

"I . . . I tried to keep up my end of the deal."

"And you have, my love. You have done well . . . but for this."

"I . . . I couldn't keep him here. I just wasn't strong enough on my own. I couldn't force him to stay."

"We cannot let him leave. We must find him. Together."

Howard tried to swallow, but his throat was too dry. He was always so thirsty.

"To . . . together," he said.

The entire cabin seemed to shudder. A deep groan echoed through the forest. The black mist coiled around Howard's legs, wrapping itself around him like a serpent.

A thin tendril moved slowly up his torso and chest, up to his face.

Howard leaned his head back slightly. His eyes closed. This was always the worst part. . . .

The mist flowed into his nostrils and mouth. A long, steady stream. Howard felt his body stiffen, then convulse. It was almost like drowning. He could feel it flowing inside him. He could feel his mind being pushed back. Locked away. Locked up inside a cell.

Slowly the convulsions stopped and Howard opened his eyes again.

They were completely white.

CONNER SLOWED DOWN AS HE approached the Bristols' driveway. He was almost overwhelmed with a nauseating sense of déjà vu. The old clapboard farmhouse stood off the highway a hundred feet or so with two big oak trees in the front yard. Behind it, Conner could see the garage, the maintenance shed, the barn, the silo. Just as he remembered.

The very idea that he'd been here before was mind-boggling. But had he actually been here? Or had the farm he'd visited been only some sort of facsimile—an exact replica that Howard had created for himself in the Interworld? In either case, the emotions it evoked as Conner pulled into the driveway were almost over-powering. His heart pounded and he found his hands gripping the wheel so tightly that they were cramping up.

He parked and took several deep breaths before getting out.

Mrs. Bristol pulled into the garage, then waved him around to the back. It was close to noon, so the sun was bright, making the whole place seem more cheery and inviting now than it had in the Interworld. Still, Conner found his legs sluggish as he climbed the back steps.

He stood in the old kitchen. The same cabinets and beige linoleum floor, with the same table in the middle. Mrs. Bristol welcomed Conner inside and told him to make himself at home while she prepared sandwiches for lunch.

Conner moved into the living room and sat down on the couch, where he could still see the kitchen. She kept talking—perhaps making up for the fact that she hadn't had her husband with her for nearly a year.

Conner didn't see any sign of her son. "So . . . how is Owen these days?"

"Oh, he keeps himself busy around the place," Mrs. Bristol said as she slathered mayonnaise onto slices of bread at the table. "I think he went to have his van worked on. I am so thankful to have him, though. I couldn't manage all of this on my own."

"Have you thought about selling the farm?" Conner ventured. "I mean what with your hus . . ."

She leaned over to give him a dour look though the doorway. "Sell the farm? Felix, this land has been in my family for four generations. I am not going to sell it off. That you can be sure of."

Just as she finished making lunch, Conner heard a vehicle pull up outside. He glanced out the window to see a black Ford cargo van rolling up the driveway. Conner could hear music blaring over the rumble of the engine. Some kind of thrash metal song with someone screaming lyrics in a shrill tone.

"Ah," Mrs. Bristol said, "there's Owen now."

Conner could see part of the van through the curtains in the living room. There was a ladder mounted on the roof and a logo on the side. The door opened and someone climbed out. Someone big.

Conner could only see the back of Owen Bristol as he walked from the van to the garage. Wide shoulders, a gray sweatshirt smudged with grease, faded jeans, and black work boots. Dark hair draped down his back in a loose ponytail.

A minute later, Conner heard steps on the porch and the screen door opened. Owen seemed to fill the entire doorway. Barrel-chested and thick-limbed, he didn't appear to have gotten his size from working out, but rather from pure genetics. Just the type of person who had been born big. He wore black sunglasses and a backward-facing baseball cap. Several strands of his long dark hair hung in his face, and his jaw was covered with a few days' worth of stubble.

Conner recalled Mrs. Bristol saying they had visited thirty years ago when Owen was two. Thirty-two? The guy's pock-marked face and beard made him look older. A lot older. That must've been a rough thirty-two years.

Mrs. Bristol was busy explaining to Owen that Felix Grady was here from Minneapolis. She had to go through a bit of history to get Owen to even recognize the name. Owen took off his sunglasses and stared at Conner with deep-set brown eyes. They were dark and very intense but slightly crossed, arousing even more uneasy feelings in Conner. As if Owen wasn't looking directly at him. But through him.

It was almost the look of a lunatic.

Conner stood nervously in the kitchen entrance and waved a few fingers. "How's it going?"

Owen just nodded slightly. "Hey" was all he said.

Conner felt a hot flash hit him. The guy wasn't buying it, Conner could tell. But then Mrs. Bristol told him to go wash up and Owen went to the sink. Conner sat down at the kitchen table. Mrs. Bristol had prepared turkey and roast beef sandwiches, chips, and a big bowl of what appeared to be leftover potato salad. She also brought out a couple of two liters of soda from the pantry. Owen had retrieved a beer from the refrigerator.

"Want one?" he muttered to Conner, holding out the Miller bottle. His voice was gravelly, almost hoarse.

"Uh . . . no thank y—" Conner choked off his sentence and found himself staring at Owen's thick arm.

A tattooed image of a large tarantula was splayed out on his forearm. Its front legs stretched up onto the back of his hand and the others wrapped down around his wrist. An identical spider graced his other arm.

A memory of the gray creatures flashed into Conner's mind. Spiderlike hands reaching out toward him. Conner blinked and cleared his throat. "Nice tattoo. You . . . you like spiders?"

Owen shrugged. "Dream I had once." He sat down but never took his eyes off of Conner.

Mrs. Bristol cleared her throat and tapped her head. Owen glanced at her, removed his cap, and dropped it on the floor.

Conner felt like he was in a sauna under Owen's persistent observation. But then again, he didn't seem to be looking directly at Conner either. And Conner couldn't keep his gaze from those tattoos.

Mrs. Bristol, meanwhile, prattled on through a whole

series of topics. Owen devoured three sandwiches in silence, crunched on a handful of chips, then downed his beer in one shot and let out a long, rumbling belch.

Conner had finished his sandwich with a glass of warm store-brand cola and wiped his mouth. "Well, it was certainly a pleasure to visit and get caught up, but I really do need to hit the road."

As he stood, Owen pushed himself back from the table.

"Mama," he growled, "you gonna let this guy leave without telling us who he really is?"

Conner froze, cursing under his breath. Someone had just turned the sauna up high.

Mrs. Bristol wiped her lips and finished chewing. Then she looked at Conner with a cold stare. "No, Son. No, I'm not."

VALLEY OF THE SHADOW

MITCH AND NATHAN TURNED AROUND, followed the freeway back to an exit ramp, and descended into the Gray City. They made their way down decaying streets, weaving between enormous chunks of stone and debris. Traffic signals were rusted and bent, and some buildings had been completely reduced to rubble. It reminded Mitch of one of those science fiction movies about a post-apocalypse world—after all civilization had been destroyed and only mutants roamed the streets.

That wasn't so far from the truth.

They traveled for another half hour, winding through block after block of the desolate city. Mitch kept an eye out for all the other souls Nathan had told him about. But so far he hadn't seen any. Then again, this was a big place. Bigger than any city from the material world. Mile after endless mile of decaying buildings, like a sober testament to all of man's endeavors. A grim reminder that everything he achieves in life will be left behind to rot and decay. All around Mitch were thousands of years of human history and accomplishment . . . and this was all that remained of their efforts. Sooner or later everything returned to dust.

The lyrics to a song started rolling through Mitch's head again. *"Dust in the wind . . . all we are is dust in the wind."*

The vast emptiness seemed to suck the energy out of Mitch. Soon the overcast sky began to grow dark and Nathan pulled into what appeared to be a parking garage. Mitch followed.

"What's up?" he said as they parked.

"We should get off the streets before dark."

Mitch raised an eyebrow. "You mean because of the Reapers? I thought you said we were safe."

"You are for now. But you still don't want to be out in the open. He can call them. Coordinate them. And he can use them to bring you back to him."

"Who? Howard?"

"Yes," Nathan said. "Well . . . the power that's controlling him."

"So they are still a threat—these Reapers. They're still dangerous. I mean . . . they'll drag me off with them?"

Nathan held up the blue chalk. "Don't worry, I've got you covered."

Mitch stared at the innocuous-looking chalk. "With that? Dude . . . the window tricks were cool and all that, but I mean,

I've seen these Reapers in action and—no offense—I don't think that's going to—"

Nathan smiled. "Mitch, you're still walking by sight, aren't you? God likes using the things you least expect in ways you'd never guess."

He led Mitch into the adjacent building through an access door. The building looked like an old hotel. Something that may have once been a five-star establishment but here in the Interworld was just a decaying shell, void of all comfort and cheer.

The front desk and concierge counters were covered with dust and debris. Without any power, the elevators were completely useless. They found a pair of couches in the lobby and pulled them closer together. Nathan drew a wide circle on the marble floor around them. Maybe fifteen feet in diameter or so. After a few seconds, it began to glow. Smoke wafted up from the chalk line, swirling in the faint blue light.

They stretched out on the couches with a low table between them. Outside the sun had set and now a pall of darkness fell over the city.

But inside the lobby, the chalk line continued to glow and faint blue tendrils of smoke reached to the ceiling.

Mitch gazed into the light. "So what is it about this chalk? How does it work? Magic?"

"Not quite," Nathan chuckled. "It's a little technical, but in layman's terms, the chalk is made of inversely charged quantum particles in a state of temporal flux."

Mitch stared at him for several seconds. "Dude, I'm serious."

"So am I."

"So what are you, some kind of physicist?"

"Nope. Plumber."

"C'mon, dude, I'm trying to have a serious conversation here."

Nathan propped himself up on an elbow. "Mitch, I don't know about you, but ever since I've been outside my body, my mind's been able to grasp concepts I never even knew about before. It all just seems to make sense somehow."

"I managed to do a little extracurricular reading myself since I've been here. Y'know, trying to expand my intellectual capacity." Mitch shrugged. "I guess I haven't gotten around to all the quantum mechanics stuff yet."

"Actually, it's transdimensional physics."

"I'll take your word for it," Mitch said. He pointed to the glowing circle. "But on another note . . . exactly how long will this last? I mean, those windows you made only lasted a few minutes."

"That's because a window's more concentrated," Nathan said. "Requires a lot more energy. But all this circle does is generate a low-level inversely charged field of quantum particles. It should last five or six hours. And the Reapers know better than to mess with it."

Mitch frowned. "But if the stuff is that dangerous, how come you can touch it?"

"Right now our spirits are in a slightly higher state of resonance than the rest of the energy in this dimension."

"Because we're not quite dead yet?"

"Exactly," Nathan said. "But as we die, our resonant state begins to enter conformity with this dimension."

"And what happens then?"

"That's the point of no return."

Mitch leaned forward. "So . . . is that what the purple rash is? Right before they drag someone off?"

"That's one of the manifestations, yes. And once it takes over, there's no hope of ever being resuscitated."

Suddenly from out in the street they could hear a low moaning sound. Like the wind had picked up and was howling through the vacant buildings. This continued for several minutes. Mitch felt a chill race down his back. This was more than just the wind.

Far off in the distance came a shrill cry for help. A human voice. A terrified shriek that lasted several seconds, echoing through the streets. The sheer terror in the scream was unnerving. Mitch had heard these before. He covered his ears.

"You hear them?" Nathan said, his voice just above a whisper. "The Reapers are coming for them."

Mitch's heart was pounding now. He sat up. "Is this going to last all night? How am I supposed to get any sleep? How could anyone sleep through this?"

"Sleep? Who said anything about sleep? I just said we needed to get off the streets before dark. You're still thinking in terms of your physical body. Your spirit doesn't need sleep."

"I used to be able to sleep. Back on the farm."

"Because you thought you were still in your body. Same with hunger or thirst. They're all just memories of what your body used to feel and require."

"So this hunger I'm feeling is all in my head?"

"Technically, your head is back in the hospital with the rest of your body. It's really all in your *mind*."

Mitch sat back and listened to the deep moaning and the occasional scream of terror. He closed his eyes. These were human beings. Souls being dragged away to a place . . . Mitch had no idea what it was like and no interest in finding out either. Still, he couldn't help but feel sickened at every cry for help. He opened his eyes.

Nathan was watching him. "There's nothing you can do for them."

"I know. But that doesn't make it any easier to listen—" Mitch stopped. Beyond the soft curtain of blue light encircling them, in the shadows of the lobby . . .

Something moved.

DEVON GRIPPED THE WHEEL as he navigated carefully through the side streets. Pale Man was lounging in the backseat giving directions and singing to himself. Something about Romeo and Juliet and not fearing the Reaper. Devon thought it was a rock song from way before his time. He thought maybe he'd heard it once or twice before, but he couldn't be sure.

"Yo, man, you mind tellin' me what that was all about back there?"

"That was about an insurance policy, chief," Pale Man said. "I just wanted you to see what kind of trouble you've gotten yourself into. In case you're thinking of doing anything stupid."

Devon felt his jaw clench. Oswald Karenga had killed Devon's bosses and Devon had no idea why. He tried to recall the events leading up to the shooting that night, but it was all a blur. He couldn't remember meeting with J.G. and Apollo. And he didn't remember any deal they were involved in for Karenga. In fact, he still couldn't remember much of anything from that entire day.

Pale Man was still singing that stupid song. Devon finally swore at him. "Man, don't you know any hip-hop or something? I'm sick of that song."

Pale Man clicked his tongue and shook his head. "Nothing like perpetuating a stereotype, chief. I think you need to expand your musical tastes a little. This is a classic rock song. Back when music was really music. When guys played real instruments instead of looping digitized segments of music that other people had recorded and calling it a new genre."

Devon swore at him again.

Pale Man chuckled. "Ah, but don't get me on my soapbox. If you want to run around with your hip-hop and your double negatives and your baggy pants hanging down around your knees, you go right ahead. You think that's some kind of ghetto culture thing, that's fine with me. Personally, I think you're your own worst enemy, but that's just my opinion."

"Man . . . whatever."

"Good rebuttal. Very articulate."

"So what is this thing Karenga wants?"

Pale Man leaned forward. "See, you're in what's called a 'need-to-know' situation. I just wanted you to understand how terribly upset Mr. Karenga is with you. So you don't stray off the reservation. As it were."

"But I didn't do anything."

"Sure you did. You just don't remember it."

"Because you're keeping me from remembering."

"See there?" Pale Man flashed his rotted teeth in a grin. "You can display such blinding flashes of brilliance—however brief. Now, I can help you get out of this little jam, but I just want to make sure I have your undivided attention. And your willing cooperation. Understand?"

Devon muttered, "Not like I got much of a choice."

Pale Man leaned back again. "Everyone has a choice, chief. Everyone."

Devon was quiet for several seconds. "So what do I gotta do?"

"You remember that lawyer who visited you yesterday? Hayden?"

Devon's hands tightened on the steering wheel. He'd been trying to forget that. Forget the whole creepy experience. "Yeah."

"You recall he mentioned a mutual acquaintance of yours. Mitch Kent. You do remember Mitch, don't you?"

"Big white guy. Tattoos."

"Exactly. Well, it seems our buddy Mitch is in a coma. His body is, anyway. But his mind—his spirit—is still in that place you're trying so hard to forget."

Devon shuddered. All he knew was that he never wanted to see that place again. Ever.

Pale Man went on. "See, that place is sort of a dimension in between dimensions. Like the hallway connecting two rooms. One room is life and the other is . . . well, not life. But poor Mitch is still kind of lingering out in the hallway. And all I want you to do is just give him a little nudge. Move him along to the next room. That's all."

"Kill him. You want me to kill him."

"Now see, that's an awfully harsh term to use. I want you

to free him. Release him. Cut his mortal bonds. Help him to . . . y'know, move on."

"Why can't you do that yourself? You seem to be able to make people do whatever you want."

Pale Man waved his hand. "Well, it's all a little compli-cated. I've got certain constraints to work within. A subject has to be conscious for one thing. Plus there's a whole bureau-cracy involved. Approvals to get. Forms to fill out. Bottom line is we generally outsource this kind of job. Go with what we call a codependent contractor. And that's where you come in."

"Yo, man." Devon was shaking his head. "I told you, man, I can't kill no one. I ain't never killed no one before."

"If you could hear yourself with my ears." Pale Man chuckled. "So, anyway, here's the thing. You cooperate with me and I'll help you retrieve your heretofore unremembered item of extreme importance for Mr. Karenga so he doesn't kill you. Now I think that's a pretty darn good deal, if I do say so myself."

Devon bit his lip and swore. Oswald Karenga probably had his entire security force out looking for him at this very moment. There was no way to be sure Pale Man would ever keep his word even if Devon did cooperate. On the other hand, if this Mitch guy was as bad off as Pale Man had described, it wouldn't really be like killing him. The guy sounded like he was half-dead anyway.

Devon was starting to feel sick inside and he knew he was in trouble.

He was in a boatload of trouble.

"Okay," he said at length. "What do I have to do?"

50

MRS. BRISTOL'S PLEASANT expression had morphed into an icy stare. Conner's heart pounded hard against his ribs and he felt dizzy.

"Now . . . now, hold on a second," he said, but his voice sounded thin and weak. "Look, I don't want any trouble. I'm not trying to cause any trouble."

"We'll be the judge of that," Mrs. Bristol said. Her grandmotherly demeanor had all but evaporated. "You see, Stewart and Anna Grady were my parents. They used to own this farm. I grew up here. Right in this very house. They passed away thirty-five years ago now. And their son, Felix, was my brother. He's gone too."

Conner felt as if the floor had dropped out from underneath him. His knees buckled and he sat down again. "Look, I'm really sorry, but I can explain."

"I'm sure you can," Mrs. Bristol said. "Start by telling me who you really are and what you want with my husband. Why were you in his room today?"

Conner opened his mouth to explain, but before he could get a word out, Mrs. Bristol continued. "Because if you think for one minute you can get me to remove that tube, you are sorely mistaken."

"I don't want you to remove his feeding tube," Conner said. "In fact if you really do love him, you should probably do everything you can to keep him alive."

Her eyes narrowed. "Why do you say that?"

"And I'm not with any insurance company or anything either. My name is Conner Hayden. I'm from Chicago. I'm not trying to get you to do anything. And I'm sorry I wasn't more forthcoming. But really . . . I didn't think you'd believe me if I told you the truth."

Mrs. Bristol folded her arms. "Try me."

Conner's mouth was dry. His eyes flitted between Mrs. Bristol and her imposing son. He needed to defuse the tension in the room. He'd been caught in a deception and didn't want to add to the mess with more lies. But he knew he'd have to be judicious with the facts. He couldn't tell her the whole truth.

"The truth is . . . I had a heart attack two months ago. My heart stopped beating for something like fifteen or twenty minutes. I had a near-death . . . an out-of-body type of experience. And during that time, I met . . . I met your husband."

Mrs. Bristol's eyes widened momentarily. She glanced at Owen, who remained silent, leaning back in his chair. Then she turned again to Conner. "You're telling me you met Howard during a . . . a what?"

"I know it sounds crazy. But I didn't even know what was happening to me. I didn't know I was dying. Everything seemed so real. I met a few other people. And Howard too. And he invited us here. We stayed in this house. Right here on this farm."

"You expect me to believe that?" Mrs. Bristol leaned forward. "I suppose now you're going to tell me that Howard said he wants me to sell the farm to you. Or that he wants me to take out his feeding tube and let him die."

Conner sighed. This wasn't going well. "I told you already, I don't want you to take out his feeding tube. And I don't want your farm. I . . . I was just curious. That's all. I just wanted to see him for myself. Just so I could know that I wasn't going crazy."

Conner decided he'd better not tell her anything about Howard's connection with the demonic creatures, how he'd been working with them and how he'd led Conner into a trap.

"After I recovered, I tried to look up all the people I had met. To see if they were real. And to prove to myself that what had happened to me was real. That's when I learned your husband was in this coma. I had to come and see it for myself. That's all. I was just curious."

Mrs. Bristol sat back for a moment, her arms still folded and her lips puckered slightly. She cast a sideways look at Owen. "What do you think?"

Owen shook his head. "The dude's crazy."

Mrs. Bristol turned back to Conner. "You see, Mr. Hayden, I've been getting a great deal of pressure from my doctor to simply accept the inevitable. That my Howard won't ever recover. They tried to operate. To relieve some of the pressure.

But now they're saying they can't do any more for him." She wagged her finger again. "But I'm not going to give up. Howard is a strong man. He's a good man. And he deserves to live."

Conner started to reply but the words caught in his throat. He tried again. "I'm sure he does. And I certainly wish you the best."

They sat in silence for a moment. Then Conner stood again. "Look, Mrs. Bristol, I sincerely apologize for any trouble or worry I may have caused you. I hope you can understand why I did it."

She just looked at him for a moment. Then at length, she nodded. "I understand. And I believe you."

"You do?" Conner raised a skeptical eyebrow.

"He's here, you know. Howard is here."

"What?"

She went on. "I can feel him here with me sometimes. I can sense his presence. I think he's trying to reach me. He's trying to come back to us."

Conner wasn't sure what to say to that. "Well then . . . I hope everything works out for you."

With that, Conner excused himself and went out to his car, followed closely by Owen Bristol.

Conner opened the door to his Mercedes as Owen leaned against the front fender.

Conner rolled his eyes and sighed. "Look, Owen, I'm leaving, okay? You don't need to—"

"Listen up, guy," Owen growled. "There's a lot of creeps like you out there, trying to scam little old ladies out of their life savings. I suppose you think that just because we live out here in the country maybe we're stupid or something. But I can—"

Conner held up a hand. "Owen, I'm not trying to scam your moth—"

"But I can guarantee you something." Owen straightened up, his expression dark. "If you ever come back here trying to pull something like that again, they won't ever find you."

"Is that a threat?" Conner tried to sound gruff, but his voice cracked and it just came out sounding pathetic.

Owen snorted and leaned in close. "I mean, they'll search for you . . . but they won't ever find you. Are we clear on that . . . *Felix*?"

VALLEY OF THE SHADOW

51

"THEY FOUND US," Nathan said.

In the darkened shadows of the lobby, Mitch saw movement. A black shape passed between two columns that framed the main entrances. Then another, off to the left.

Mitch's breath came in choppy rasps as he watched several dark figures approach the circle. He could see their black shapes now, grotesquely thin, crouching low and moving slowly—as if with caution. Then against the darkness, Mitch could see white eyes glowing.

They stood around the entire perimeter of light, sniffing it. Inspecting it. Their mouths gaped open in low growls. They pressed close to the circle but did not cross it.

"Don't worry, Mitch; they won't cross the line," Nathan whispered, his voice barely audible above the hisses and growls. "Their hate for you is tempered only by their instinct for self-preservation."

"Will it kill them?"

Nathan managed a grim chuckle. "No. Death doesn't have the same meaning to them as it does to us. There's no finality for them. But there are things worse than dying. They would be . . . severely disrupted for some time before regaining any semblance of their current form."

"What are they . . . like, demons?"

"Not exactly. They're the multiplied manifestation of the being that inhabits this dimension. They're its collective mind and will."

"What being?"

"Death," Nathan said. "Death itself ushers lost and dying souls through this dimension to the other side. And it has only one overriding desire: to consume. It's an end-less hunger that feeds on all life. It's savage and insatiable, even though there's a steady stream of human souls to feed from."

"What about all the hallucinations? all the weird stuff I've seen?"

Nathan shrugged. "Some of it people create themselves. Some of it Death creates just to generate terror. To heighten the experience."

Mitch couldn't take his eyes off the creatures. "But me and Howard—these things never bothered us much. Not on the farm."

"Because he wanted to keep you here. Keep you from leaving. He tried to make you feel safe and lull you to sleep so you wouldn't begin to get curious and venture off."

"Why would Howard be working with these things? What's in it for him?"

"Nothing." Nathan shook his head. "I assume he made some kind of deal. Maybe to be set free and returned to his body. I don't know. Whatever it is, I can guarantee you, Death has absolutely no intention of keeping up his end of the bargain."

Mitch closed his eyes and tried to block the sounds and even the thought of the Reapers from his mind. He could feel their presence just a few yards away.

And then he heard something else.

"Mitch!"

Mitch's eyes snapped open. He turned to see someone walking toward him from the darkness.

VALLEY OF THE SHADOW

52

CONNER BACKED OUT of the driveway as Owen stood by, watching him. Conner put the car in gear and tore off down the highway. He wasn't sure where he was going exactly, but he wanted to put some distance between him and that farm.

His jaw was clenched so tight that his teeth hurt, and he cursed himself for being so stupid. Every instinct had screamed at him not to go with Mrs. Bristol to the farm. He should have just explained everything to her there in the nursing home. His heart was still pounding. And that crazed-looking monster of a son could have killed Conner with his bare hands.

Conner glanced at his watch. It was nearly two o'clock. He drove a few miles farther and finally pulled onto the shoulder to collect his thoughts.

His forehead was damp with a cold sweat. Owen had made a clear threat to him. He could kill Conner and dispose of his body where no one would ever find him. Conner glanced at his cell phone, still off. But there was no sense calling the police. From their perspective, Conner would have been in the wrong, looking as if he'd tried to take advantage of an old woman. Her son would have been justified in threatening him in that case.

He leaned his head back and tried to clear his mind. Let his adrenaline level subside. He closed his eyes and tried to pray. But his thoughts were too jumbled and conflicted. Why was he even here? This whole trip had been a result of a dream. Just a stupid dream. And now he'd made a fool out of himself again.

More than that, he'd been dishonest with Marta and Rachel. He'd left without explaining where he was going. At the time, he'd rationalized it away as being for their own protection. But protection from what? Conner had been feeling that he was up against some sort of ethereal menace. An enemy not of flesh and blood. Really just a general impression of danger. Or that someone he knew was in danger.

But in the end, that was all he'd had to go on. He'd come all this way based on nothing more than a feeling.

He started the car and pulled back onto the road. He'd had enough excitement for one day. For an entire month. And it was high time for him to go home and start to focus on his own family.

He pulled into an old gas station to fill up. The station was so old the pumps weren't even outfitted for credit card payment, so Conner had to pay inside when he was done. He stood at the counter while the gray-haired man swiped his card through the reader.

The old man was leathery and grizzled with white hair and glasses perched at the edge of his nose. The reader had apparently not scanned Conner's card properly, so he began tapping the card number into the keypad with a gnarled finger. Conner chuckled to himself.

The old man grunted. "Forty-seven years and I still can't get no one to work for me on Saturdays."

Tap, tap.

"Forty-seven years, huh?" Conner frowned as a thought struck him. "So . . . you must know the Bristols up the road."

The old man looked up and his face crinkled as if Conner had just insulted his wife. "You a friend of theirs or something?"

"Nope, I, uh . . ." Conner wasn't sure exactly how to describe it. "No, I just met them actually."

The old man snorted and went back to his tapping, muttering to himself.

Conner's curiosity was piqued. "So you do know them."

"Not personally. I know of them," he said finally. "Nobody round here really knows them all that well. The whole family's a bit creepy, if you ask me. But that kid of theirs sure is a piece of work."

"Owen? Why? What's he done?"

The old man shook his head. "Oh, he's just . . ." His voice trailed off and he sucked in a wheezing breath.

"What?"

"Just a bad seed."

Conner slipped his credit card back into his wallet. "You know, now that you mention it, he did seem a little odd."

"Odd?" The old man inspected Conner through narrowed eyes. "My wife used to teach sixth grade years back and had that boy in her class. She used to say he was like a grown man inside a child's body. And not because he was smart. Because he was mean. Not little kid mean. *Grown-up* mean. Things he'd say to other kids. He never had any friends. And nobody who ever spent more'n five minutes with him ever wondered why."

He leaned forward and lowered his voice. "Once they caught him in the field out back of the school. He'd killed a cat and her litter of kittens. Choked 'em all. Said he'd done it just to see what it felt like." He shook his head and snorted. "Like some kinda dang experiment. I mean, what kid does something like 'at?"

Conner frowned. None of this information surprised him. If Owen was killing cats as a kid, what kind of things had he gotten into as an adult? "Has he ever been in trouble with the law?"

"Well, he never did anything anyone could prove. Couple years back, though, we had a young guy from town just up and disappear."

"What do you mean?"

"I mean he disappeared. Dale Edwards. Couple years ago he left for work in the morning but never showed. A few days later, they found his car up near Gary, like it'd run outta gas. They looked all around up there, but no sign of Dale. Nowhere. Folks said he'd run off with some woman. But no one's seen him since."

"So you think Owen killed him?"

The old man just raised an eyebrow and shrugged.

Conner went on. "Well, did they know each other?"

"I think they went to school together."

"But I mean, did they have an argument or something? Was there any kind of motive?"

"Motive?"

"Yeah. Usually for a murder, there's some reason for it. Some kind of motive."

"Beats me," the old man snorted again. "He didn't need no motive to kill them cats."

"Yeah, but you can't just arrest somebody because they're creepy. You need to establish motive, opportunity, and intent. And without a body, there's no evidence that a murder even took . . ."

Conner's voice trailed off as he recalled his encounter with the Bristols. A chill washed down his back. Owen had made no uncertain threat to Conner's life if he ever showed up there again.

"They'll never find you."

Owen definitely seemed ruthless enough—perhaps capable of such an act. After a moment, Conner shook his head and forced a chuckle. "Well, I guess I'm glad I made it out of there alive, then."

He returned to his car and turned on his cell phone. Three messages. He quickly dialed his voice mail and listened. The first was from Nancy at the office. She must've called yesterday after he'd left.

"I saw you left early today. Just wanted to see if everything was okay. Call me if you need anything, Connie. Okay? I mean it."

The second message was from Marta earlier that morning. *"Connie, call me when you get this please. I think it's important."*

The third was also from Marta at around noon. *"Connie, why do you have your phone off? Call me as soon as you can. I got a call from a Jim Malone. He says he knows you. He said he needs to talk to you. Right away."*

VALLEY OF THE SHADOW

MITCH STOOD AND WATCHED his
father elbow his way through the crowd
of Reapers to stand, hands on his hips,
at the edge of the circle.

"Dude," Mitch whispered to Nathan,
"do you see this too?"

"I see him."

"He's . . . he's real then, right? Or
is this another hallucination?"

"He's probably a manifestation
of your thoughts and memories.
Were you thinking about him just
now?"

"No. At least I've been trying
not to."

Nathan stood. "Then I would say
they're trying to deceive you again.

They obviously know the issues you had with him and they're trying to use that against you."

"But how? I'm not going out there."

"I'm not sure what they're trying to do. Just try to ignore him for now."

"Yeah." Mitch rolled his eyes. "Like that's gonna happen."

Mitch was turning to sit down when his father bellowed, "Don't you turn your back on me!"

"Whatever." Mitch put his feet up on the coffee table.

"I'm not paying for your school so you can goof off."

"Yeah, I know."

Nathan sat down again, across from Mitch, his forehead puckered. "Just don't respond."

"And that," his father went on, "that right there is the problem. The kind of friends you're hanging around with. They're the ones getting you into trouble all the time."

Mitch sighed. Nathan motioned him to ignore the comment, but he couldn't not respond. His anger was growing. The man was always dictating. Always setting some new rules to obey. And not for Mitch's good. Not out of love. These rules were designed solely to keep Mitch from embarrassing him. To keep the congressman's son out of trouble. And out of the news.

"They're like bad pennies, Dad. They just keep showing up wherever you send me."

"Well, not while you're under my roof. Not while I'm paying the bills."

Mitch popped up off the couch again and turned to face his father. Somewhere in the back of his head, Mitch knew this wasn't his father, but he couldn't help himself. He was angry and he was going to vent. All the rage that had been pent up for so many years was starting to explode out of him in short bursts. Rage over the man's political obsessions, with getting reelected every two years, with his career and his reputation. And rage over the loss of the only good thing in their family.

His mother had been the glue that had kept them together. And she had been the insulation that kept them apart. She maintained an uneasy peace and was always trying to reconcile her husband and son.

But now that she was gone, it was metal on metal. There was no more buffer. No quiet voice of calm and reason. No faithful partner and no hope for peace. Her death had driven them farther apart than Mitch could have imagined. His father had not let the news of Mitch's role in her death leak out. He'd not told a soul. But not for Mitch's sake. Rather for his own reputation. Mitch was sure the old man would've gone public with the story if it could have bolstered his career in some way.

Indeed, his mother's illness had already garnered an out-pouring of public sympathy. It was just the thing his father had needed in a close race that year. Mitch had watched his father make her illness a central focus in his campaign by steadfastly maintaining in every speech that he would not use her illness for political purposes.

Mitch's jaw clenched. He stood nose-to-nose with his father. The blue veil of light was all that separated them.

"You're paying the bills?" Mitch sneered. "You're paying the bills? You're a politician, Dad. Remember? You live off the public dole like a leech. Bloodsucking the taxpayers and getting kickbacks on the side!"

"Mitch, stop!" Nathan's voice sounded too late.

Mitch reached through the light and grabbed for his father's throat, but his fingers closed on empty air. His father's image had dissolved into nothing.

Mitch pulled his hand back through. The Reapers hissed

and growled, baring their teeth and puffing out their chests. But then—as if by some unseen or inaudible cue—they began to back away from the light. On every side, they moved back into the shadows and disappeared.

Nathan stood beside him as they peered into the darkness. Outside, the faint trace of gray morning light began to filter through the front double doors.

"Is that why they left?" Mitch whispered. "Daylight?"

Nathan shrugged. "I . . . I don't know."

They stood in silence for several more seconds.

The circle of light crackled a bit, flickered, and then began to fade.

Mitch heaved a deep sigh. "Well, wherever they went, let's hope they stay—"

He never finished. The building shook with a deafening noise from outside. A thundering roar that Mitch recognized immediately. The ground trembled as a massive shadow passed by the window.

CONNER DIALED MARTA'S CELL while
still parked at the gas station. He
hoped he wasn't too late to get ahold
of Jim Malone. Maybe it hadn't been
a coincidence that they'd run into
each other at the juvie center the day
before.

"Connie? I've been trying to call
you all day."

"I'm sorry, sweetheart. It's kind of
a long story, but I left my cell phone off.
I felt like I had to come down here and
see Howard for myself."

"Howard Bristol?" Marta's voice
seemed to go up an octave. "Why
didn't you tell me? I would have come
with you."

"That's why I didn't tell you. Look, I just felt like I had to do this myself."

"Why? That doesn't make any sense."

"I know it doesn't, and I can't really explain it, either. Besides you and Rachel had plans today and I didn't want to derail everything you had going on."

"I'm your wife, Connie. I'm supposed to be helping you, but how can I do that if you keep shutting me out?"

Conner rubbed his eyes. "Marty, I'm not shutting you out. I just had to see him and I didn't want to drag you all the way down here for that."

There was a pause on the other end. "So did you see him?"

"Yeah. He was in a nursing home, still in a coma. Completely unresponsive."

"Are you on your way back, then?"

Conner hesitated. He didn't want to go into all the details of his visit with Mrs. Bristol and Owen. Frankly, he wasn't sure what he was going to do. He wasn't quite ready to leave. He felt like he was following a trail of bread crumbs now that was leading him somewhere. And he couldn't give up.

"Soon. I want to check one last thing first and then I'll head back."

He could hear Marta sigh on the other end. "Well, I got the strangest phone call this morning."

"From Jim Malone?"

"He said he was a client of yours."

"Almost a client. Actually, I just ran into him yesterday morning." Conner winced. He hadn't told Marta about going to see Devon. Not that it was a big deal. She knew he'd been trying to track the kid down for the last several weeks. But after the whole Pastor Lewis fiasco, this wouldn't go over well. He'd look like he was trying to keep more secrets.

There was another pause. "Yeah . . . well apparently you have a mutual friend."

"What do you mean?"

"Apparently this Jim knows Devon Marshall too. He said he had found Devon and his friend, Terrell, in a car the night they'd been shot. The same night you were having your heart attack. Just like you told me. Anyway, he said he performed CPR on Devon until the police arrived."

Conner moved the phone to his other ear. "He said that? Is that what he told you?"

"Yes. He said he'd gone to see Devon after you had left. And somehow Devon escaped."

"Escaped?"

"Yeah, from prison. Connie, what's going on? You didn't say anything about going to see Devon yesterday."

Conner sighed. Everything was happening too fast. "I know. I just wanted to try to make contact. To see if I could help him somehow. I had managed to get permission, but we didn't even get a chance to talk. He freaked out when he saw me. He wouldn't talk to me. Did Jim say how he escaped?"

"He didn't give me a lot of details, but he said he needed to talk to you."

"Did he give you his number?"

"Connie, are you going to tell me what's going on?"

"Yes, but not right now. I think Devon's in a lot of trouble."

"Is that why you went to see Pastor Lewis?"

"No! Look, I'll explain everything when I get home. I promise. Just give me the number."

Marta relayed the number and Conner reassured her that he loved her, that he wasn't in trouble, and that he'd explain everything as soon as he got home. Whenever that might be.

VALLEY OF THE SHADOW

SHORTLY AFTER TWO O'CLOCK, Jim Malone's phone rang. It was Conner Hayden.

"Do you believe in coincidence or providence?" Conner said.

Jim chuckled, feeling a bit relieved. "I'm sorry if I gave your wife too much information. It's just that she started giving me the third degree and I didn't want to lie."

"Don't worry," Conner said. "She has a way of dragging things out of people. She should work for the CIA."

"I know the type. I married one too."

"So tell me what happened to Devon."

Jim recounted the events of the

previous day, Devon's seizure and subsequent escape. He felt a little foolish at first, talking about their suspicions of something supernatural at work.

But Conner didn't seem the least bit incredulous. "I think we have to try to figure out what he might be up to. Where he might be going. He's potentially very dangerous, and I doubt the police are equipped to handle something like this. This could end very badly for Devon."

"To be honest with you, I was having a hard time believing the whole thing. I mean, I believe in supernatural things— spiritual things—but the idea that you two met during your near-death experiences is . . . well, a little bizarre."

"You don't know the half of it."

"What was it like? I mean, where were you? What did it look like?"

"That's what was so strange," Conner said. "For a while, we didn't know what was happening to us. Everything all seemed so normal and so real."

Jim listened to Conner explain the details of his experience and how he'd come to meet up with Devon. He also told Jim about Mitch Kent and Helen Krause. And a farmer named Howard Bristol. He described terrifying creatures that had hunted them and how this Howard had turned out to be working with the creatures.

Jim scrawled down notes so he'd be able to follow up on his own to verify the facts. This lawyer could be making up the whole thing. Maybe just to write a book and get rich. Jim noticed there were conveniently no eyewitnesses to back up his story. None except Devon. And now Devon was conveniently unavailable, not that he would have been a reliable witness anyway.

When Conner had finished, Jim remained silent.

"Look, I know you probably think I'm crazy," Conner said after a moment. "And I wouldn't blame you. I don't expect you to believe anything I've said. But I think if you want to try to help Devon . . . I just thought you should know the whole weird story."

"*Weird* doesn't begin to describe it," Jim chuckled. "But what can I do? I mean, I don't know where Devon is or where he's going."

There was a long pause, and then Conner spoke up again. "Yesterday, I told Devon about Mitch. I think I even told him what hospital Mitch was at. If Devon is even half as curious as I've been, I'm guessing he may try to see if Mitch is really there."

Jim frowned. "You think so?"

Conner sighed. "It's just a hunch. I don't know anything for sure. But if you feel like you want to pursue it, I'd encourage you to go see for yourself. And feel free to get in touch with my wife again. I'm not so sure she fully believes me either."

"So what are you doing in Indiana?"

There was another pause. "I don't know if I can explain this either. But I had to come down here and see Howard myself. I went to his farm, met his wife and son."

"Did you tell them what you told me?"

"Sort of. But I have a bad feeling about those two."

"What do you mean?"

"I'm not sure. I'm not sure of anything right now. I just have to check something out before I come back. It's something I have to see for myself."

Jim hung up and went to the kitchen, where Annie was sitting at the table. She had heard only one end of his conversation with Conner, so Jim relayed the details as best he could. Annie's frown grew deeper.

"You okay?" Jim said.

"Yeah." She took a long breath. "Do you believe his story?"

Jim shrugged. "Before yesterday, not in a million years. But now? I'm starting to see how . . . sheltered I've been."

Annie nodded. "I remember a missionary coming to our church when I was a kid. He had worked for years down in South America—Colombia or someplace. And I remember him telling us that demonic activity down there was so much more visible and direct. He said that Christians in America have been lulled into thinking demons aren't real. That Satan is subtler here. That he comes as an angel of light." She shuddered. "And I guess he was right, because I'm still having such a hard time believing this is real."

"Well, I don't know if what I saw was something supernatural or not, but I can't figure any other explanation."

Annie sighed. "So what do we do now?"

Jim drummed his fingers on the table, holding the same inner debate he'd had the day before. On the one hand, he could go into the other room, turn on the TV, and forget about the whole thing. That would be the easy thing to do. The safe thing. It was the weekend, after all.

But on the other hand . . . Well, the other hand held an option that offered none of those things. Finally he said, "I think we've come too far to quit now. It's like God's been giving us a trail of bread crumbs. And I have to keep following it."

56

A SECOND DEAFENING BELLOW shook the building.

Nathan clutched Mitch by the arm and said, "We need to go. Now."

The glass doors along the front of the hotel exploded inward, showering the lobby with glass. A long, black limb—thick as a tree trunk—extended through the shattered doors. Gnarled claws unfolded and stretched out toward them.

Nathan pulled Mitch back, out of the way, as the claws impaled one of the couches, smashing it into splinters. A second arm burst through the doors. Mitch could see the nightmarish, faceless head of the Keeper, its jagged maw opened wide with another earsplitting roar. The beast was forcing its way into the building like a dog burrowing after its quarry.

"Come on!" Nathan pushed Mitch toward the stairwell that led to the parking garage.

Rusted metal groaned and bent; concrete and bricks broke away as the massive creature forced itself through the entrance.

They ran down the stairs and through the exits into the adjacent parking garage. Mitch jumped onto his Harley and started it up. Nathan was digging behind the seats of the Ferrari and produced the rocket launcher he'd used on the beast the last time.

He loaded a new rocket into the feed and climbed on the back of Mitch's bike. Twenty yards away, the Keeper was smashing through the wall from the hotel into the garage.

"Go! Go! Go!" Nathan ordered. Mitch gunned the throttle and tore off through the garage.

They emerged onto the street and Nathan tapped Mitch's shoulder. "Hold up here!"

He hopped off, spun around, and aimed.

The missile screamed out of the launcher and disappeared into the garage entrance. Moments later an explosion rocked the building. A ball of flame and smoke rolled out toward the street. Nathan dropped the launcher, jumped back on the bike, and they tore off.

They stopped again at the end of the block. Smoke billowed up the street toward them. The building seemed to groan and shudder. A moment later, the entire lower level collapsed onto itself, bringing the rest of the parking garage—and the hotel next to it—down in an expanding cloud of dust and debris.

"Whoa!" Mitch swore. "One rocket did that?"

Nathan smiled grimly. "You just never know in this town."

Mitch shook his head. "Man . . . that was such a nice Ferrari."

"I can't take it with me," Nathan said. "Not where I'm going."

They rolled through the city, weaving down side streets and alleys. They drove the rest of the morning and into the afternoon but still had not found the edge of the Gray City.

"Dude, how big is this place?" Mitch said when he stopped to stretch his legs. Now with the two of them on the motorcycle, the ride was not nearly as comfortable. They had driven for hours and had found themselves on a wide plaza overlooking what may once have been a park. The trees were black and barren. And what grass remained was brown and dry. In the center of the plaza was what appeared to be a fountain, though it was completely devoid of water. The statues in the center were cracked and broken. Decapitated, with their large, concrete heads lying at their feet. On the rim of the fountain sat a slender, middle-aged woman, holding her purse. Mitch had almost overlooked her completely.

The woman stared off into the distance.

Mitch couldn't help himself; he went over to her. "Hey . . . ma'am?"

She did not appear to notice him.

Mitch waved his hand in front of her face. "Yo, lady."

The woman wore a long black coat and clung tightly to her purse. She looked around but still didn't appear to see him. Her hands were stained purple with the rash. The rash he'd seen so many times before on so many others.

Nathan walked up. "Some souls are so wrapped up inside themselves, they don't even notice anyone else."

"She can't even see us?"

"She could if she wanted to." Nathan sighed. "But people delude themselves. They create their own theology. Trust their own intellect. And when they come here, their delusion continues. They see what they want to see. And only what they want to see."

"She's not going to make it, is she?" Mitch said, nodding to the woman's hands.

"She's like so many others here. They live their lives, make their choices, and suffer the consequences."

"Consequences? What'd she do to deserve this?"

Nathan's voice grew stern. "Mitch, He gave everything for her. He offered His grace for free, and she turned her back on it. She didn't think she needed it. She thought she was good enough."

"Is that so evil?"

Nathan rubbed his jaw for a moment. "Well, I don't know, Mitch. How bad would she have to be to go to hell?"

Mitch stood with his arms crossed and stared at the woman. She looked down at her hands. Felt the purple, spotted skin. Then she sighed and looked around again, completely oblivious to Mitch.

"So you're telling me this lady and some mass murderer will both end up going to the same place? they get the same punishment?"

"Everyone's judged according to their works. God may not punish all sin the same, but He does punish it all."

Off in the distance a low rumble echoed through the streets. The sky was growing dark. To the east, between the buildings, they could see an enormous black patch inside the clouds. It seemed to creep across the sky, spreading outward like an ink stain soaking through a gray sheet. It fanned out black tendrils and moved westward on a slow but steady course.

Mitch momentarily forgot about the old woman and climbed onto the fountain for a better look. "Dude . . . what's that?"

Nathan's lips were tight. He shook his head. "That's what I was afraid of."

"What's wrong? What's going on?"

"He's found us. He's coming."

VALLEY OF THE SHADOW

CONNER RETRACED HIS PATH and drove past the Bristol farm one more time. The van was still there, now moved to the garage. But no one was in sight.

Conner drove up the road roughly a quarter mile before he came upon an access drive into a field. There were some trees and brush where he could park out of sight. Conner looked across the highway, over another open field, to a line of trees several hundred yards back. The woods on the Bristols' property.

Then Conner turned around and followed the highway back into West-ville. His mind was still buzzing with the bizarre conversation he'd had with Jim Malone. Somehow Jim had been drawn into Conner's story, and Conner knew it had been for a reason. And that gave him at least some sense of peace.

For two months Conner had felt too inadequate for whatever God wanted him to do. He'd felt like he was alone in his struggle. Now he knew he wasn't. God had let him see that there were others being brought together to help.

He hoped he'd done the right thing by suggesting Jim drive up to Winthrop Harbor to check on Mitch. He'd given Jim his cell phone number and his home number as well. Then he contacted Marta again to fill her in with the new information.

On one hand, he was making a wild guess that Devon would try to see Mitch at all. On the other, he'd felt there was a certain logic to it as well. That somehow it had been the right thing to do. Conner still wasn't sure what was going on, but he felt that they were all interconnected in some way.

And so were Howard and his family.

Conner came across a sporting goods store along the main business route through town and stopped to purchase a few items. A flashlight, a compass, hiking boots, and a camouflage hunting jacket. He also purchased a hunting knife and a Smith & Wesson pistol with a box of ammunition.

"Let me guess," the clerk said with a wink. "Possum?"

Conner forced a grim smile and nodded. "Something like that."

By now it was close to five o'clock. This late in October, it would be getting dark before too long. Conner decided to wait until just before dusk, when it was dark enough to remain unseen but not so dark that he'd get lost. He changed his shoes and slipped on the jacket.

At six o'clock, Conner returned to the field and parked

behind the trees. His stomach was tight with fear. He paused for another prayer before getting out of the car.

"Lord . . . it's me again. I just wanted to ask for whatever kind of protection You can provide. It'd really be nice to get some kind of sign . . . y'know, something to let me know I'm doing the right thing. That this is really what You want me to do. And also, just to let You know that I'm scared. Really scared. But I'm sure You probably knew that already. And if anything happens to me tonight . . . well, at least this time I know where I'm going. And . . . well, I want to thank You for that."

Conner loaded the revolver and stuck some extra ammo in his jacket pocket. Then he tied the hunting knife to his belt, got out of the car, and crossed the highway. He crouched low as he crept across the open field. All the corn had been cut, leaving rows of dried stubs jutting up from the ground. It made his passage easier but unfortunately left him no cover during his trek toward the woods.

Conner kept an eye on the farmhouse to his right. There was a light on in one of the upstairs windows. Maybe that was a good thing. Maybe they were settling in for the night. But Conner's main thought now was just to make it to the cover of the trees. After that, he would try—as best as he could remember—to locate the old cabin.

The sun had dipped behind the clouds along the horizon. This was good, Conner figured, in that he wouldn't cast a long shadow on the ground as he moved across the field. But now he wished he'd been more of an outdoorsman. At least then he might be better prepared for whatever he might find tromping around in the woods. Conner glanced at the sky and estimated he had maybe a half hour of usable daylight left.

Finally he drew up to the line of trees. He looked at the

branches and another wave of déjà vu washed over him. His mouth was dry. He'd been here before. He'd been here in the Interworld, and he'd been here several times in his dreams.

And now he was here. Again.

Conner took several deep breaths, steeling himself against his fear. He glanced back at the house, now shadowy and menacing in the gloomy light. Then he turned and pushed his way into the brush.

58

JIM AND ANNIE KISSED their children good-bye. Annie's mother had come over to watch them while Jim and Annie headed out, hopefully to find Devon. Jim's mind was still spinning and he couldn't believe he was actually going along with this whole idea.

Conner seemed fairly confident that Devon was headed to Winthrop Harbor. Maybe just to confirm his near-death experience by actually seeing Mitch in person. Or maybe there was some other purpose. If in fact Devon was being influenced by some kind of spiritual force, who knew what that purpose could be.

Conner was convinced they were

all interrelated somehow. That Mitch and Devon and Conner himself were connected by a common thread. And that was why he had gone down to Indiana. To try to determine what that thread was.

For his part, Jim—despite any lingering doubts—couldn't just leave Devon to himself. Or to whatever forces might be at work.

But Winthrop Harbor? It was nearly in Wisconsin. It'd take a good sixty minutes just to get up there, and it might all be a complete waste of time. There was no guarantee Devon would show up after all. Frankly, chances were better that he'd been there already. The kid had escaped yesterday and had been on the run all night. But his life might be in danger. So if there was still a chance to track him down, Jim knew he had to take it.

They headed north but needed to make a stop first.

Annie spoke up after a minute. "I can't help feeling this is just a little crazy. I mean . . . what are the odds he'll even show up there?"

Jim shrugged. "I'd tend to agree. But after talking to Conner, I'm becoming more convinced there's something else going on."

"So why not just call the police up there and have them keep an eye out for Devon?"

"We may eventually need to do that, but I doubt they'd move on that kind of tip unless they get a compelling reason. And I'm guessing the police don't find supernatural scenarios too compelling."

Jim had stopped believing that he'd been drawn into this whole story through a completely random set of events. There was a reason he'd been there to save Devon the night of the shooting. There was a reason he'd been on that street at just that particular time.

He and Annie had been contemplating the malpractice lawsuit for the stillbirth of their infant daughter. It was Hayden himself who'd pushed the suit in the first place. But they'd decided to take the weekend to think it over and pray for direction. Annie was always big on prayer, while Jim was more prone to action. Together they normally balanced each other out. But that night, Jim had been frustrated. The thought of a large settlement had him salivating. They could've potentially won a million dollars or more. A lot more if it'd ever made it to court.

But Annie wasn't convinced it was the right thing to do. She felt her doctor had done everything humanly possible to save their daughter. Jim had argued she could have done more. Their discussion had grown so heated that night that Jim had lost his temper. He'd said some things he regretted. But rather than apologize, he'd gone out to fume. To stew over the predicament.

Annie had decided God ultimately had some reason for their tragedy, but Jim couldn't swallow that. What purpose could God have for bringing a woman through nine months of an uneventful pregnancy only to take her child at the last moment? What possible purpose could something so terrible serve?

Jim had been angry with a doctor who wasn't able to save his daughter. He was angry at himself for being more con-cerned with the money than with the loss of their child. He was angry with his wife for accepting the tragedy without question. And he was angry with God for allowing the whole thing to occur in the first place.

But ultimately that event had led him here. Led him to Conner, to Devon, and now to Mitch Kent. Jim wasn't sure what the outcome was going to be. Or what God's ultimate purpose was. He wasn't sure when or if he'd ever know. But he was beginning to see that every event in their lives—good or bad—offered them a choice. And every choice led to other events. And more choices.

But one thing he was growing sure of. None of them were accidents. Annie was right. Everything did have a purpose.

"WHO'S COMING?" MITCH SAID.
"Howard?"

"Death." Nathan stared at the black sky in the east. "Death himself is coming. We need to leave."

Mitch turned back to the old woman and waved his hand in front of her face. "C'mon, lady. Wake up!"

Nathan seemed to be growing agitated. "Mitch, there's nothing you can do for her. She can't even see you."

Mitch shook the woman gently, but she didn't notice him.

Nathan grabbed Mitch by the shoulder and spun him around. "We need to leave now!"

Mitch glanced back at the sky. The

black patch inside the clouds was spreading wider, stretching north and south and creeping slowly westward. Soon it'd be overhead. Soon it would fill the entire sky.

Mitch started up the bike, Nathan climbed on the back, and they roared off down the deserted street.

Nathan pointed out turns and directions as they went.

"We're not far now," he said in Mitch's ear. "Once we get out of the city, the two mountain ranges converge. That's where we need to go. That's the edge of the world."

Mitch gritted his teeth. "What do we do when we get there?"

"Go into the mountain."

Within five minutes, they arrived at a narrow street leading between two enormous, decaying skyscrapers. Their lofty peaks were jagged and broken against the gray sky. Behind them, the darkness was approaching. Beyond the towers, the land stretched out wide and flat toward a looming mountain range. It reminded Mitch of the salt flats in Utah.

Nathan tapped his shoulder. "Haste is a virtue here, my friend."

Mitch nodded. "Hang on."

He opened the throttle and the Road King lurched ahead. The engine thundered louder as the RPM gauge climbed higher. Cold air blasted Mitch as he accelerated faster.

98 . . . 100 . . . 105 . . . 107 . . .

The mountain range before them grew steadily larger. The jagged, black rock looked as if it was jutting straight up out of the sand. The peaks were hidden inside the clouds. The sky in the east continued to grow darker. The wispy leading edges of the phenomenon were now directly overhead, stretching out like fingers toward the mountains. Inside the darkness, flashes of lightning erupted. Red, blue, and yellow.

Soon the road dissolved beneath them and Mitch found himself navigating the motorcycle across the hard, packed sand. He could feel the Harley wobbling as its tires slipped on the surface. His grip tightened. One mistake could send them skidding sideways across the sand. At that speed, it would grind away their flesh in moments.

But they had entered a narrow canyon now, as the two great mountain ranges converged toward a single point. Nathan pointed straight ahead.

"There it is!"

The canyon came to an abrupt halt. Mitch rolled to a stop at the base of a sheer cliff. He could see the dark opening of a small cave a hundred feet or so straight up. A narrow trail wound along the jagged rock face. There was no way to get the bike up that ledge. They'd have to go by foot. And that would be precarious.

Mitch shook his head. "We're not going up there, are we?"

The clouds were nearly shrouded by the darkness. The eastern sky was completely black. The lightning flashed, illuminating the landscape below it in brief glimpses. A gusting wind moaned through the canyon, driving eddies of sand along in swirling vortexes.

Mitch swore softly. They were trapped.

VALLEY OF THE SHADOW

DENSE BRANCHES PRESSED back against Conner as he fought his way through. Every step brought a cacophony of sounds. Crunching and snapping of dry leaves and twigs underfoot. There was even a strange sort of zipping sound as the smaller branches scraped across his jacket. And moving at a slower pace only prolonged the noise, making it more noticeable; it even seemed to amplify the sounds.

At this point, Conner couldn't have snuck up on a dead cat. He checked his compass but could only guess he was headed in the right direction. After several minutes the lower brush seemed to thin out and he was able to move a little more freely. And quietly. Also, he was able to see a little farther into the woods.

There was no path that he could make out. The gloom of dusk was starting to encroach on his vision, but he didn't want to risk using the flashlight. At least not yet. The temperature had also dropped considerably, and now Conner wished he'd purchased a hat and gloves as well.

He wandered farther through the woods. He thought he'd had a fair idea where the cabin lay from the satellite images he saw on his computer. It looked roughly a hundred yards in from the edge of the woods. Straight back from the silo next to the barn. Conner had entered the woods roughly fifty yards to the left of that position and so was estimating the direction and distance he would need to cover.

But he knew both could be deceiving in a setting like this. He was thankful for his compass but wished he had some way to determine the distance he'd come. Then he stopped and cursed himself again. He should have been counting his steps. If one pace was roughly a yard, he'd be able to calculate his position close enough. But he'd been slogging his way for several minutes now and had no idea how many steps he'd taken so far.

He stopped to get his bearings. He couldn't see the field or any of the farm buildings. He decided to take a wild guess that he was maybe thirty yards in from his original point of entry. His initial plan had been to head straight in to the woods along a parallel route until he thought he was deep enough and then cut over to the right. That would make it more difficult to find the cabin. But he figured it was safer than cutting over any sooner. That way he would stay clear of any path—if there was one—directly from the house to the cabin. Conner guessed he would be less likely to run across Owen if he avoided the direct route. And that was one thing he absolutely wanted to do.

He continued on for several more minutes, counting roughly seventy paces. Then he cut to the right and started counting again. Now that the woods had thinned out a bit, his visibility was better, and that at least raised his spirits a little. He'd have a better chance of spotting the cabin. Of course it also meant he'd have a better chance of being spotted, as well.

Conner plodded along as slowly and quietly as he could manage, counting his steps. *Forty-one . . . forty-two . . . forty-three . . .*

Then he stopped. Ahead and to the left, something was visible among the trees. He crouched down and crawled forward slowly. He drew up behind the trunk of a toppled tree and peered into the gloom. There it was. Not twenty feet ahead. Dark, sagging, and huddled in a small clearing.

He'd found the cabin at last.

VALLEY OF THE SHADOW

NATHAN CLUTCHED MITCH'S ARM
and thrust a finger in the air.

Mitch glanced up the looming cliff
and shook his head. "Dude," he said.
"I . . . I don't do so well with heights."

Nathan wasn't smiling and he
didn't appear to be in any mood to
argue. "Now's as good a time as any
to learn."

He shoved Mitch toward the base
of the cliff. Mitch swallowed hard and
found a few openings in the rock. He
grabbed hold and pulled himself up.
"This is crazy. I hate heights."

"Get moving!"

They scrambled up several yards
until they came upon a narrow ledge.

It was less than a foot wide, steep and uneven. Mitch stood, pressing his back flat against the rock, and slid sideways up the ledge. The wind gusted harder now, screaming at times through the canyon. The flashes of light blazed around them, illuminating the mountain in alternating hues of red, blue, and yellow. Sand whipped at Mitch's face. He could barely see the ledge in front of him. He could hardly tell where to place his feet.

The ledge sloped upward, zigzagging across the narrow cliff face. All the while, the wind pushed and tugged at them. Swiping at them from all angles. On several occasions, Mitch felt himself stumble and almost fall, only to feel Nathan's hand on his shoulder, pressing him back against the rock.

On the canyon floor, the wind continued to kick up sand in rising eddies. The sight was dizzying. At times there was so much sand flying, Mitch could barely tell which way was up. Unable to see more than a few feet in front of him, he was forced to feel his way, inch by inch.

After what seemed like hours, he felt the ledge widen and level off. He turned to see the cave entrance behind him. He knelt down, pressing his face against the rock. A wave of relief swept over him.

Nathan crouched inside the entrance, breathing heavily. His hand clutching his chest.

The wind raged harder now, and after a few moments, Mitch gathered the nerve to peek back over the edge.

"Whoa."

They had climbed more than a hundred feet up from the canyon floor. Below them something odd caught Mitch's attention. The sand was spraying straight into the air as if from underground. Pouring upward like some sort of fountain.

Nathan grimaced and coughed. "We need . . . to go."

The undulating pillar of sand grew taller, like a geyser

erupting from below. And Mitch could see a lone figure standing on the very top, as if a huge serpent were rising up, balanc-
ing him perfectly on its head.

Mitch knew who it was before he could even recognize
the face.

"Howard?" Mitch moved away from the edge and grabbed
Nathan's arm. "Uh . . . dude?"

But Nathan's breathing grew labored. He winced again.

"Hey, dude." Mitch grabbed him by the shoulders. "You
okay?"

Nathan coughed. "I don't have much . . . time."

At that moment, Howard Bristol rose over the edge,
standing on the swirling fountain of sand. His eyes were
white, inhuman.

Howard shook his head. "Well, this is a happy surprise.
At last, I've found my wayward sheep."

Mitch stood. "Look, I don't want any trouble. But I'm not
going back to the farm, so why don't you just—"

"I opened my home to you, and this is how you repay me?"

Mitch's lips tightened in a scowl. "You lied to me. All
those years were just a lie. We weren't in Indiana."

Howard smiled. "Reality here is whatever you choose to
make it. And I can show you how to make it into whatever you
choose. You can create your own world here. Entirely from
scratch."

Mitch shook his head. "Why should I trust you now?"

Howard only smiled and nodded toward Nathan. "Your
friend here has shown you things. Things that perhaps you've
had some trouble believing."

"I don't know what to believe anymore."

"You've seen sights that have shaken your entire view of
the world."

"Which world?"

Howard chuckled. "This world, Mitch. The old world you knew, the world of flesh and bone, is only a cheap imitation of the real thing. Like a dim shadow of a deeper, greater reality."

"I just want to go back."

"Back?" Howard repeated. "Back to your miserable flesh? You stand at the brink of a realm more amazing than you can even imagine. What you saw was only the dimmest edge of what truly lies beyond. I can show you more of it. I can show you everything."

Nathan struggled to his feet. "We need to go."

Howard's eyes glowed. "He wants to lead you back into darkness and pain. Sickness, frailty. Trapped inside a broken body. You may never even wake up."

"Mitch, don't listen to him."

Howard held out a hand. "I can help you become what you were meant to be. Everything you were meant to be. It's your choice."

Mitch shook his head. "You're a liar."

"Liar? Me?" Howard said. Then he looked at Nathan. "And you think he's been honest with you?"

"He showed me the truth. He let me know what was really going on."

"Truth?" Howard's mouth twisted into a lopsided grin. "Do you think he's shown you the whole truth?"

Nathan coughed. "Mitch . . ."

Mitch frowned. "What are you talking about?"

Howard just shook his head and sighed. "He hasn't told you, has he."

"Told me what?"

Nathan tugged at Mitch's arm. "Don't . . ."

Mitch looked from Nathan to Howard. "What are you talking about?"

Howard seemed to loom closer, rising on the current of sand beneath him. "About what happened to you. About how you got here."

Mitch stared at Howard now. What was the old guy trying to do? This was some kind of a trick. Howard was just trying to confuse him. To keep him from leaving. "He showed me. He told me what happened."

Howard raised an eyebrow. "Ah, yes. You were in an accident of some sort."

"On my motorcycle."

"Yes, yes. You were on your way to pick up . . . Linda, was it?"

An image flashed inside Mitch's head. The lights shining in his face. The headlights coming toward him. "I got hit by a truck."

"And now you're in a hospital. In a coma. Barely clinging to life."

Mitch said, "He told me all of that."

"Did he now?" Howard chuckled softly. "But did he happen to mention who was driving the truck?"

VALLEY OF THE SHADOW

AT LONG LAST, Devon pulled into the hospital parking lot in Winthrop Harbor. His palms were sweating, his heart pounding.

Pale Man sat in the back, humming a song. Devon thought it might've been "Hotel California" but he couldn't be sure.

Pale Man had led him on an erratic, seemingly haphazard route up from the city through the northern suburbs and nearly to the Wisconsin border. They had avoided most of the major highways, partly to evade police, but also to avoid any of Karenga's people who were most certainly out searching for him. They had occasionally hidden the car in several construction sites and parking lots for up to an hour at a time before continuing on. It was as if Pale Man knew where every police cruiser in the greater Chicagoland area was located at any given time and he was meticulously directing Devon to avoid each one.

As the day wore on, Pale Man himself was growing increasingly irritable. He kept referring to other "projects" he had going on and an overall schedule he needed to keep. Like he was some corporate executive with all kinds of irons in the fire.

Devon's mouth was dry as he and Pale Man slipped across the lot toward the hospital. "So, man, how am I supposed to kill this guy? A gun won't exactly be subtle."

Pale Man snorted. "Use your imagination, chief. The gun was for your protection. Just in case we ran into any cops or other unsavory types. Our friend is in a vegetative state. I don't think it'll take much."

"How am I supposed to get up to his room? They ain't gonna let me just walk in and see him."

"What, you don't think they'll believe you're a doctor?" Pale Man led Devon down a quiet hall to a supply room and shut the door. "ICU is on the third floor. Let's get you out of your gangsta costume and into something more appropriate."

Several minutes later, Devon emerged in green scrubs, head down and pushing a supply cart. He made his way to the elevators, trying to appear as nonchalant as possible. But his forehead was beaded with sweat. He felt more out of place here than at any time in his life. His gun was hidden inside the cart.

"Relax; you're a natural." Pale Man chuckled as he walked beside Devon. "Y'know, I think if this whole gangbanger gig doesn't pan out for you, you should try your hand in the medical profession. I can always use you there."

"Shut up."

They rode the elevator to the third floor. The doors opened and Devon's jaw dropped. Pale Man swore.

They were staring at a corridor full of police.

Pale Man pulled Devon back into the elevator and exploded in a stream of profanity as the doors closed. Devon's heart was pounding at the close call. There were at least a half-dozen cops lounging around in the hallway. They hadn't noticed him standing in the elevator. No one had recognized him—or so he hoped.

"Hey, man," Devon said. "I thought you knew where all the cops around here were. What's up with that? You nearly got me caught."

Pale Man just raised a hand. His eyes shone bright yellow. "Don't . . ." He took a deep breath and calmed himself. "Don't get all up in my face right now, chief. I'm not in the mood."

"Hey, I'm just saying, you're not all-knowing after all."

They returned to the first floor and went back to the supply room. Pale Man paced around the room, still fuming. "It's your friend Hayden. This guy's really starting to get on my nerves."

"What'd he do now?"

"He's messing with things he shouldn't be. He must have found out somehow that you escaped. He must have figured out what I'm trying to do. Now shut up; I need to formulate a new plan."

Devon leaned against the cart. He almost sighed with relief. "So that means I don't have to kill the dude?"

"We'll get back to Mitch." Pale Man continued pacing. He looked at his watch. "But for right now, we need to make a slight alteration in our schedule."

"Alteration? What are you talking about?"

Pale Man stopped pacing. "Hayden is like an obnoxious kid. He gets something stuck in his head and he just can't let it go. Usually I can get people to ignore the things I want them to ignore. Rationalize them away and forget about them. But this guy's like the spoiled brat who just doesn't give up."

"So why don't you go bug him and leave me alone."

Pale Man let out a long sigh and closed his eyes. "It doesn't work like that. He's out of my . . . jurisdiction. But not entirely out of my influence. If he wants to mess with me, let's see if we can't make it as painful as possible."

"What are you talking about?"

But Pale Man was already grinning. "Let's get back to the car, chief. We have another stop to make."

Devon rolled his eyes and swore. "Now where?"

"Lake Forest. Hayden has a wife and daughter. And I think we should pay them a visit." He chuckled. "More accurately, I think you need to pay them a visit."

63

CONNER WATCHED THE CABIN from the cover of the trees for several minutes. The window was darkened and the sagging porch shrouded in shadows. It was exactly as he remembered it—except there was no light glowing inside.

With his gun held ready, Conner slipped across the small clearing and up onto the rickety floorboards of the porch. The glass window was almost completely encrusted with dirt from years of exposure to the elements, and the wood was soft and gray with rot. The little paint that was left was chipped and peeling. Like the few, flaky remnants left after a snake sheds its skin.

The cabin looked to have been built on a foundation of odd, misshapen bricks. Almost as if they'd been collected from various sources and used in random arrangement. It appeared to have been lived in at some point. Conner guessed maybe it had been used for a hunting shack or for field hands. The roof was bowed and stratified by at least three sets of shingles. As if the solution to any leak was to slap on another patch of tar and shingles to cover the hole. Just enough to get by.

Conner peeked inside the front window but saw only motionless black shapes. A table and some chairs. The fading daylight had cast the interior in a pall of shadows that seemed to suck all color from the furnishings within.

He tried the door and discovered it was unlocked. Not that it mattered; a lock wouldn't have kept anyone out with the wooden doorjamb rotted as it was. It creaked open on rusted hinges and Conner slipped inside.

The flashlight beam swept across the front room and set shadows dancing along the walls. It was cluttered with old furniture, a chest, and an iron stove in the center.

He stood perfectly still and let the silence cover him. There was no movement inside. Conner moved the light across the far wall and spotted two doors along the back of the main room. He checked to see if they were both unlocked as well. His boots made dull clops across the floorboards and he could feel himself sag a little. As if the cabin had settled on its makeshift foundation, making for an uneven surface.

The first door was unlocked and revealed a tiny bedroom. The bed was more of a cot, really. A stained and lumpy mattress situated on a rusted bed frame. Next to the bed was an antique dresser. Several knobs were missing. Dozens of spiderwebs dangled precariously in the corners of the room, having captured more dust over the years than insects.

Conner returned to the main room and swept the light slowly around the perimeter. The cabin itself seemed suitably empty, but Conner knew where there was a foundation, there may be a crawl space or a cellar. And where there was a cellar, there was a way down into the cellar.

He opened the second door and saw a narrow wooden stairway leading down into darkness. Conner caught a cool whiff of moist earth and swore under his breath. He'd been ready to call it quits and go home. He'd come so close. His stomach churned now and he knew that he wasn't going home any time soon.

He descended halfway down the steps and looked around the cellar. Low brick walls and a rough concrete floor. Cans of paint were stacked against one of the walls and a pair of homemade two-by-four shelving units stood along the other. Other than that and a few centipedes, the place was empty.

Conner Inspected the stack of paint cans, moving them to see what might lie behind. Nothing but the brick wall. He shone the flashlight along the entire perimeter until he came to one of the shelving units. It was mounted to the wall and the floor with masonry bolts. The shelves contained an assortment of bolts and screws and a few rusty chains.

He moved on to the second unit. This one seemed to be looser than the other. Conner inspected it more closely. The legs of this shelf were set into shallow holes, cut right into the concrete floor, not mounted with bolts like the other shelf. The top of the unit was bolted to the floor joists of the cabin. Conner frowned and jiggled the shelving unit again. The bolts weren't fully tightened. Conner loosened the bolts by hand and lifted the entire shelf up, out of the holes in the concrete. Then he set it aside and inspected the wall behind.

Conner could see that the floor under the shelf was worn.

Numerous scratches marred the concrete. He focused the light on the bricks and could see an outline along a section of the wall where the masonry work had crumbled away. He pushed against that section of the wall, but it wouldn't budge.

Then he noticed two of the bricks had small holes cut into the surface, an inch or two in diameter. Conner knelt down and felt inside with his finger. He could feel something metallic inside. A metal bar, running vertically through the bricks.

Conner sat back for a moment and stared at the wall. The holes were about two feet off the floor and roughly eighteen inches apart. It looked like some kind of door, he knew. But how to move it? How to open it?

Then it struck him: the chains on the other shelf. He grabbed them and discovered hooks at each end. Conner took a moment to catch his breath. He flipped open his cell phone. This was clearly enough evidence to get the police involved.

But his phone could not get a signal in his current location. He considered heading back to the car to call, but before he did, he needed to be sure. He inserted the hooks into the holes in the bricks. He twisted them and felt them catch the metal bar inside. Then Conner wrapped the chain around his wrists and pulled.

At first nothing happened. Conner braced himself and pulled again.

He felt the wall move slightly. He clenched his teeth and leaned back. Inch by inch, a three-by-four-foot section of the brick wall slid toward him. Conner grunted and pulled until he had created enough of an opening to look through.

He shone the flashlight into the hole and caught his breath. A powerful stench wafted toward him. He gagged and covered his nose with his sleeve. A small passageway, four feet high, was cut through the dirt and clay. At the far end, maybe ten yards away, it seemed to widen. And in the darkness, a dim orange light glowed.

Conner felt a wave of fear uncoiling inside him. Death lurked at the end of that tunnel. Death and decay. He could smell it. He could feel it. Just like in his dreams. Conner turned immediately and headed for the stairs. He had to get out of here. He had to get back to his car before Owen showed up. He had to . . .

Conner stopped at the stairs. A thought came to him. Like a still, small voice.

Why was there a light at the end of the tunnel?

VALLEY OF THE SHADOW

MITCH COULD BARELY SEE HOWARD amid the sporadic flashes of lightning. It took a while for the words to sink in.

"Did he happen to mention who was driving the truck?"

What was that supposed to mean? Howard gazed back at him, a half grin on his face, as if he was enjoying watching Mitch grapple with this news. Mitch looked to Nathan, whose face was almost expressionless. Just a hint of regret in his eyes.

"No!" Mitch turned back to Howard. "You're lying. Everything you've told me over the last five years has been a lie."

Howard only chuckled, a cold and hollow laugh.

"He's right, Mitch." Nathan's voice came softly behind him.

For a moment, Mitch found himself at a loss for words. He could only shake his head with his mouth hanging open. Finally he turned to Nathan. "Are you serious? You were driving that truck?"

Nathan nodded. "I was going to tell you when the time was right. I was afraid you wouldn't have trusted me otherwise."

"You did this to me?"

Howard interjected himself. "How do you think he knew so much about you? Why do you think he was so desperate to help you? To ease his conscience."

"Mitch," Nathan said, "you have to believe me. I was going to tell you."

Mitch suddenly felt dizzy, like the ground was shifting beneath him. He'd come all this way for nothing. He had trusted Nathan and all the while the guy was hiding this secret. Keeping the truth from him.

"I trusted you. And you're the whole reason I'm here!"

"It was an accident," Nathan said. "It was late. I'd been working a double shift and I was on my way home. I was just so tired."

"That's no excuse!" Mitch's anger exploded. He shoved Nathan back against the side of the cave. "You did this to me! You killed me!"

"I'm trying to help you." Nathan didn't raise his voice. "God knew you weren't ready to die yet. He knew you were trapped in this place. He sent me to save you, to bring you back."

"Save me?" Mitch shoved him against the rock again. "I wouldn't even be here if it wasn't for you!"

Anger now flared up in Nathan's eyes. He shoved Mitch backward, breaking his hold. "I tried to swerve out of the way, but it was too late. After I hit you, I lost control, drove into the ditch, and smashed into a tree. You're in a coma? I'm the one they're pulling the plug on. I've got a wife and kids I'm leaving behind. You don't think I'm paying a price?"

Mitch's chest was pounding, but his anger quickly gave way to despair. He suddenly felt the loss of all the plans he'd been making. All of his hopes had been shattered in that one instant. On that one section of asphalt.

"I was going to propose to Linda," he said. "I was going to buy a business. . . ."

If only he'd left a few minutes sooner. Or if he'd just taken a different route. But his father had called to talk. That had delayed him those few precious minutes. Three minutes that changed his entire life. Three minutes he'd never get back.

There were so many things that had happened that night. So many choices he might have made differently. If only he hadn't answered the phone. He would've passed Nathan on another stretch of highway. And he . . .

Mitch shuddered.

He wouldn't be here now, clinging to whatever life he had left.

Mitch grimaced at that thought. Maybe it was his father's fault after all. In spite of the man's best intentions, he had caused this tragedy. Even in his attempt to reconcile with Mitch, his father had ruined Mitch's life. Dashed all of his plans to pieces.

Nathan regained his composure. "Mitch, everything happens for a reason. I know you don't think God takes any interest in us, but He does have a plan. For each of us."

Mitch grunted. "Not anymore."

"No, Mitch. He still has a plan for you. You've strayed too far for too long, and now He's trying to bring you back."

Howard stood atop his column of sand, arms folded. Grinning. "Ah yes. The Almighty's ever-elusive, top secret plan for the universe." He shook his head and laughed. "It's funny, though, how things never seem to go quite how He wants them to. Too bad He gave you each your own will. Your freedom to choose. But I guess when you're God, even if something doesn't go your way, you can still say it was all just part of the plan. And no one's the wiser, eh?"

Mitch could hear whispers on the wind now. He looked over the edge. Amid the flashes of light, the entire canyon floor seemed to be moving. And Mitch could see why. Hundreds of the Reapers—thousands of them—were marching across the sand toward them. They reached the base of the cliff and began scaling it like a horde of insects.

Howard's white eyes glowed in the darkness. "Plan or no plan, I'm afraid you're not going anywhere, Mitch. Not for a long time."

Nathan winced, clutching his chest. He grabbed Mitch's arm. "Listen to me. I'm out of time. I wish I could've gotten you farther than this." He doubled over.

The first wave of the Reapers had nearly reached the ledge.

Nathan caught his breath. "Go through the tunnel. You'll know it when you reach the other side. Your time is nearly ready. Don't be afraid of what happens. Don't be afraid of the tunnel. Fear will lead to anger. . . ."

His breathing came in deep gasps now. He took Mitch's hand and pressed something into it. "Remember . . . you're not alone."

Nathan's lips tightened and he pushed Mitch away from the ledge, into the cave entrance. Then, turning to Howard, he said, "You know, I would've thought you'd have learned a little humility by now."

Howard only laughed. The first of the Reapers reached the top of the ledge—dozens of them. Mitch backed away, farther into the cave.

Nathan tore his shirt open, exposing his chest. A large patch of his skin had changed color. It was . . .

Mitch blinked and looked closer.

It was glowing. Like the rash he'd seen on all the others, only instead of a sickly purple tinge, this had a warm, yellow glow. Like sunlight. It seemed to grow more intense every second as it spread across the rest of his body.

Howard reeled back and hissed.

Nathan straightened up. He no longer seemed to be in pain. He spread his hands out to his sides and they flared with a bright light. His back arched, his head flung back, lost in the brilliant glare.

Howard threw his hands up in front of his face. The Reapers, too, hissed and writhed, tumbling backward off the cliff. The circle of light exploded out from Nathan, slamming into Howard's column of sand, dissolving it into dust. Mitch caught a glimpse of the old man plummeting down.

The light blazed into the cave as well, flooding over Mitch. Warm and clean, it seemed to have a physical force that knocked him to the ground.

Nathan's form was transfigured into pure light. As if light itself had become a solid, living thing. Like the spirits Mitch had seen from the mountaintop. Mitch could feel the pure energy radiating outward from Nathan, passing over him and through him almost like an electrical charge.

Nathan flung his arms upward and leaped into the air, ascending higher and higher, until at last he disappeared through the clouds and was gone.

VALLEY OF THE SHADOW

"I MUST BE CRAZY."

Conner squeezed through the opening into the tunnel. The sound of his own hushed voice was of little comfort. His hand sank into the cold mud as he crept through the passage. His other hand held the gun in front of him. The sides of the tunnel were braced with old timbers every three or four feet.

The odor was overwhelming. Conner felt nausea growing inside him but swallowed hard and forced himself on. *Just a few more feet. Just a little farther. Take a look and then get out quick. Get back to the car. Call the police.*

He could see that the tunnel opened into a tiny room up ahead.

Just an alcove with pea gravel on the ground. He could see a small orange light wired to a car battery. Conner crept closer still. He could see . . .

His eyes widened.

A pair of corpses lay motionless under a clear plastic tarp.

The stench was overpowering and Conner couldn't fight it any longer. He vomited the contents of his stomach into the dirt.

"Oh . . . dear God," he said, coughing. Choking on the horror. "Dear Jesus . . . help me."

Conner's heart pounded, beating against his ribs like a sledgehammer. He wiped his sleeve across his mouth and tried to calm himself. He couldn't lose it in here. He had to get out.

He started to back away when one of the corpses sat up straight.

Conner cried out and dropped his gun. In the dim light, he could make out the vague features of a human face behind the loose tarp.

He looked closer and saw rope and duct tape wrapped tightly around the shoulders, chest, and legs. He pulled the plastic down from over the head and was met with a pair of wide blue eyes. A girl's eyes. Crazed with fear. Like an animal.

"It's okay; it's all right," he whispered as his hands tore at the tape around her chest. "I'm not going to hurt you. I'm going to help you get out of here."

Several layers of tape covered her mouth and wrapped around her neck. Conner reached up to peel it away but the girl flinched and jerked back, as if trying to move away from him.

Conner held up both hands. "Listen to me! Listen!" His voice was hoarse with hushed urgency. "I am not going to hurt you. I promise. I want to get this tape off."

She had pushed herself back as far as she could against
the wall of the underground prison. Conner reached for the
hunting knife and slid it out of its sheath. The blade glinted in
the dim light, sending the girl into another spasm. Squirming
as she was, Conner knew he wouldn't be able to free her. He
tried again to calm her down but to no avail. Finally he tugged
her bound feet toward him and leaned his weight on her legs.
Then he wrapped one arm tightly around her upper torso and
began slicing the layers of tape.

"Please don't be afraid," he whispered in her ear. Her hair
was drenched with sweat and moisture. She reeked of body
odor and feces. But he could feel her shaking in his grasp.
Thin and frail. Trembling fiercely.

Conner paused and set the knife down. He wrapped his
other arm around her and held her close to him. His bizarre
dreams were making sense now. God had brought him to
this cabin in the Interworld . . . and now had led him here
again. "I'm not going to hurt you. My name is Conner. God
brought me here to save you." He continued whispering
softly to her for several moments. He could feel her weeping, her eyes pouring tears. He held her a few moments longer until her trembling receded. Then he picked up the knife
and cut the bonds.

He peeled the tarp away and as her arms got free, she
began clawing at the tape over her mouth, pushing herself
back again into the corner.

Conner took a breath and turned his attention to the other
body. He gently pulled the tarp down from her head and saw
another pair of eyes. Brown and wide open. Staring straight
back at him.

"Can you hear me?"

The eyes moved and Conner felt a wave of relief sweep

over him. "I'm not going to hurt you," he whispered. "I'm here to help you. Do you understand me?"

She nodded.

Conner reached again for the knife but found the other girl wielding it in front of her, her thin hand white and shaking. Her eyes were fierce. Filled with hate. She had peeled the tape from her mouth and cursed at Conner in a weak, sobbing voice. "Who . . . are . . . you?"

Conner held up his hands. "Please, I'm not going to hurt you. I've come to help you."

"Where are . . . we?"

Conner tried to keep his voice calm. "On a farm . . . Indiana. These people—I don't know what they want. But we have to get out of here before someone comes." He reached out his hand. "I need the knife to free your friend."

She was still trembling. She swore at him again.

"Look," he said, debating whether he should just make a grab for the knife. He didn't have time to reason with someone half-crazed with fear. But he didn't want to make things worse. "My name is Conner Hayden. . . ." He couldn't think of how to begin explaining how he had found them. "Please . . . what's your name?"

Her blue eyes narrowed a moment. "Katie," she hissed at him through clenched teeth.

Conner tried to smile. "Good, Katie. I have to help your friend. I have to cut her loose. We have to get going. We can't stay here. He could show up any minute."

She lurched forward. "Don't touch her! I'll do it."

"All right. Okay." Conner moved away slowly, back into the tunnel. He felt the gun in the gravel, where he had dropped it. As Katie slid over to free her friend, Conner slipped the gun into his jacket pocket.

After a few moments, the other girl was free as well. The two hugged and sobbed on each other. Their jeans were stained with sweat and urine. Their shirts as well were covered in mud and grime. Tape still clung to their matted hair. Conner heard Katie call the other girl Amber.

After a moment, Conner said, "Can you move okay? You think you can make it through the tunnel?"

"We're okay," Katie said.

Conner turned and crawled back through the passage and out into the cellar. He flipped on the flashlight as the girls emerged.

They had stopped sobbing now and straightened up slowly, rubbing their joints. Finally Amber spoke up. "Where are we?"

"A farm. Just outside of Westville."

They both looked confused. "Westville?"

"Indiana. Where are you from?"

"Purdue," Katie said. "We're freshmen at Purdue."

Amber ran a trembling hand through her matted hair. "What day is it?"

"Saturday, October 30," Conner said.

"The thirtieth?" Katie glared at him. She turned to her friend. "How long have we been here?"

Amber seemed to think for several seconds. Conner could see they were both disoriented. She shook her head. "I think it was the twenty-fourth."

Katie looked up. "Six days? It felt like six weeks."

"Who did this to us?"

"A guy named Bristol. Owen Bristol. I think. Big guy. He lives here on this farm with his mother."

Amber shuddered. "He looks like Satan."

Conner aimed the light at the stairs. "He's got you in a cabin in the woods out behind their farm."

Amber's strength seemed to be returning. "I was leaving work Sunday night. It was late. A van had parked behind my car, blocking me in. I went to see if anyone was inside and then he just . . . he came out of nowhere. When I woke up, I was inside the van. All tied up."

Katie nodded. "And I was leaving a bar that night. He did the same thing. He had his van blocking my car."

"He had a Taser or something," Amber said. "I saw him use it on her. Then he pulled her into the van and tied her up."

Conner frowned. "So he abducted you both on the same night at different locations. Had you seen him around the campus before? Did you recognize him at all?"

Katie shook her head and seemed to fight back tears.

"We didn't even know each other before this," Amber said.

"Did he tell you why he kidnapped you?"

"He had us tied up most of the time. He'd give us food and water once in a while, but he never said anything to us. We tried to escape once, and he wrapped us up like that. I couldn't move. I could barely breathe."

"If you think you can walk okay, we should go," Conner said. "We have to head back through the woods and it's dark. My car is down the road a ways."

Katie was still holding the knife. "How did you know where to find us?"

"I didn't," Conner said. "I didn't even know you were here. I just felt like I needed to see this place for myself. This cabin."

"What are you, psychic or something?"

Conner offered a grim chuckle. "It's a long story. And I'll be happy to tell you once we're out of this place. But right now nobody knows where we are. We have to get out and call the police."

Katie held the knife out further. "If no one knows where we are, how did you find us?"

Conner took a deep breath. "I . . . I don't think you'll believe me."

"Try me."

"God sent you," Amber spoke up. "You said before that God brought you here."

Conner shrugged. "That's the only way I can describe it."

"I knew it." Amber managed a hint of a smile. "I was praying that God would send someone to find us."

"It worked," Conner said. "It wor—"

Suddenly they heard a muffled thump in the cabin above them. The sound of heavy footsteps on the porch outside.

Conner froze. He had left the cellar door open. Whoever was upstairs would know something was wrong. He didn't have much time to react.

Conner held his finger to his lips and motioned for the girls to move back to the corner of the cellar, behind the stairs. Conner moved back as well. He slid the gun from his jacket and flipped off the flashlight.

Upstairs the door squeaked open. Through the cracks between the floorboards, Conner could see a light sweep across the room upstairs. Footsteps entered the cabin and moved slowly across the room. The floorboards bowed and groaned with each step.

Conner pressed the girls farther into the corner. He could hear their breathing grow quick and shallow. He had to keep them quiet.

The footsteps halted at the top of the steps. A light shone down into the cellar. The figure stood at the top of the stairs. For several moments nothing happened. It felt like hours.

Then the stairs creaked. Conner could see a large, shadowy figure coming down.

He had only seconds to formulate a plan, but his mind was a pinball of fear. He couldn't concentrate. He held out the gun in front of him but his hand trembled.

The figure reached the bottom of the stairs and Conner heard a high-pitched screech behind him. Katie pushed past Conner—the knife clutched in her quivering hand—and lunged toward the figure. He spun around, sweeping the light up in Conner's eyes. Conner stepped backward, momentarily blinded. He heard a deep grunt and a stream of curses. Both girls were screaming now. He pointed the gun but couldn't be sure he wouldn't hit either of the girls.

Conner glimpsed one of the girls fly across the cellar and land in a heap near the wall. The light flashed back into Conner's face. He couldn't wait. He had to act. He squeezed the trigger.

Nothing happened.

Conner didn't have time think. Something hard smashed into his jaw. His head snapped to the side. Jolts of pain streaked through his neck and down his spine. He could feel himself falling. His head slammed against the cold, hard concrete. His mind reeled and he knew he was losing consciousness.

But with his fading thoughts came a moment of clarity. He had made a fatal mistake and he knew what it was.

He had forgotten to take the safety off.

66

MITCH NOW FOUND HIMSELF ALONE on the ledge. The dark clouds seemed to loom ever closer. Sporadic flashes of multicolored lightning illuminated the mountains and the surrounding desert. There was no sign of Howard and no sign of his vast army of Reapers on the desert floor. Even the wind had died away.

Mitch looked down at the object in his hand. It was the stump of blue chalk. Nathan had given it to him just before his final transformation.

Mitch suddenly felt an almost overwhelming sense of loneliness standing there. As if he were the only man in the entire universe. Nathan's words came back to him.

"Remember . . . you're not alone."

But it gave him little comfort. Mitch's anger was still roiling inside him. He couldn't help feeling betrayed. That Nathan had kept his true identity hidden this whole time. And that he was the real reason Mitch was here in the first place.

And yet Nathan had warned him about Howard. He had saved Mitch from the Keeper. Twice. Nathan had shown him the incredible vision at the top of the mountain and had explained all of what was going on—because he had been experiencing it too. The guy had left a wife and three children behind.

Mitch shuddered. He had nowhere to go but onward. Into the cave.

He knelt down to scrawl a heavy chalk line across the entrance to the cave, then stepped back. In moments, it began to glow and smolder. A soft blue light filled the entrance completely. He figured if and when the Reapers returned, this should keep them out at least for a while. Then Mitch turned and headed deeper into the cave.

His journey was slow in the darkness. He kept one hand against the cool rock wall and the other in front of him. At one point his foot kicked a rock and he suddenly got an idea.

He bent down to pick it up and felt that it was roughly the size of a softball. He took out the chalk again and scrawled several lines on one side. In moments it began to give off a dim glow. It wasn't much, but it lit the tunnel for two or three yards ahead of him. Enough to see his immediate surroundings anyway.

Now holding the rock aloft, Mitch was able to move a little more quickly through the passage. Nathan had not indicated how long it was or if it split into other tunnels along the way. If that happened, Mitch would have no clue which way to take.

But he told himself there was no use worrying about things that hadn't happened yet.

After what felt like half an hour, the tunnel opened quickly into what Mitch guessed was a large cavern. He couldn't see the sides or the ceiling, if there was one. But the ground seemed to twist and turn between boulders and outcroppings, providing a sort of winding path for Mitch to follow. All he could hear was his own breathing and footsteps echoing back off the distant walls. He could only guess at how large the cavern was.

Then suddenly a light appeared up ahead. It was dim but distinct, and Mitch paused for a moment to decide whether he should avoid it or head toward it. Nathan had instructed him not to be afraid. But then again, Mitch had good reason to doubt how trustworthy the guy really was. In the end, Mitch decided to continue toward the light. If it was something dangerous, he'd know soon enough.

After several more minutes of walking through the dark, Mitch climbed a steep rise and found himself standing on a wide, level patch of ground, staring at something that—despite all the bizarre things he'd seen over the last five years—he was still amazed to find inside a cave.

It appeared to be a room. A dining room to be exact. With hardwood floors and a long, polished table. And several chairs parked around it. All of this stood on an ornate area rug with tan and crimson designs embroidered on it. There were plaster and paneled walls that faded off into darkness and stone. Mitch's lips tightened against his teeth.

It was the dining room in his father's house.

Mitch stepped onto the wooden floor. It creaked beneath his weight like the dining room floor back home. In the corner stood the old grandfather clock his grandmother had brought from Germany. Its pendulum swung slow and methodically, ticking away the seconds. Mitch recalled so many times when that clock had been the only sound in the entire house. It was a chilling, disturbing memory from a childhood he wished he could forget.

On the far wall stood an arched entrance into the spacious formal living room. And beyond that lay the expansive foyer with the winding staircase. Mitch could see the stairs from his position in the dining room.

His heart was pounding. Was this another illusion? Behind him was the cold darkness of the cavern, but here before him stood a replica of his father's house. Mitch moved into the living room. Then looked back from where he'd come. The dining room was completely enclosed. He could see no evidence of the cave beyond it. The bay windows opened to bright daylight. The sun was shining outside.

Mitch closed his eyes. Every scent, every sound told him this was his father's house, yet he knew—he kept telling himself—this was an illusion. Or . . . what had Nathan said? This place could take your memories and give them form. Even Howard had said as much.

He stood now in the foyer and saw the door to his father's study closed. A strip of daylight shone beneath the door. The floor creaked as a shadow passed by, momentarily blocking the light.

Mitch's mouth went dry. His hands grew cold and his heart thudded harder in his chest. Forcing his legs to move, Mitch crossed the foyer, turned the knob, and opened the door.

DEVON APPROACHED the Hayden house, clutching the gun in sweaty palms under his sweatshirt. Pale Man followed at his shoulder. The house was huge and the front entrance was all lit up.

"Yo, man, this is crazy," Devon said. "Look how bright that is."

"Go around back, *yo*." Pale Man shoved him forward. "Do I have to do all your thinking for you?"

Devon swore as he crouched behind a row of bushes lining the front yard. "Man, why do I got to kill these people? They didn't do nothing to me."

Pale Man sighed and rubbed his yellow eyes. "See, when you keep using double negatives like that, it makes you sound like an illiterate thug. 'Didn't do nothing' means they did in fact do something. Good communication skills are vital if one wishes to become successful in any arena of life."

"Whatever. I still don't got no reason to kill them." Devon was fed up with Pale Man's sarcasm, but for now he couldn't do anything about it.

"How's this for a reason: If you don't, Mr. Karenga will kill you. And I can guarantee he won't be the least bit conflicted about it."

Devon was sick inside. He'd done a lot in his few years working for Karenga, but he had never actually killed anyone before. That was a whole new level of crime. Underage or not, he'd be sent up with the big boys on this one.

He stared at the house. His breathing grew more rapid. "I . . . I don't know if I can go through with this."

Pale Man's eyes flared bright and he sank his hand into Devon's chest, piercing both flesh and ribs. His voice growled deep and full. "You will do what I tell you to do. You'll kill who I tell you to kill or I'll turn you back over to Karenga so fast, your head will spin."

Devon convulsed, his eyes wide. He struggled for breath but couldn't suck any air into his lungs. Darkness crowded in around the corners of his vision. Endless, terrifying darkness.

Pale Man released his grip and his eyes dimmed to their pale yellow hue. "I think I've made my point, yes?"

Devon could not speak but managed a stiff nod.

Pale Man smiled, showing a mouthful of brown teeth. "Well, that's just super! Now, like I've told you before, I have some other commitments tonight, so let's get this over with and I'll get out of your hair. So to speak."

Devon crawled on his hands and knees around to the

back of the house. The kitchen area was dark but it looked like there was a light on in the front room. Devon crept up to the glass door.

It clicked and opened.

Devon's heart was pounding but he felt like a man completely tied up. He was out of options and at the mercy of a power he couldn't fight. A power with absolutely no mercy. Pale Man would certainly turn him over to Karenga if he didn't comply. He'd probably do it anyway. An overwhelming sense of hopelessness struck him at that moment. Nothing good was going to come out of this night. Nothing.

"Kill the wife and daughter," Pale Man said, stepping back from the door. "Make it quick and get out."

"Aren't you coming in with me?"

"It's complicated—a jurisdictional thing. You're on your own here, chief. But I'll be waiting right outside."

Devon slipped inside the house. He'd taken off his shoes so as to move without noise. He found himself inside a large kitchen. A hallway straight ahead ran all the way to the front entrance; then a living room was off to the right.

"Hurry it up," Pale Man whispered.

Devon heard the sounds of a television in the living room. He slipped through the kitchen and down the hall. In the living room, on the couch, sat two women. They were engrossed in some cable news program.

Devon could kill them both from his vantage point in the hall. They hadn't seen him. They were completely unaware. Devon looked back into the kitchen. Pale Man stood outside the glass door, watching. Eyes glowing. He made a gun with his fingers and thumb and mimed the act, mouthing the words *Boom! Boom!*

Devon nodded and took aim.

VALLEY OF THE SHADOW

CONNER FOUND HIMSELF LOST in darkness. Far off he could hear muddled sounds. He couldn't make out what they were. But they seemed to be coming closer.

He heard footsteps and soft whimpering.

He groaned and tried to lift his head. New shards of pain stabbed his neck and shoulders. Wincing, he opened his eyes and saw a blur of light and shadows. Something—or someone—was moving in front of him. Slowly everything came into focus.

He was still in the cabin. A lantern sat on the table beside him. He couldn't move his arms or legs. As he looked around, he could see he was strapped to a wooden chair. Coils of rope wrapped tightly around his chest and arms. His hands were bound behind him. His feet were immobilized as well.

Conner could see someone beside him. One of the girls was tied up like he was. Her head hung down, hair covering her face, and she was whimpering.

Conner's jaw was throbbing; he could feel that one of his back teeth was loose and could taste his own blood. "Hey, are . . . are you okay?"

She lifted her head. It was Katie. Her blue eyes were wide and fearful still. "We're going to die."

Conner craned his neck but he couldn't see any sign of the other girl. "Where's Amber?"

Katie only shook her head.

A voice came from behind him. "She managed to get away. But we'll find her. Don't worry."

"You?" Conner strained to look behind him. "You knew about this?"

Mrs. Bristol stepped into view, smiling. "Owen's out looking for her now."

"What's going on? Why are you doing this?"

Mrs. Bristol drew up a third chair and sat down. She wore a wool coat, trousers, and galoshes with a scarf over her head. She smiled at him, looking like someone's grandmother. "I know what you're thinking, Mr. Hayden. I can see you judging me with your eyes. You're thinking I'm some kind of monster."

"You're crazy. Why would you do this?"

"I have my reasons."

"People know I'm here. They'll call the police."

Mrs. Bristol nodded. "In fact, you were here. You came under false pretenses and we asked you to leave." She shrugged. "And we never saw you again."

"What?" Conner couldn't believe what he was hearing. Who were these people? What kind of family was this? "They'll search the premises. They'll find this cabin. They'll find the room down there. They'll find out what you've done."

"Maybe. Maybe not. But that won't save you now, will it?"

Katie spit at the old woman and hurled a stream of curses at her.

Mrs. Bristol's eyes flared with anger. "You see?" She wagged her finger at Katie. "You see there? This is why you're here. You beast. You selfish, spoiled, worthless beast. This is why you're here."

Conner wrinkled his forehead. "What are you talking about? What did she do to you?"

At that point, Conner heard footsteps approaching, onto the porch. The door opened and Owen entered, muttering to himself. He glared at Conner as he entered, then back at his mother.

Mrs. Bristol seemed to look past him out the door. "You didn't find her?"

"I don't know what direction she went."

"We can't let her get to a phone."

"I know, Mom; I know."

Mrs. Bristol glanced at her watch and shook her head. "She can't have got far."

Owen paced around the cabin. "She could wander through these woods for hours and not find her way out."

Conner could sense Mrs. Bristol's concern now. He breathed a sigh. If Amber was able to find her way back to the road, she might be able to wave down a passing car or something. She'd call the police. That was clearly something these people needed to avoid.

He managed a grim smile. "Looks like things aren't going quite like you planned, eh?"

Owen leaned into Conner's face. His yellow teeth clenched and his eyes seemed to bore right through Conner. "I'm gonna kill you nice and slow. And I'm gonna enjoy it, too. Every minute of it!"

Conner tried to back away. Fear gave way to anger and a rush of adrenaline. "I believe it, big guy. And the cops will put you away for life. Or, come to think of it, doesn't Indiana have the death penalty?"

Owen cursed him again and straightened up. "Let's just kill 'em now and I'll go find her."

Mrs. Bristol checked her watch again. "We'll wait until he gets here."

Conner turned to her. "You're meeting someone else here? Who?"

"I'm afraid you'll have to wait until he gets here."

THE DOOR SWUNG OPEN into Mitch's father's study, revealing two walls covered with bookshelves and a massive desk of burnished oak. Mitch pushed the door a little farther to find a figure in dress slacks and a sweater, standing with his back toward Mitch, reading a book.

Mitch's throat was still dry. "Dad?"

Walter Kent turned. His eyes narrowed for a moment; then his shoulders seemed to slump a bit and he sighed, as if seeing Mitch was some sort of disappointment.

Memories flooded back to Mitch at that sight. This was the day Mitch had left home. He'd moved his things out earlier and then had come for one final confrontation with his father before leaving for good. Mitch could recall every detail of that day. Every nuance. He had relished the memory. It had brought a sort of joy to finally have it out with the man. To release all the hate and anger in one torrential rush.

His father snorted. "So this is it, huh? You're leaving?"

"Just wanted to, y'know, say good-bye." Mitch found himself back in his memory, speaking the same words he'd said on that day. He couldn't help reliving, reenacting, the moment. He had savored it so much. He couldn't resist the urge.

"Right." His father shook his head. "Well then, no need to drag it out."

"Oh no, Dad," Mitch said, smiling. "I wanted to take my time with this. I've been thinking about it for quite a while—planning out exactly what I wanted to say to you."

His father just rolled his eyes, but Mitch knew better. He knew his father's ego. The tremendous sense of disappointment with his son. Everything he'd ever done for Mitch, he'd done to keep Mitch from being an embarrassment. It was always, always about the congressman.

So that had become Mitch's sole motivation in life: to embarrass his old man.

Every fight, every disciplinary incident at school, every speeding ticket, every drunken or drug-induced exhibition, every sexual escapade. Everything. Mitch wanted to be nothing but a public embarrassment to Congressman Walter Kent.

Mitch would not be deterred. "I know you're trying to pretend you don't care anymore. Or that you've given up. I bet you've even convinced yourself that you actually cared about me at some point in your life."

"You think too highly of yourself, Mitch," his father said through tight lips. "I have given up on you. I have done

everything I could to help you. You had every opportunity in
the world, but you just frittered it all away. So I'm done. You're
eighteen. You're on your own. I'm through with you. Have a
nice life."

Mitch moved farther into the room. "Everything you ever
did for me was ultimately about you. My whole life revolved
around improving your image as a politician. If you could've
gotten away with trading me in for some other kid, I have no
doubt you would've done that."

"Yeah, well . . ." His father shrugged, not looking up from
his book. "Maybe I could've found one who knew how to show
a little appreciation."

"For what? For turning him into a stage prop?"

His father seemed to ignore that comment. "You know,
in a way, I'm glad you're leaving. I was starting to worry that
maybe you'd try to kill me in my sleep too."

Mitch laughed. He remembered laughing even though
that comment had physically stung in his chest. But he knew
he couldn't let on. "You have no idea how bad I was tempted.
I mean . . . just to put you out of my misery." He went on, not
wanting to leave his father any further room for comment.
"Because some people make the world a better place with
their lives and others with their deaths. And you? You're just
a waste of oxygen. The world will be a much better place after
you're dead."

His father's eyes widened momentarily; then he burst
out laughing. "That the best you got? You took all that time
to think of something to throw at me and that's all you could
come up with? A waste of oxygen?"

Mitch smiled. He had something better. "I just can't figure
out why I've been such a disappointment. I've turned out to be
so much like you."

Mitch could see his father's jaw tense. But the congress-man only shook his head. "Right. That's lame too, kid."

"No, think about it. That's how I've lived my life. I ask myself, what would Congressman Kent do? You know? The apple never falls too far from the tree, does it, Dad?"

"You're lazy. You have no ambition in life. Zero." His father snorted as if in disgust. "You're nothing like me, Son."

"No?" Mitch moved closer, trying to get into his old man's space. "Think about it. I'm abusive, arrogant, selfish, ungrateful, and narcissistic. Dude—I'm your clone!"

His father snapped the book closed. His eyes flared. Mitch knew he'd struck a nerve. Maybe *the* nerve. "You forgot one thing," his father said through clenched teeth. He pointed a trembling finger into Mitch's face. "You're a murderer. Now there's something you didn't get from me. All I did was try to cover for you. To keep that stigma from following you the rest of your life! I did it to give you a chance!"

"Give me a chance?" Mitch leaned in close to his father's face. He was no longer a child. Now he stood toe-to-toe with the man. Eye-to-eye. His lips peeled back. "You did it to save yourself from embarrassment. That was the only reason. It would have cost you the election. You didn't care about justice or me or Mom. You never did. It was always only ever about you!"

At that the house shuddered. Somewhere outside a ter-rifying but familiar sound thundered. It was deep and hideous, and Mitch recognized it immediately. He blinked as if waking up from a dream. He stood alone now in his father's study. Daylight was no longer shining through the windows. Outside was only darkness.

The Keeper.

The walls vibrated with a second roar. Then a long, black

limb smashed through the window. Glass shattered, wood splintered, furniture flew across the room as the beast's appendage blasted into the house. Enormous claws spread open, sank deep into the floor, and raked backward, tearing up the carpet and the floorboards beneath it.

Mitch dove to the side and rolled back to his feet as another gnarled limb crashed down through the roof, through the second floor, nearly impaling him where he stood.

Mitch scrambled out of the way again and tried to formulate some kind of plan. Nathan had said they couldn't kill this thing. He had said all he could do was disrupt it or disunify it or something. They had last left it buried under a thousand tons of rubble—Nathan had brought an entire building down on it.

An overwhelming sense of hopelessness grew inside Mitch. He struggled to fight it back. But what could he do if the thing couldn't be destroyed?

His mind raced with more questions. How had it even gotten into the cave? How had it made it past the chalk lines Mitch had drawn at the entrance? That stuff was supposed to keep all those creatures away. According to Nathan, anyway.

Regardless, the beast was clearly going to demolish the house and Mitch along with it. He dashed for the back door— no idea where exactly he was going or what he was going to find when he opened it.

But one thing was clear: he'd have a better chance of survival outside the house than in it.

Or so he hoped.

VALLEY OF THE SHADOW

DEVON HAD A CLEAR SHOT at Hayden's wife and daughter. He raised the gun and stopped. He suddenly felt a presence—someone standing behind him.

"Devon?"

He turned to see another woman behind him. Devon blinked. This had to be some kind of hallucination. His mother stood in the shadows of the hallway.

Juanita Marshall only shook her head. Her eyes were moist. She'd been crying, yet she didn't seem surprised to see him. At least not as surprised as he was to see her.

"M-Mom?" Devon stammered. "Wh-what are you—?"

"Oh, Devon, baby," she whispered. "Don't do this. Please come back to me."

A thick hand came out of the shadows and clutched his wrist like a vise, forcing the gun down. An arm wrapped around his chest from behind and squeezed.

Devon swore. The grip on his wrist was so strong his hand went numb. The gun dropped out of his grasp and clacked onto the tiled floor of the hallway. Devon struggled against the force holding him. But he didn't feel the rage or the power he'd felt on previous occasions. Where was Pale Man when he needed him?

Devon caught a glimpse through the glass door. Pale Man just stood there, a stunned expression on his face. Slowly his lips peeled back, baring his teeth and gums. His eyes glowed bright yellow against the darkness outside. He looked more like an animal now than a man. He opened his mouth and roared.

It was deafening. Devon felt his ribs shake with its fury. His entire body trembled and convulsed.

Pale Man drifted backward, away from the door. Moving into the shadows of the yard. Soon, all Devon could see were his yellow eyes, glowing like flames. Then they disappeared as well.

Meanwhile, someone had turned on the hallway light. Devon felt dizzy; his knees buckled and his body fell limp.

A voice said softly in his ear, "I've got you, kid. I've got you."

Devon fought through a haze of images and memories. He wondered if he had passed out. He found himself lying on the couch in the living room. There was a bustle of activity around him. A figure loomed over him. A stranger.

But he looked vaguely familiar. A big white guy. Devon

thought he might have recognized him, but the memory was hazy. And there was Hayden's wife and daughter, along with some other woman. A redhead. Their faces seemed concerned.

And his mother sat beside him, her eyes red and her hands trembling. "Baby? Are you okay?"

"Mom?" Devon tried to sit up. "What are you doing here?"

"We've been looking for you." Her tears began again. "We had to find you before you went and did something stupid."

The big man spoke. "You know where you are?"

"Yeah . . . I think so." Devon tried to recall the specific events that led him here. Much of it was a jumble. "I . . . uh, I was in juvie."

"You escaped yesterday. You remember any of that?"

Devon groaned. His head was throbbing. "Some dude . . . was . . . He made me . . . wanted me to . . . to kill . . ." Devon felt the room spinning. He lay back and felt himself sinking into darkness. He tried to tell them that he hadn't wanted to hurt anyone. He had to tell them about the Pale Man. It was his fault. He had to tell them, but he was too tired.

". . . ghosts . . . in my mirror . . ."

"WHO?" CONNER'S MIND was spinning. "Wait until who gets here?"

Owen moved behind Conner. "Let me kill him, and then I'll go back out and find the girl. Either way, we'll still have two of 'em."

Conner craned his neck, trying to see if Owen had a gun or if the guy was just planning to kill Conner with his bare hands. "Uh . . ." He tried to sound nonchalant but his voice was still shaky. "If it's all the same to you . . . I just as soon wait."

Mrs. Bristol stared at Conner for a moment. "I know you saw Howard. Met him like you said. During your heart attack. I believe you."

"You do, huh?" Conner said.

Mrs. Bristol seemed to get a glow in her eyes. A smile spread across her face. More like a psychotic grin. "You see, Mr. Hayden, I have a kind of sixth sense."

"Sixth sense?"

"Ever since I was a young girl. Sort of an insight into the next dimension."

"I kind of got the feeling you were a little paranormal."

Mrs. Bristol smiled but ignored his comment. "When I was twelve, I nearly drowned in the pond we had out back. Out here in the woods. It was in the winter and I fell through the ice. I don't know how long I was under, but my father pulled me out."

She went to the window and peered into the darkness. "I remember seeing the whole thing as it happened. I could see my father running with me in his arms. I could hear his frantic calls for help. I could see him crying. Tears, big and fat on his red cheeks. He made it here to the cabin. Farmhands used to stay here during harvest time. And he tried to breathe life back into my lungs."

Conner felt a strange tightness in the pit of his stomach. He took a breath. "I take it he succeeded."

Mrs. Bristol twirled a strand of hair as she stared out the window. Like a schoolgirl. "It was all so clear. I could see every detail. Hear every sound. I found myself outside in the snow, though I wasn't cold. I wandered through the forest until I saw him."

"Him?" Conner frowned. "Who?"

She turned and looked at Conner, her eyes almost alive with excitement. "The pale man. Out in the woods. He called to me. Said he was waiting for me."

"The pale man?" Conner said.

Mrs. Bristol nodded. "He was beautiful . . . like a guardian angel. He said I had to go with him. But I didn't want to. I could hear my father weeping and I wanted to go back to him."

"So what did he do—the pale man? He just let you go?"

She looked down. "He said I could go back if I chose to. He said he'd let me live but that there'd be a reckoning some-day. Someday he would come again. And if he did, I would have to do what he said."

Conner glanced at Katie. Her face showed complete dis-belief, but she didn't say anything. He looked back at Mrs. Bristol. "So is this why you're doing this? Your pale man? He's telling you to do this?"

"Yes," she said. Then her face grew solemn and she shook her head. "Oh, but it's not what you think."

"How do you know what I think?"

She turned back to the window. "You see, twenty-four years ago, when Owen was just a boy, he got sick. Very sick. And that's when Pale Man showed up again. He was outside, at the edge of the woods. He said he was coming for my son. He said that was the price I had to pay for my life all those years ago. He was going to take my son."

She looked at Owen and her eyes welled with tears. "But I couldn't let him. I couldn't give him my son. So I begged him. I pleaded for him to take me instead, but he wouldn't. He wouldn't do it."

Conner glanced up at Owen Bristol, towering over him like a grizzly bear. Two months ago he would have written the old woman off as a superstitious, ghost-chasing nutcase. Or certi-fiably psychopathic. But not now.

"So what did you do?" Conner's voice was trembling. "I mean, obviously you talked him out of it."

Mrs. Bristol stared at Conner, her lips tightening. Almost

as if struggling within herself. Probably debating how much to tell him. Conner could sense the battle. That part of her wanted—maybe needed—to tell someone. But part of her resisted the urge, warning her to use caution.

"He said I needed a substitute for my son."

Conner's voice grew shakier. "What . . . what do you mean?" Was this why the girls had been kidnapped? Some kind of sacrifice? Was that what he was going to be now?

"A substitute, Mr. Hayden," she said. A kind of calm had come over her now, as if letting an outsider in on their dark family secret had given her a sense of peace. "Someone . . . someone to die in his place."

"Someone to . . . So . . . so you killed someone else to save your son?"

"What would you have done?" She moved toward Conner and leaned her face close to his. "Hmm? What would you have done faced with that choice?"

"You're a murderer," Conner said. He looked from her to Owen. "You can try to explain it any way you want, but you're . . . just murderers."

"Really?" Mrs. Bristol's eyes grew cold. "What would you do if your child was about to die and you could save him by some horrible deed? What would you do to save him?" She straightened up again. "What wouldn't you do?"

Conner felt his breath leave him. The question hung in the air like a noose, wrapping around his neck. His thoughts flashed to Matthew, drowning in their pool. What would he have done to save his son? If someone had offered him the same kind of bargain, what choice would he have made? At the time, he knew, he would have jumped at such a deal. He would have done anything to get Matthew back. Anything.

Mrs. Bristol was chuckling now. "No need to answer. You

know you would have done exactly the same thing. You're no better than me."

Conner blinked. "So who did you kill?"

"Carter." Her eyes traced a path around the cabin as if barely able to recall the name. "Morris Carter. He was a drunk and a wife beater and he didn't deserve to live."

"I see. And you determined that?"

She looked at Conner and smiled. "Some folks, the world's just better off without."

"So, what? You just brought him here and killed him?"

"We didn't have much time. We needed to bring Pale Man a substitute before the day was over. October 30. Twenty-four years ago. He met us here. He wanted to see it done. He wanted to watch."

Conner closed his eyes and fought back a wave of nausea. He was getting light-headed. His voice was weak. "But that was twenty-four years ago."

"The price was higher. Pale Man had demanded only one life for mine, but it was to be the life of my son. So now he had increased the price. Morris Carter's death bought my son just one more year of life."

"A year? You've been doing this for twenty-four years? Kidnapping innocent people and . . . and you bring them here to . . . to kill them?"

"Innocent?" Mrs. Bristol pointed a trembling finger at Katie, who was hissing profanities at the Bristols through her tears and spitting at them. "There are no innocent victims here, Mr. Hayden. We've been very careful to find only those who deserve to die. Thieves and drug dealers. People who peddle in filth. People who abuse their children and go free on some technicality!" She closed her eyes a moment and took a breath. "We're doing the world a favor by getting rid of these sorts of people. And there's plenty of them left. We never seem to run out!"

Owen moved behind Katie, grabbed a handful of her hair, and snapped her head back. "You know what this one did? You think she's just an innocent victim?" He grimaced. "She's a partier, this one. Just loves to drink. Can't get enough. Trouble is she likes to drive after she's had a few too many. She nearly ran me off the road last spring."

"That's no reason to kill her." Conner tried to stay calm.

"It's good enough for me," Owen said. "She's got no sense in her. No common decency. It's only a matter of time before she kills someone."

Conner shook his head. "If you just need one life to buy you another year, why did you have two girls here?"

"My Howard," Mrs. Bristol said. "We needed to bring two souls this year. One for Owen and one for my husband. He's been in that coma for nearly a whole year, and Pale Man said they would give him back to me."

"You better hope so," Conner said. "Because I've seen what's waiting for him if he dies. What's waiting for all three of you."

Owen swung an arm and backhanded Conner across the face. Conner's head jerked backward. His jaw throbbed. Blood dripped down onto his jacket. The room seemed to swirl as he teetered on the brink of consciousness.

"He'll be here soon," Mrs. Bristol said. "Pale Man. And when he comes, we'll be done with you."

As if on cue, Owen hushed them all and went to the window. Conner could hear Katie's soft sobs, but beneath that, outside . . .

He heard the faint crunch of footsteps.

THE HOUSE SHIFTED under Mitch's feet, as if the Keeper was trying to pick the entire structure up. Mitch burst through the back door and tumbled out into the darkness of the cavern. He crashed onto the cold, hard rock floor and rolled as far as he could, then crawled away on all fours.

He glanced back to see the black shape of the Keeper thrashing about in the midst of a pile of rubble that was once his father's house. It used its enormous claws to dig through the wood and stones as if searching for Mitch.

Mitch felt his way up a rocky incline, smashing his hands and fingers against the stones. A light was coming from somewhere. Maybe the light he'd seen earlier when he'd first come upon the room inside the cavern. But then somehow the one room had morphed into an entire house with Mitch inside it.

The whole thing had seemed like the shifting realities inside a dream. But the light seemed to be coming from the house—or what was left of it. And it was quickly growing dimmer. Mitch could see a small opening, maybe three feet in diameter, about ten feet farther up the incline. He scrambled up the rocky wall and tossed another glance back at the beast.

The Keeper rose up. Mitch heard the horny protrusions on whatever head it might have had scrape against the top of the cave. He suddenly felt exposed. The beast turned toward Mitch and opened its jaws in another deafening roar. It lumbered toward him as Mitch pulled himself up and into the small opening.

Mitch found himself crawling through utter blackness. The rock beneath his hands was cool and relatively smooth. The cavern shook as the beast pounded against the wall. Rocks broke loose and tumbled around Mitch. He could hear the sound of scraping and pounding behind him.

Suddenly the darkness was pierced again by a soft glow up ahead. The tunnel began to descend sharply and Mitch felt himself sliding down while the beast raged behind him.

He tumbled out of the tunnel into a second, much smaller cavern. The light was coming from somewhere above him. Scraped and bruised, Mitch climbed to his feet and looked up. And gasped.

This cavern was maybe twenty yards across and in the middle stood a large, wooden cross. Its base was buried in a mound of rocks and dirt. A dim, bluish light seemed to shine around the cross and filled the cave. And Mitch could see the arms and torso of a figure on the other side, suspended on the wooden crossbeam.

The cavern shook and rocks crashed down. On the other end of the tunnel, the Keeper roared and pounded against the rock wall, hunting its prey.

Mitch circled the edge of the cave to the other side of the cross. There he could see the figure more clearly.

If the man had a face, Mitch couldn't make it out. Partly because it was shrouded in shadows and long, blood-soaked hair, and partly because it was misshapen by bruises and lacerations. Blood soaked his beard. His lip was swollen. The flesh of his chest, abdomen, and thighs was torn open, and strips of skin hung off like ribbons, dripping with blood.

He was held to the wood with thick iron spikes through his hands and feet and by coarse ropes lashed around his arms. His whole body seemed to quiver, as if convulsing. After a moment, the man's arms shook and he pulled himself up slightly. Mitch could hear a gurgled rasp of a breath. Faint. Then the body fell limp again.

The vertical timber dripped with long trails of blood. The rocks at its base were covered as well.

The muffled pounding and roars of the Keeper grew louder. The fury of the beast was dislodging larger chunks of rock from the cave ceiling. Mitch knew it would be only a matter of minutes before the creature brought the entire cavern down.

But Mitch couldn't turn away from the image before him. He had no idea if this was a hallucination or if it had physicality like the house in the adjacent cavern had. He wasn't about to climb up to the cross and touch it.

The sense of pain, of agony, was palpable, however. It hung in the air and stung Mitch's ribs. He winced. But he couldn't look away.

Then he felt a presence behind him and he spun around.

Someone was standing in the shadows, just outside the ring of blue light.

Mitch backed away. "Who are you?"

"Do you know why you're here?" The voice was soft. Feminine. Mitch recognized it immediately.

"Mom?"

His mother stepped out from the shadows. Her hair fell in soft, blonde locks onto her shoulders. Her skin was so white it seemed to glow all on its own. "Oh, Mitch, can you see me? Do you know where you are?"

Mitch's eyes stung. She looked so beautiful. Like she did before she got sick. Back when he was a kid. But now he was at the end of his rope. He'd been through too much. His emotions tumbled around inside him. He was relieved. He was frightened. He was angry.

He backed up farther. "Stop doing this to me. Please, just leave me alone."

"Don't be afraid of me." She pointed to the tunnel. "Do you know what that is?"

The cavern shook with another roar.

Mitch shook his head. "The . . . the Keeper?"

His mother nodded. "Yes. The Keeper. Do you know what it is?"

The roars grew louder, more ferocious. Mitch looked back at the tunnel, his chest pounding. The rock wall behind him cracked. Rocks and dust flooded into the cave.

"That thing is . . . they sent it to try to keep me here."

"No, Mitch. It's you."

Mitch stared at his mother—or at the image of her. "I don't . . . I don't understand."

"It's all of your anger. Your hate. This place gives it form.

It becomes like a living thing. But it's all from you. You're giving it its strength. You're giving it life."

"Hate?" Another tremor shook the cave. Mitch fell back onto the rocks in the shadow of the cross.

"For your father. For God. You've let it fester and grow and now it's become this monster. That's what is keeping you here."

Mitch blinked, his mind reeling. "What are you saying?"

"It's been following you, appearing every time you think of your father. That's why they keep making you think about him. They're using your memories against you. All those visions. They've been trying to keep your hate for your father alive. To keep you trapped here."

Mitch's thoughts raced. She was right. The visions of his father started up again the same day Mitch had met Nathan. After he'd first mentioned to Howard that he wanted to leave. And the creature appeared when Mitch made his first attempt at actually leaving the farm. And ever since then—in the garage and at the hotel and now here in the cave—each time it was preceded by another vision of his father. Each time, Mitch's anger had grown more intense.

Mitch nodded. "That's why we couldn't destroy it. That's why it kept coming back."

"You're feeding it. You're making it stronger."

"But I can't help it! I can't stop hating him. It's been too long."

His mother shook her head. "Oh, Mitch, don't. My only prayer was that you and your father would mend your relationship."

"It's too late for that, Mom. I killed you. He won't forgive—"

"He has. He called you. He wanted to redeem what little time you had left."

"He can't forgive me," Mitch said.

The Keeper roared again. It had almost broken through the wall.

His mother stood quietly amid the crashing rocks. "He can. Mitch, I love you. I never stopped loving you. Your father loves you. Even now he's tried to tell you."

Mitch's eyes began filling with tears. He wiped them away fiercely. "I couldn't stand it, Mom. I couldn't take watching you suffer."

"I know. And I know you blamed God for it. I know you hated Him. But God's power is made perfect in weakness. I was suffering, but it was for a reason."

"What? What reason could there possibly be for you to suffer like that?"

"For you. To show you what real faith was like. I know you only saw your father's faith as empty religion. But I wanted you to know mine was real. It was more than belonging to some church. It was a real relationship with the Creator of the universe. I never complained. I never blamed God for taking me from you. He took me so you and your father would need to work out your relationship together."

Mitch could not keep himself from weeping now. "It's too late for that."

"No, it's not. You can still let it go. You can leave it here and move on. Get back to your body. But you have to leave your hatred behind."

"I can't. . . . I can't just leave it behind. You don't understand. . . ."

His mother pointed to the cross. Mitch turned. The man was still hanging there, struggling for another breath. The cave trembled again.

"Let it go, Mitch. Give it up. There's still time."

The creature roared again. But it sounded different somehow. Instead of a blind, animalistic rage, Mitch could hear words. He could hear his own voice echo through the cave. It was a stream of profanity.

The man on the cross grimaced. His body stiffened, as if Mitch's words drove another lash, tearing into his flesh.

I hate you!

The man groaned and threw his head back against the wood. Mitch could see His bruised and beaten countenance, contorted with pain. One eye was swollen completely shut. Blood dripped from the multiple lacerations along his forehead.

The Keeper roared again in Mitch's voice. More profanity. More hate.

More pain racked the man's body. His head drooped forward again. Blood, sweat, and saliva dripped from his face.

Mitch shook his head. How could he stop the raging beast? How could he just will himself to give up his hate? It had been with him for so long. It was a part of him now. An extension of who he was. It felt . . .

Mitch sobbed at the foot of the cross.

It actually felt good.

The tunnel gave way. Huge chunks of rock fell away. The beast had broken through and was reaching its clawed appendage toward Mitch.

Mitch rolled away from the cross. His mother had vanished. The creature's claws wrapped around Mitch. Constricting his chest. He couldn't breathe. The cross seemed to be fading into darkness as well. Mitch could see the man gazing down at him as the Keeper dragged Mitch toward the tunnel. It was going to take him back to the farm. Back to his prison.

He had come so close. He'd come so far. Only to fail.

He clawed at the rocks, but the beast was too strong. The sounds grew muffled. Time seemed to slow down. Mitch caught one final glimpse of the man's face. His expression unrecognizable.

"Please," Mitch gasped with all of his strength. "Help . . . me."

The man on the cross flung his head back against the wood and struggled to pull himself up. Teeth bared and straining against the gaping wounds in his wrists and feet, he sucked air deep into his lungs and with the last of his strength, he cried out.

Thunder shook the cavern. The ground shook. The walls shook. A light blazed inside the cave, white and clean. It flooded over Mitch, blinding him. Burning inside him. He could feel the massive claws around his chest dissolve. The pressure released.

Wind rushed past him, roaring in his ears. He clung to the rocks to keep from being blown away himself.

Then it passed.

Silence hung in its place. The wind receded to a steady, cold breeze. Mitch lay on his back, gasping for breath.

He opened his eyes.

MRS. BRISTOL DIMMED THE LIGHT
while Owen pulled Conner's gun from
his jacket and held it ready as he
peered through the window.

"Is it him?" she whispered. "Can
you see him?"

Owen shook his head. "It's too
dark. I can't tell. . . ."

The slow crunching of leaves
grew louder. Conner struggled against
his ropes. His breath came in shallow
puffs. His heart raced. His mind reeled
as he struggled to come up with a
plan. If he could try to talk his way
out of their execution, if he could just
delay until Amber managed to find
help . . .

Beside him, Katie was sobbing, mumbling to herself.

Conner heard one of the porch boards creak.

Mrs. Bristol gasped and her eyes moved to the door. "He's here! He's here! Let him in." Conner caught a hint of fear in her words.

Owen went to the door and pulled it open.

A flash of light and a crack of thunder rocked the cabin. Owen staggered backward and toppled over at his mother's feet. His head bounced on the floorboards. His limbs splayed out, quivering, with a gaping hole torn out of his chest. Crimson fluid gushed up over the charred remnants of tattered flesh and soaked his shirt. His eyes stared—wide open—at the ceiling; his breath came in shallow, gurgled rasps.

Chaos filled the room. Katie screamed, twisting in her chair. Mrs. Bristol fell onto her son's body, wailing with a high-pitched shriek.

Conner looked up to see Amber in the doorway, a massive shotgun in her grasp. She dashed across the room and slammed the butt of the shotgun into the back of the old woman's skull. Mrs. Bristol shuddered, then fell across her son's body and lay still.

Amber dropped the gun and rushed to Katie, who was still screaming. She scooped Conner's knife from the table and began sawing at the ropes, whispering words of comfort.

Conner's mind was a fog. He could see and hear everything clearly, yet he felt oddly detached, like he was watching a movie. Owen Bristol lay motionless on the floor in a growing pool of blood. His old mother crumpled on top of him.

Conner blinked and said to Amber, "You . . . you okay?"

Amber nodded, her hands trembling as she worked to free Katie. "I . . . I got to the farm . . . and I was hiding in the barn.

And I—and I found this gun in the barn. I had to come back—I couldn't let them kill you."

"You did the right thing."

Katie's arms were finally freed and they embraced, weeping and laughing. Conner could only imagine their sense of relief, having been locked inside this cabin, in a hole in the ground, tied up in dirt and filth. He could only imagine the terror they'd felt over the last few days, not knowing what was going to happen to them. Knowing death was imminent.

"Umm . . ." Conner cleared his throat. "Little help here?"

Amber slid over and began sawing at his ropes. "God sent you to save us," she said. "He . . . He told me to come back and save you."

"I think they were getting ready to kill us both," Conner said. "I don't think we would've made it if you'd gone for help. You did good. You did real good."

Once freed, Conner stood and rubbed his arms and wrists. They'd gone numb from lack of circulation. Katie was huddled by the doorway. Conner slid an arm under her and helped her to her feet again.

"My car's just up the road a bit."

Then Conner sensed something moving behind him. He turned to see Mrs. Bristol standing there, the shotgun in her grasp.

Her hair was matted with blood, and it dripped down her face as well. Her eyes were wide. A crazed, animal look in them. Her lips pulled back in a twisted grimace. She hissed at them, and Conner could barely discern the words through her throaty snarl.

"You killed him. You . . . you killed my baby!" She unleashed a torrent of profanity as she brought the gun up.

Conner pushed the girls out the door and down off the

porch as the gun blast exploded behind them. The shot bit a chunk out of the doorframe. Pellets whipped past them. Conner could feel the heat on his face. He tumbled to the ground and rolled to his feet again as Mrs. Bristol moved to the doorway and cocked the gun.

Amber pulled Conner's arm and they rushed into the woods as a second blast echoed behind them.

Conner felt white-hot razors slicing into his back just under the shoulder blade. The force of the gunshot hurled him forward. Blistering pain knifed through his ribs. He cried out and collapsed into the dirt.

74

MITCH FOUND HIMSELF GAZING up
at a clear sky. An endless black canopy
stretched out above him, shimmering
with a myriad of stars.

He sat up and saw that he was sitting on a wide, flat ledge. It was as if
the walls and ceiling of the cave he'd
been in had simply dissolved away,
leaving the floor open and exposed to
the sky. Behind him, the mountainside
rose another three hundred feet or so;
in front of him, the cliff—in fact the
whole world—dropped away. Mitch
crawled to the edge and peeked over.
The gray rock of the mountainside fell
into emptiness. More stars and galaxies shimmered below him. There was

no sign of any land beyond the edge. Nothing but open, end-less space.

Mitch stood. There was no sign of his mother or the cross or the man hanging on it. Behind him was a small opening in the wall. Probably the tunnel through which he had crawled earlier to escape the Keeper. But there was no trace of the Keeper, either.

Mitch stood at the edge of the cliff, his heart still pound-ing. He felt a sense of weightlessness. As if he'd been wear-ing a coat of sandbags and just now had taken it off. He could breathe easier. He sucked a lungful of cold, clean air deep into his lungs. He felt incredible. And he knew why.

His hate was gone. His anger and rage. His sense of self-righteousness. He'd let it all go. . . .

No. He had been unable to get rid of it himself. He had been caught in the grip of a monster of his own making. And he wasn't able to free himself.

The man on the cross had done it. Mitch recalled his last act of desperation, crying out for help. And forgiveness.

But he hadn't let go of his hate. It had been taken from him.

And it felt beautiful.

Mitch closed his eyes and breathed in again and thought of his father. He remembered the phone call he'd gotten just before his accident.

"I just don't want us to be enemies anymore. I . . . I love you, Mitch."

That call had come out of the blue. Out of nowhere. His father had dropped the news that he was dying of cancer. At the time, Mitch had tried to block it out of his thoughts. He was too occupied with his own plans to be bothered.

But his father had wanted to mend their relationship

and Mitch had not wanted anything to do with that. He'd gotten comfortable hating his father. It had felt too good to give up.

Now those words stung in his memory. He would never be able to respond to them. He'd never be able to tell his father that he'd forgiven him and that he was no longer filled with hate.

That beast was dead. Killed at the foot of a cross.

Though now his peace was invaded by something else. Regret. All those years wasted in self-righteous anger and the harboring of a grudge. And he'd blown the one chance he'd had to fix it. His eyes stung and his chest ached.

Mitch also wondered at the vision he'd had of his mother. Had that been real? Had he actually spoken with her? Or was it something else?

He'd never know for sure. But he thought of all the things he wished he had said to her as well.

How sorry he was.

Mitch found himself weeping now. But in his sorrow came a quiet feeling of peace. That maybe some good might still come of all this.

He gazed out over the field of stars, trying to recall Nathan's words. This was the place dying souls appeared. There was some kind of portal here. And he would have to pass through it when it opened in order to get back into his own body. If he was to ever have a chance.

Then a cold wind gusted from the tunnel behind him. And on the wind came the sounds of whispering.

Mitch turned to see the shadowy forms of Reapers emerging from the tunnel. Dozens of them. They lurched out into the open, fanning out on either side of the tunnel.

Mitch searched his pockets and found the remaining stub

of chalk. He scrawled a quick line with the last of it on the ground between himself and the growing crowd of Reapers. In moments he had sectioned off a twenty-foot area at the edge of the cliff. The blue line smoldered and glowed. But now he was trapped. The Reapers gathered around the wall of light, baring their teeth and hissing.

Then a voice echoed from the darkness.

"Just when you thought you were free," it said, "the harsh reality of truth comes crashing down on you."

Howard stepped out from the tunnel, smiling.

"How did you . . . ?" Mitch stammered. His peace had dissolved into fear. "How did you get past the chalk?"

Howard shrugged. "You didn't think that would keep us out forever, did you? I think you overestimate the power of that substance."

"Well, it'll hold you off a little longer."

Howard laughed and shook his head as he shouldered his way through the crowd of Reapers. He stood at the edge of the chalk line for a moment. "Yes . . . and no."

Then he stepped over the line. Nothing happened.

Mitch gasped, backing to the edge of the cliff.

Howard patted his chest. "Mr. Bristol's accommodations have proved helpful in this regard. You may recall his spirit is in the same state as yours. Not so affected by this defense as the rest of us."

Mitch struggled to control his fear. That night in the hotel, Nathan had explained the physics behind the chalk. Or tried to. Most of it was over Mitch's head, but he did recall Nathan had said there was a reason why the chalk had no effect on them. It obviously held true for Howard as well. He had not yet entered that final stage of death either.

Mitch glanced over the edge of the cliff. He had no idea

what he was waiting for. He didn't know what these portals would look like. He just assumed he'd know when he saw it.

"Come now, Mitch," Howard said. "I've pursued you over a great distance. Doesn't that indicate my intentions? My concern is for you. We all need a little companionship."

"You want to keep me here. You lied to keep me here."

"Careful not to throw too many stones in your house of glass. Are you so pious now that you can't forgive an old man his indiscretions? Come back with us, won't you? It's been so long since we've had a good game of cribbage."

"I don't think so. I think you can just find yourself someone else to trap."

Howard's expression darkened. His eyes glowed white against a deepening scowl. His face continued to contort into a mask of malice. So much so that now it no longer looked human. He spread his arms out and his clothes darkened. A black mist swirled around his limbs, coiling around him like a cloak. He rose, too, growing taller until he loomed over Mitch. His arms elongated and spread out like great wings. His lips peeled back and his jaws opened. Black saliva dripped down and Mitch found himself staring at Death face-to-face.

"I am the lord of this world. I am sovereign here." A deep, inhuman voice rolled like thunder. Like a thousand voices speaking as one.

A dark terror clutched Mitch's heart. As if Death had somehow reached into his mind and filled it with dread. Mitch shrank back, his heart pounding. But in his terror one memory returned to him. Something Nathan had said. That Mitch was safe until he entered the final stage of death—the purple rash. Until then they couldn't touch him. They couldn't do anything.

"Until then, it's all just a show."

Then he recalled what Howard had said moments earlier. A good game of cribbage. Mitch gathered his strength again and straightened up. In all the years he'd played cribbage with Howard, the old farmer had never won a game.

Not a single game.

Mitch braced himself against the demonic creature's fury. "You don't have any authority over me," he said. "You can't touch me."

Death reared back and roared. A stream of black mist blasted down from its elongated claws, striking Mitch squarely in the chest.

Mitch's body seized, racked with pain. His mind flooded again with darkness and terror. Thick and heavy and impenetrable.

Death leaned its head down. "I have more power than you can possibly imagine," it growled. "I can show you what lies beyond this place. What you are destined for. Darkness so deep and endless that you will never find your way out. You have no concept of the horrors of hell."

Death released its grip and Mitch sank to his knees, gasping for breath. The image was more than Mitch could handle. The terror of it left him physically shaken and paralyzed. His limbs felt heavy, and though he struggled, he couldn't move.

Then below him, a light began to shine. A small spark appeared amid the stars, spinning in the darkness of space. It grew and spread until Mitch could see it clearly. A spiraling vortex of light. The center glowed brilliant white.

It was beautiful, and for a moment, it drew Mitch's gaze further inside. There in the middle, Mitch saw something moving.

Something was emerging.

CONNER LAY, DAZED, IN THE DIRT. His upper back burned like someone had taken a white-hot branding iron and seared his flesh. For a moment, his arms and legs went numb. The ground was spinning and he could hear himself groaning.

A torrent of curses continued from the cabin behind them. Conner swore at himself. How could he have been so stupid as to take his eyes off the old woman or the gun? He'd been so relieved to see Amber that he'd lost all sense of caution. Pain racked his body and he struggled to get back to his feet.

Suddenly Amber was there, tugging at his arms. Pulling him up again.

Unable to move his arm and not knowing how serious his wounds were, Conner hobbled on through the forest. His breath came in painful, sharp gasps. He pointed with his left hand, in the direction of the farm, but Amber seemed to remember the way.

"Come on!" she shouted at him, wrapping her arm around his waist. "Keep moving!"

Behind them, now a little more distant, came a third blast. The old woman's shriek echoed in the darkness like something inhuman.

Conner's mind flooded with thoughts as he stumbled forward. His lungs burned and he felt like he might collapse any moment. They pushed on through the darkness— no lantern, no flashlight. Branches slapped at them, clawing at their faces. Conner hoped that Katie might be somewhere ahead. He hoped she was going in the same direction.

Their flight through the woods seemed to take forever. Three more shots blasted from the forest behind them. Conner could hear the pellets cracking into the wood of the trees around them.

Then they were free. The trees and brush gave way to the open field so suddenly that Conner lost his balance and stumbled into the dirt. A sharp bolt of pain seemed to slice through his ribs and he cried out.

For a moment, he lay facedown in the field. The ground was spinning and muffled noises echoed far off. He could hear someone pleading with him, and he knew Amber was tugging at his arm again, trying to get him back on his feet. He sucked in agonizing gasps of air.

Branches snapped somewhere behind him.

"Come on! Come on!"

Conner rolled to his side, planted his one good arm on the ground, and pushed. First to his knees, then to his feet.

The next thing he knew, he was hobbling across the open field. He could see the porch lights of the Bristol house ahead. He suddenly felt exposed. They were free targets here in the open. Once Mrs. Bristol emerged from the woods.

He hurried, pushing his legs harder. His thigh muscles cramped. Conner stumbled and felt himself falling.

Then another arm slid under his, propping him up again. He looked over to see Katie now, holding him up as well. The three of them shuffled across the field, past the barn, the house, and down the long front drive.

They came at last to the road and Conner motioned in the direction of his car. They hurried off down the highway as fast as Conner could hobble. He barely managed the last several yards. He could no longer move his legs. His arms were numb as well. And he knew why.

He was bleeding. In the dark, he couldn't see it, but he could feel the warm wetness of his shirt beneath his jacket. He could feel blood trickling down his spine, dripping down his legs.

They came to the spot where he'd left his car. Conner had half expected it to be gone—that maybe Owen had discovered it during his search for Amber while Conner had been unconscious. But it was still there.

Every breath brought a new jolt of pain to his back and ribs. He fumbled for his keys but could barely move his hand.

"Pocket . . ." he gasped. "Keys."

Amber found the keys, unlocked the doors. Conner collapsed onto the backseat, growing numb and cold. His head swam and he now felt himself sinking into darkness.

"Bleeding . . . ," he thought he heard himself say. "Bleed- . . . ing . . ."

The interior of the car seemed to dissolve away, and darkness folded around him like a curtain closing on a stage.

Then suddenly he saw Marta in front of him. Rachel was standing beside her. Only Rachel looked younger—like during those years when she wore pigtails. The sun was shining again and . . .

Conner gasped.

And Matthew jumped out from behind them. Tousled blond hair. Mischievous grin.

"Boo!"

Conner laughed. Matthew just stood there, hands on his hips, grinning back at him. Sunshine felt warm on Conner's back, and he was suddenly aware that he no longer felt any pain. His family was all here, smiling. And he felt the distinct sensation of being home. Then they all looked up, beyond Conner. Past him. Behind him, the sunlight was growing brighter.

And Conner turned around. . . .

76

MITCH WATCHED AS THE OBJECT emerged completely from the glowing vortex directly below him. It was another spirit passing into eternity. It shone brightly against the background of stars and glided straight up the cliff face toward him.

As it drew closer, it seemed to slow down, as if it saw Mitch lying helpless on the ledge. It was a being of pure light. It ebbed and flowed as it approached Mitch. As it did, it seemed to congeal. The light formed itself into a human shape.

Mitch watched, unable to move. The spirit's figure took on more detail until Mitch sucked in a gasp. A face was forming.

But . . . but Mitch had seen it before. He recognized it. He knew this man.

Strength returned and Mitch forced himself to his knees. The spirit hovered in front of him, within arm's reach. Mitch stretched out his hand.

"Conner?"

The spirit's face smiled. A voice emerged. "Mitch."

Mitch sat, stunned. A thousand emotions flooded over him and he couldn't find the words to express them. The spirit of Conner Hayden reached out a hand to touch Mitch's outstretched fingers.

Mitch felt the rush of power flow into him. Through him. He felt strength returning to his limbs. Surging into them. He stood. All the effects of Death's attack burned away like a morning mist in the heat of the risen sun.

Tears flowed down his cheeks.

Conner's countenance shone as if bathed in sunlight. Mitch could barely stand to gaze on it.

"Mitch," the spirit said, "the way is open."

Mitch looked down at the swirl of light glowing against the field of stars. The portal Nathan had told him about.

As Conner's spirit rose upward, he glowed brighter. His last thoughts and feelings entered Mitch's heart with explosive power.

They were not words—Mitch knew words could never describe the experience. He could feel Conner's emotions wash over him. They broke on him like ocean waves, crashing on the rocks and spraying foam high into the air. They filled Mitch. Flowed through him and around him. Successive explosions of joy and awe. Of anticipation and . . .

Home.

It was an overwhelming sense of someone who had been gone a very long time and was now finally coming home.

Mitch knew this must be the way spirits communicated once free of their mortal shells. It was a depth and wonder he could not grasp, and he felt a sudden urge to follow Conner. To see for himself. To experience what lay beyond that great door of heaven.

But below, the vortex—the doorway back—was closing. Mitch gathered himself and turned again to face the darkness behind him.

"I'm not afraid of you anymore."

Death sneered and raged. "You will be lost in darkness forever."

Mitch shook his head. He didn't know what was going to happen to him. But he knew God had not brought him all this way—through all these things—for nothing. He felt the peace only a repentant man could feel. He felt the freedom of a man forgiven. His hate was gone.

Buried at the foot of a cross.

Mitch leaned backward and plunged into the emptiness of space. Death thundered in mindless, openmouthed, and impotent fury.

It all receded rapidly as Mitch plummeted. Swallowed at last by the great vortex, he felt himself accelerating, spinning. The cliff, the stars, and all the majesty of the heavens shrank into a single point of light that glowed brightly for a moment.

Then it faded into darkness.

VALLEY OF THE SHADOW

77

LIGHTS OF THE POLICE CRUISERS
flashed red and blue against the house
and through the windows. Jim was giving a statement to one of the officers
while another led Devon out to the
waiting car.

Annie sat with Juanita in the
Haydens' living room. Marta Hayden
stood in the hallway with her arm
around Rachel.

Jim and Annie had stopped to pick
up Juanita before heading north. Even
though her relationship with Devon had
been broken for a long time, she was
still his mother, and after their visit that
morning, somehow Jim felt God was
compelling him to bring her along.

But the hospital had refused to let them see Mitch. Apparently his father had imposed a strict rule against any visitation. So Annie had suggested calling in an anonymous tip, just in case Devon was in the area.

Then Jim had called Marta Hayden once again to see if Conner had gotten home yet. Marta had said she thought he'd be home soon and invited them over to wait.

Jim finished giving his statement. "Conner and I had been trying to help the kid. Y'know . . . to get his life on the right track. I think that's why he came here. He was looking for help."

Jim shot a glance at Marta, who nodded. Before the police arrived, they had put the gun somewhere out of sight. There was no need to add attempted murder to Devon's crimes, believing as they did that he was being led along—pushed into a corner by something evil.

Devon would need to go back to corrections, but he would need prayer and counseling more than anything. At least now he seemed open to it.

Devon had looked exhausted by his ordeal but grew suddenly agitated when the police arrived, begging them for protection. Jim overheard Devon telling them about his gang affiliations and about some deal he had witnessed the night he'd been shot. The officers took notes and scheduled him to speak to one of their detectives.

Jim could only shake his head at the kind of life this kid had been leading prior to all of this. Though only a teenager, Devon had already gotten involved with some serious criminal organization. Jim didn't catch all the details and, frankly, wasn't sure he wanted to know.

He just wanted to get back home. Back to his kids and his life. The life he'd had before he'd met Devon. And Conner

Hayden, for that matter. Though something told him his life was not going to be the same after this night.

One of the officers came in from outside with a grim look on her face.

"Mrs. Hayden, may I speak to you in private please?"

Marta led the woman into the kitchen. Jim could see her listening to the officer for a moment. Suddenly her eyes widened and her hand went to her mouth. Her face turned white and she staggered backward. The officer caught her before she collapsed.

She was shaking her head and sobbing. "No, no, no . . ."

Jim felt his stomach sinking. Somehow he knew it was about her husband. About Conner. Something terrible had happened. Jim's vision grew tunneled. He had to sit down. He hardly knew the man but he'd spoken to him only a few hours earlier. What had happened to him?

Rachel ran into the room and Marta tried to tell her the news. The police officer gave her the details calmly. Rachel's reaction was different from her mother's. She straightened, turned away, shaking her head.

"No," she said. "I don't believe you. He . . . he said he was coming home tonight. He just went down for work. For a deposition. You must have made a mistake."

The officer shook her head. No, there was no mistake.

Then Rachel began to cry.

Jim watched them from the hallway. His mind felt numb and he steadied himself against the wall. He watched their pain as they held each other, sobbing onto each other's shoulders. After a moment, the officer left them. Marta and Rachel stood there, holding each other. Alone in the kitchen. Weeping.

Weeping.

VALLEY OF THE SHADOW

78

LINDA WILSON SAT at Mitch's hospital bedside as she had done most evenings for the last two months. It was late and she knew she should be getting home. She had stopped by on her way home from work just to spend a minute to pray over Mitch, like she always did when she sat with him. But she was starting to feel it was a futile exercise. She had prayed for him for two months with no results. She wasn't sure what exactly she was expecting. Maybe some sign that Mitch was getting better. Or at least that he wasn't getting any worse.

The nurses told her she had missed quite a ruckus earlier in the evening.

Half a dozen deputies had combed the entire hospital looking for someone. Apparently, an anonymous caller had tipped them off to the possibility of an escaped convict in the area or in the hospital itself. Something like that. Linda didn't get all the details.

The deputies had hung around for a while but were now gone, and the halls were quiet again. Linda sat in the darkened room with Mitch.

"I keep praying for you, Mitch," she whispered, taking his meaty hand in hers. "I keep asking God to send you back to me. But I have to admit . . ." Her voice cracked. "I'm starting to think He's not listening or something."

She wiped her tears and squeezed Mitch's hand. "I just need you to hear me. I love you. Can you just give me some sign that you hear me?"

She began to cry harder and laid her head against Mitch's arm. It wasn't fair. They had so much to live for. So many plans. And all of that had been wiped away in an instant. She thought back to that night, as she had so many times. If only he'd taken the car instead of his motorcycle. He'd been so eager to get it running. To show it off to her. If only he'd left a few minutes sooner. Or later.

But it had to be on that stretch of highway. Just at that moment in time. The other driver swerved into Mitch's lane. Just at that second. She had begged God for some answer. Some reason why it had to have been Mitch and not someone else.

The other driver had gone off the road completely and struck a tree. He'd been in a coma too, and he and Mitch had even been in adjacent rooms. But when Linda arrived tonight, the other man's room was dark. His bed was empty.

The nurse had said they'd disconnected him earlier in the

evening. His wife had held out hope for two months. Linda had met her. Prayed with her. Cried with her. Whatever loss Linda might have felt, the other man had left behind a wife and children.

The news that he had died hit Linda in the pit of her stomach. It was as if Mitch had run out of time as well. She had no idea what Walter Kent's plans were. He wouldn't talk to anyone. Not even the nurses knew.

She whispered a prayer. "Oh, Jesus, please don't take him too. He's not ready. Just . . . please, just give him another chance."

It was all she could say. All she could think of. She felt like she was running on an empty tank. Like any hope she might have had was finally used up with that last prayer.

Then she felt it.

A gentle press of flesh from Mitch's hand against her fingers. Soft—almost imperceptible. Linda thought she'd imagined it. She popped her head up.

"Mitch?" she whispered. She leaned up to his ear. "Mitch, can you hear me? Squeeze my hand again if you can hear me. Squeeze my hand."

He lay still for several seconds. Then she felt it again. The soft squeeze of his fingers against hers.

Linda's heart rose. She sat up. "That's it, baby. I can feel you! I can feel you! Can you hear me?"

This time—a third time—Mitch's fingers squeezed firm around her hand.

Linda was laughing now, full and loud through her tears. And her laughter filled the darkened room, spilling out into the corridor beyond.

VALLEY OF THE SHADOW

79

FIVE DAYS LATER

AN ICY NOVEMBER DRIZZLE soaked the crowd of black-clad mourners, peppering umbrellas, overcoats, and hat brims. Jim Malone wrapped his arm around Annie and pulled her closer underneath his own umbrella. Through the gathering, he could see Marta Hayden, seated beneath the temporary pavilion with her daughter beside her. Their expressions seemed vacant as they stared at the coffin, glistening with droplets.

The pastor beside them opened his Bible and read from Psalm 23. "'The Lord is my shepherd; I shall not want. He makes me to lie down in green pastures . . .'"

Jim felt an ache in his chest over the events of the previous week. He had barely known Conner Hayden, and yet he found himself unexpectedly intertwined in the man's life and in the lives of his widow and daughter.

News of Conner's death had come as a shock. But as the grim details of the deeper and darker story surrounding his death came to light, it grew into a full-blown media frenzy, even gaining some national attention.

The two girls Conner had rescued—Katie Polchek and Amber Bronson—had contacted the police on Conner's cell phone. They drove to a nearby gas station, where the police and an ambulance met them. Conner had suffered a gunshot wound to the upper back but had already lost too much blood. He was dead by the time the paramedics arrived, reportedly with a look of peace on his face.

The two girls were treated for dehydration and severe trauma, and they gave statements to the police. The authorities descended immediately on the Bristol farm, where they discovered Mrs. Bristol sitting in the old cabin in the woods, cradling her dead son.

She had said nothing, but after a thorough search of the premises, the police took her into custody. And her son to the morgue.

The pundits debated Conner's involvement and how he had managed to know the girls' whereabouts. Had he been involved somehow with the Bristols? Or was he psychic? Had his near-death experience two months earlier given him some supernatural abilities? There were those who called it a clear act of God. And as always, there were others who doubted. Who would always doubt.

But the girls related quite a harrowing story, saying there could be bodies buried around the farm. The Bristols were named as suspects in the disappearance of another young man from Westville two years earlier. The police indicated they were considering opening a whole slew of missing persons cases from all around the state, dating back more than twenty years. Even now they were searching the farm for remains.

And Howard? Howard still lay comatose at the nursing home in Indiana. The news reports indicated that Mrs. Bristol had been fighting for months to keep him alive. Now the debate swirled as to the old man's fate.

Jim gazed again at Marta and Rachel, alone in their pain among their friends. And yet in all their sorrow, Jim thought there might still be some comfort. Some small, faint hope, awash in tears and the pain of loss, like a candle flickering in the rain, fighting to cast its light yet a little farther. And after a time, Jim knew the flame would still be burning, growing brighter as the storm waned.

The pastor's voice cracked with emotion as he read the psalm. "'Yea, though I walk through the valley of the shadow of death, I will fear no evil; for You are with me; Your rod and Your staff, they comfort me. You prepare a table before me in the presence of my enemies; You anoint my head with oil; my cup runs over. Surely goodness and mercy shall follow me all the days of my life; and I will dwell in the house of the Lord forever.'"

VALLEY OF THE SHADOW

JULIE HARRIS WENT THROUGH her morning routine at the LaPorte County Nursing Home. There were a few minor housekeeping chores and some paperwork left over from the night shift. Then she loaded up the supply cart and headed out on her normal rounds. She flashed a smile at the state trooper posted outside Howard Bristol's room.

"Hi, Gary," she said. "Just need to load up a new feeding bag."

The trooper tipped his hat and stepped aside.

Julie rolled the cart inside, humming softly.

"Good morning, Howard," she said. She always talked to him. Comatose or not, she decided it couldn't hurt. And it'd been known to help in some cases.

"Would you like some breakfast?" she said. "You look a little hungry."

She disconnected the old feeding bag from the IV pole; then she laid a hand on Howard's forehead and glanced out the door at the trooper. Gary was sitting in a chair, his nose in a newspaper.

Julie produced a small photograph from her smock and stared at it a moment. Then she leaned close to Howard's face, holding the picture in front of his closed eyelids.

"Thought you might like to see a picture of my boyfriend, Dale," she whispered. "Dale Edwards. I think you might remember him. He disappeared a couple years ago. And as you can imagine, we've all been worried sick."

She leaned closer. Her voice became a low hiss. "You and your psychopathic little family killed him for no reason." She shook her head as disgust washed over her. "What kind of a sick freak are you?"

She paused again to make sure Gary the trooper was still engrossed in his newspaper.

"Oh, wait, I know. . . ." She gently pinched the old man's nostrils shut and his lips together. "The dead kind."

The body of Howard Bristol lay motionless for a moment. Then it quivered slightly and tensed. Julie kept her eyes on the door the whole time.

The seconds ticked by. . . .

Four and a half minutes later, Julie Harris rolled the cart back out of the room, softly humming a pleasant tune.

"All done," she said. "Thanks, Gary."

HOWARD BRISTOL SAT on his back porch, chewing a Slim Jim, staring out at the yard, the field, and the woods beyond. It had been a quiet few weeks since Mitch had gone. Howard had left the cribbage board out on the table, ready for another game. Just in case. He still held out hope that Mitch would be back someday. He was always hopeful.

Everyone has to die sooner or later.

A gust of wind blew through the yard, carrying fine dirt off the field. It swirled and scattered along the driveway.

Howard caught sight of someone standing at the entrance to the barn.

A silhouette. Tall and thin. He noticed a second faceless figure standing by the maintenance shed.

Howard frowned. "What now? I don't have any visitors. There's no one here to grab today."

A second, stronger gust of wind rattled the door and the shutters behind him. A soft voice whispered.

"Beloved."

Howard stopped chewing. "What?"

Two more gray creatures appeared at the corner of the house and one on the other side by the tree. They approached the porch from all directions. Some walked upright; others crouched. But they all moved with quiet, deliberate strides.

Howard stood. Something strange was going on. They rarely came out so early in the day. He was starting to get annoyed. "I told you, I don't have any visit—"

A sharp pain stung his flesh. He clutched his chest and doubled over. It was a pain he'd never experienced before. His skin tingled.

"What the—?"

He tore open his plaid shirt and examined his chest. It was the sagging, mottled chest of an old man. And it was covered with a purple rash.

Howard shook his head. "Now . . . now wait a minute. We had . . . we had a deal."

He tried to move inside, but a second bolt of pain stung him. The skin on his hands was turning purple as well.

He staggered back into his chair. "Hold on a minute. Please . . . listen to me. . . ."

The creatures climbed onto the porch.

"We had a deal!" Howard's eyes flared in anger. "I did everything you asked of me! Every last thing!"

They reached out long, spiderlike fingers and grabbed him

by the arms. He pleaded; he begged. He cursed them. But they hauled him down off the porch. He struggled but he was no match for them. His arms grew numb.

They pulled him across the yard, out into the field.

Howard screamed now, full-throated, kicking his feet and fighting in mad desperation as they dragged him over the open field, leaving a haphazard trail of footprints and ruts in the dirt. They disappeared finally into the embrace of the black forest. But his screams continued several minutes longer, echoing amid the trees.

Then, at last, they stopped.

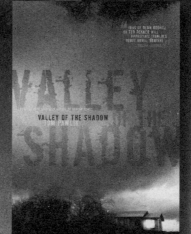